Julie Wassmer is a professional television drama writer who has worked on various series including ITV's *London's Burning*, C5's *Family Affairs* and BBC's *Eastenders* – which she wrote for almost 20 years.

Her autobiography, *More Than Just Coincidence*, was Mumsnet Book of the Year 2011.

Find details of author events and other information about the Whitstable Pearl Mysteries at:
www.juliewassmer.com

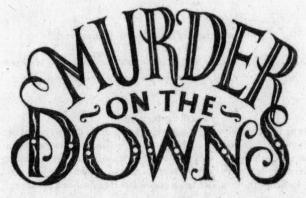

MURDER ON THE DOWNS

A Whitstable Pearl Mystery

JULIE WASSMER

CONSTABLE

CONSTABLE

First published in Great Britain in 2020 by Constable

Copyright © Julie Wassmer, 2020

7 9 10 8 6

A CIP catalogue record for this book is available from the British Library.

ISBN: 978-1-47213-009-9

Typeset in Caslon Pro by SX Composing DTP, Rayleigh, Essex
Printed and bound in Great Britain by Clays Ltd, Elcograf S.p.A.

Papers used by Constable are from well-managed forests
and other responsible sources.

MIX
Paper from
responsible sources
FSC® C104740

Constable
An imprint of
Little, Brown Book Group
Carmelite House
50 Victoria Embankment
London EC4Y 0DZ

An Hachette UK Company
www.hachette.co.uk

www.littlebrown.co.uk

For Ashley Clark,
the Friends of Duncan Down,
and in loving memory of
Keith Dickson of Harbour Books

There is a pleasure in the pathless woods,
There is a rapture on the lonely shore . . .

'Childe Harold's Pilgrimage'
Lord Byron

CHAPTER ONE

Whitstable, June

It was early morning at Seaspray Cottage and Detective Chief Inspector Mike McGuire was standing behind Pearl Nolan, the palms of his strong hands shielding her eyes. He leaned forward and gently whispered: 'Keep them closed . . .' Then his voice trailed off as he moved towards the kitchen. Pearl resisted all temptation to take a glimpse of whatever lay in front of her until, moments later, McGuire returned. 'Okay!'

Pearl opened her eyes to see her dining table laid for breakfast. As McGuire set a plate down before her, and a second one for himself, she glanced at him, astonished. 'But you said you were going to rustle up some bacon and eggs.'

'And I did.' He smiled proudly, indicating Pearl's plate on which a poached egg sat on top of a toasted muffin, smothered in a buttery sauce and latticed with two rashers

I

of Pearl's finest pancetta. He handed her some cutlery. '*You* said you were hungry? Tuck in.' He nodded for Pearl to begin, waiting expectantly for her verdict.

Taking her first bite, Pearl's eyes closed once more, this time to appreciate fully the silky consistency of a rich Hollandaise sauce, enlivened by a hint of citrus – just sufficient to lighten without producing any over-acidity or curdling. The English muffin base was suitably firm and the crisp pancetta offered an exquisite scorched contrast to a perfectly poached yolk. As the sum of all parts melted in Pearl's mouth, a sigh of satisfaction, coupled with the look on her face, told McGuire all he needed to know.

Pearl's eyes narrowed with suspicion as she now asked: 'How long have you known how to make perfect Eggs Benedict?'

McGuire checked his watch. 'Since around eight fifteen this morning.' The Canterbury police detective tapped his smartphone. 'There's a recipe for everything on here and I knew you'd have all the ingredients.'

He nodded towards Pearl's well-stocked kitchen then began to enjoy his own breakfast while Pearl considered how conscientiously he must have obeyed the instructions of a cookery website to have achieved such a result. But that was McGuire all over – he was a man who liked to follow a well-trodden path and always put his faith in procedure.

Pearl, by contrast, trusted her instincts – especially when it came to cooking. Having long ago learned the basics of good cuisine, she now preferred to improvise and experiment rather than to follow doggedly any recipes

– other than her own, that is. It was a tactic that had paid off well, because Pearl's restaurant had become one of the most popular eateries in her native north Kent town of Whitstable. Although there were some swanky establishments near the beach, The Whitstable Pearl remained a popular and precious gem – full of charm – and with a reputation for providing some of the best seafood in town, for locals and visitors alike. Fresh oysters and tapas were always available at the bar, but the restaurant also offered a selection of signature dishes, ranging from marinated *sashimi* of tuna, mackerel and wild salmon in summer to a year-round menu of squid encased in a light chilli tempura batter and sautéed scallop dotted with ginger and breadcrumb.

Pearl's reputation was built on simple dishes created with the finest ingredients, each course having been perfected over time. Now, with a new and very able chef in place, her presence wasn't always needed at the restaurant, but the quality of her food remained constant – guaranteeing a steady if not growing trade.

The business had supported Pearl while she had brought up her son as a single parent but old ambitions had reawoken once Charlie had disappeared off to university in nearby Canterbury, convincing Pearl that it was high time for a new challenge. Starting up Nolan's Detective Agency had offered her the chance to use the police training she had abandoned on discovering she was pregnant at the tender age of nineteen, and to test the detective skills she felt sure she still possessed twenty years later. It was true that she had put her life on hold for her son, eschewing opportunities, even for romance, but she had never given up on the idea of, one day, finding the right partner. She had simply found nothing among the sparks of a few short-lived liaisons to match the white heat of her first love for Charlie's father, Carl, not until she had found herself pitted in a murder investigation against a Canterbury police detective by the name of DCI Mike McGuire . . .

At that very moment, McGuire was sipping his coffee and enjoying not only the satisfaction of having prepared a perfect chef-y breakfast – but also the sight of Pearl there beside him, dressed only in a vintage red silk dressing gown, as she tucked into her Eggs Benedict. Not long awake, her beautiful features were devoid of make-up and her long dark curls still glistened wet from the shower. McGuire noted that her moonstone-grey eyes were the very same shade as the sea beyond her window on this fine summer morning.

Sensing his gaze upon her, she turned to him, leaned in close and whispered, 'Thank you.'

'For breakfast?'

'For everything.'

Her eyes lingered on McGuire's handsome features, her gaze tracing the lines of his strong chiselled jaw and fine cheekbones. She smiled at his tousled 'bed-head' blond hair then lost herself in his ice-blue eyes as he gently framed her face with his hands – and kissed her . . .

They had returned the night before from Bruges, late enough to allow themselves to believe they might still be there, lost among the winding lanes and cobbled squares of a romantic medieval city. McGuire had booked a 5-star hotel – a sixteenth-century landmark building, just 200 metres from the Burg Square and the Markt, the main market, but close enough to the canals to enjoy the sight of white swans gliding past their window. A carriage ride had taken them through the city's fabled streets and on to Minnewater Park. There they had discovered the Lake of Love and heard from an old couple who had been crossing a bridge that spanned it the story of a girl named Minna, who, in love with a warrior of a neighbouring tribe, had run away rather than marry the man of her father's choice. Escaping into the forest, the girl had finally died of exhaustion just as her lover had found her, so the area and bridge had been named in Minna's honour. 'If you walk across this bridge and kiss your loved one,' the old couple had explained, 'that love will last.' Pearl and McGuire had waited until the couple had disappeared before doing just that, each considering they might have entered the pages of a fairy tale – somewhere, at least, far from the stress of their hectic working lives.

Three nights only – an all-too-short break – but long enough to enjoy an unfamiliar landscape, when, in spite of Pearl's fear of heights, they had climbed over three hundred steps in the Belfry of Bruges for a panoramic view of the city. The building had once acted as an observation post for identifying fires and other dangers but now it served as the location for Pearl and McGuire to recognise that in spite of all their differences, their relationship might finally be given a chance to develop into something more . . .

Breaking away from McGuire's kiss, Pearl glanced back at the breakfast table noting that, with characteristic attention to detail, the detective hadn't forgotten a thing. There was a cafetière filled with rich French coffee, sugar bowl, milk jug, napkins and even a small glass vase containing a sprig of honeysuckle blossom – the fragrance of which now flooded the warm room. Glancing towards the window, Pearl realised that McGuire had cut the shoot from a plant that climbed the walls of the lilac-painted beach hut in the garden, which she now used as an office for her detective agency. After savouring her last mouthful, she looked down at the empty plate before her and smiled teasingly at him. 'I can see I've got some competition. You'll be opening a restaurant next.'

McGuire shook his head. ''Fraid not,' he replied. 'I've never much liked the idea of us being in competition.' He winked, but then held her gaze and Pearl's smile faded as she looked away, as though in need of a distraction. Her thoughts drifted back again to the short break they had just spent together while she considered how easy life had seemed when they weren't at loggerheads over one of McGuire's cases. For three days they had left behind The Whitstable Pearl, McGuire's police work at Canterbury CID and Pearl's own cases at Nolan's Detective Agency – not that there had been much in her in-tray recently, apart from a few credit checks, a hunt for a stolen bicycle and an appeal to find a lost Russian Blue cat by the name of Sergei.

'It was wonderful,' she whispered, leaving McGuire unsure if she was referring to their recent trip, his breakfast or perhaps even the agreement they had reached not to allow work to come between them again. He felt a need to clarify but the urge to kiss her was far greater. He leaned closer, but before their lips could meet, the sound of his smartphone broke the silence between them.

Checking the caller ID, he seemed to struggle with himself before answering the call. Terse, he gave only his surname, and as he did so, Pearl remembered that in spite of their close relationship, she still referred to him in just the same way – McGuire – which was how he was mostly known to his colleagues. He listened carefully to the voice at the end of the line, then gave a cursory nod and checked his watch before offering a brief reply. 'Okay. I'll be there in twenty minutes.' Ending the call, he paused for a moment as though finally aware that he was no longer in a fairy-tale city but back on police duty.

Pearl reached out to him and rested her hand on his strong forearm. Her look was questioning and McGuire seemed torn before responding. 'Sorry, Pearl. I have to go.'

At this, she gave a resigned smile. 'Of course,' she said. 'It's begun already.' McGuire looked back at her and she offered a stark reply: 'Work.'

'Life,' said McGuire.

Pearl knew that as far as McGuire was concerned, they were one and the same, but before she could voice this, her own phone sounded with an incoming text. Glancing quickly down at it, she saw that it was from her mother, Dolly.

Hope you had a nice time. You can tell me all about it at the restaurant. PS Charlie's done quite a few shifts in your absence. He's got a favour to ask. Bye. Mum x

Pearl continued to stare at the message as McGuire asked: 'Everything all right?'

Pearl nodded and quickly pressed a napkin against her lips before checking the time on her own phone. 'I'd better get ready for the restaurant. Call me when you get a chance?'

'Of course, but . . .' He hesitated for a moment as he got up from his chair. 'How about I come back later – take you out for dinner?'

She looked up in surprise. 'But it's your first day back. You probably won't get time.'

McGuire was snatching his jacket from the back of his chair. As he slipped into it, Pearl got up and eased the collar of his shirt over his jacket lapel, before gently raking her fingers through his blond hair. Caught suddenly in her gaze, he leaned in to her, kissing her hard before he reminded her: 'We said we'd make time, remember?'

Pearl nodded. Returning his smile, she watched him head towards the front door, where he grabbed his suitcase from the small pile of luggage that had been dumped there the night before. He looked back at her, gave a wink and said: 'Tonight.'

As the door closed after McGuire, Pearl's tabby cats,

Pilchard and Sprat, stared up at their owner, as if for an answer. Pearl had none. Instead, she turned back to the breakfast table and decided to clear away the plates, wondering what kind of favour Charlie needed to ask of her, and whether he might be in some kind of trouble – with his grandmother covering for him, as Dolly was apt to do. She looked again at her phone lying on the table, and was just considering calling her mother when a sound began echoing from the beach: a man's strident voice distorted through a loudhailer.

Pearl was unable to make any sense of what was being said but after opening a window, she could see people hurrying along the promenade as though summoned by a clarion call. It was the kind of racket that was frequently heard by residents during the town's annual oyster festival in July – advertising events on the beach like the epic tug-of-war that took place on the muddy flats of the shore or the blessing of the first catch of the new season's oysters – but the festival wasn't due to take place for another six weeks. Pearl's curiosity was piqued. As the volume grew louder, she hurried to her kitchen ready to head out through her sea-facing garden to join the crowds on the beach . . . until she suddenly remembered she was wearing only her red silk dressing gown. Pulling it tightly around her slim waist, she rushed back inside to get dressed, keen to discover what all the commotion was about.

CHAPTER TWO

A short while later, Pearl closed the wooden gate behind her that led from the foot of her garden on to Whitstable's promenade. To the west lay the Old Neptune – the white clapboard pub that stood on the beach itself, audaciously some would say, because several times throughout the centuries the right, or maybe wrong, conditions of wind and wave had created seas to threaten 'the Neppy's' existence. Instead, Pearl headed east, following a warm sea breeze and the sound of the man's voice that was still booming through a loudhailer. It wasn't long before she caught sight of figures milling around a familiar landmark.

The Peace Bench, as it was known locally, had been placed on the beach in memory of Brian Haw, a campaigner who had spent some of his childhood in Whitstable before conducting a highly conspicuous protest against the Iraq War in a Peace Camp based in London's Parliament Square. Made by a local craftsman, and carved with slogans, the bench was used as a location for various events, as well as serving as a structure on which children climbed or lovers sat staring out to sea, especially on a clear day like this.

But today was different because as Pearl approached, she saw that the bench was in fact surrounded by a great number of people. DFLs – the town's acronym for Down From Londoners – were easily identifiable by the selfies they were taking, while the local people in the crowd were giving their full attention to the speaker, a slightly built middle-aged man who was standing on top of the bench itself, addressing them in a well-spoken voice through the loudhailer. Pearl inched her way forward, recognising some familiar faces: a few fishermen from the harbour and some shopkeepers from the nearby High Street, all listening carefully to what the man had to say.

'We have never suggested that local people have opposed these plans just for the sake of it,' the man said. 'What we have always maintained is that this particular development deserves special attention. It must be better situated – and proportionate to the environment. As to the houses that are planned for this site, there needs to be adequate infrastructure and reasonable access to services – to nurseries, schools and GPs' surgeries – or the whole development will be nothing more than a white elephant.'

Heads nodded and Pearl turned to the woman beside her, recognising her as the owner of a new pet store in the High Street. She leaned in to ask: 'What's going on, Gloria?'

Gloria Greenwood, an attractive woman in her early forties, tugged the dog's lead in her hand to prevent her Jack Russell terrier from jumping up at Pearl, before tilting her head towards her as she explained. 'Seems they've just lost their case – the campaign group fighting that new development near the downs?' With this, she gave a disgruntled shake of her head and returned her gaze to the man on the bench who Pearl now recognised as Frederick Clark, chairman of an organisation called the Whitstable Preservation Society. He had just come to the end of his speech and was lending a hand to a woman who joined him up on the Peace Bench.

In contrast to Clark, she was dressed casually in a loose bright batik shirt over faded blue jeans and trainers, and appeared a striking figure, with a shock of thick, dark, shoulder-length hair streaked white at a deep widow's peak. Lean and spry, the woman's age had been disclosed in numerous local press stories as somewhere in her mid-fifties, but to Pearl she now seemed at least ten years younger. The loudhailer was passed to her but she refused it, clearing her throat before she continued without it – more than adequately, since her voice was as powerful as her tone was authoritative.

'My name is Martha Laker,' she announced. At this, a trickle of applause sounded, together with a few whistles of support. Martha put up her hand for silence before continuing. 'I'd like to give thanks to Frederick here, and to everyone at the Whitstable Preservation Society, for their support in helping the Save Our Downs campaign with our legal challenge. As you know, the judgement has gone against us, but that doesn't mean to say we are beaten.' A murmur spread among the crowd. 'Far from it,' Martha went on. 'We now believe we have even *more* reason to continue our fight.' Vigorous nodding of heads expressed support for this. 'The developer, Invicta Land, and our own local council will no doubt issue a statement that building work can now begin. But any such statement would be highly premature. Not a single brick has been laid since planning permission for this scheme was granted two years ago and the council has yet to issue the required formal approval notice.'

She paused as she noticed some were looking confused by the planning jargon she was using, so she took a deep breath, and some time to reorganise her thoughts, before continuing with a far simpler message. 'We are not protestors but protectors,' she said. 'Protectors of clean air and green space for residents; protectors of our right to cross that land freely and to use it for traditional purposes and customs – as has been our right for centuries. We may well decide to take an appeal to the Supreme Court and we can also challenge the planning approval notice when it is released. We've campaigned, so far, and on your behalf with a fighting fund backed not only by you but by a legal team sympathetic to our cause. And with your help we have raised tens of thousands – while Invicta Land claims the delay has cost them millions.'

A cheer went up at this but Martha raised her hand for silence. 'I don't believe that's true. It's simply crying wolf on their part. What they're referring to are the millions they stand to lose in *profits* – the money they will never receive unless the project goes ahead as planned. *That* is an entirely different matter. So we will continue to fight for all the reasons we've set out during our campaign. We'll delay this development further and if the company does go out of business—'

'Good riddance!' yelled an old fisherman, his comment followed by a loud murmur of approval.

'Yes!' called out Gloria suddenly. 'Let them go to the wall!' Gloria's Jack Russell terrier, Teddy, barked his own agreement.

But as the crowd began to applaud, another voice suddenly shouted: 'You don't know what you're talking about.'

Heads turned as a man stepped forward. Casually dressed in a T-shirt and jeans, he wore a sun visor, which he tilted back off his forehead before raising his arm in the air. 'And what about the people who work for that company?' he asked. 'Are you happy to see them all lose their jobs?'

Gloria Greenwood frowned. The crowd fell silent until the man went on: 'We need homes to live in, don't we? Houses that local people can afford to buy? *That's* what this development is all about.'

He now looked directly at Martha Laker but before she could respond, another woman spoke up, this time from the edge of the crowd. Wearing a pink jacket, and with her blonde hair tied up in a high ponytail, she pushed her way forward, raising her voice as she pointed an accusing finger at Martha. 'You know what? I think you're in this for yourself.'

A murmur of disapproval spread through the crowd, but the woman continued, nonetheless. 'That's right.' She turned again to Martha. 'You like being in the limelight, don't you? But you've tried to prevent this and failed, so why don't you stop moaning and give up? Let it go ahead, I say!'

Pearl noted confused expressions among those in the crowd but someone called out pluckily: 'Why should she?'

'Why?' responded the woman in pink. 'Because I, for one, would like a chance to *buy* one of those houses. Because I *love* that area and I want to live there – with my family.' She looked away from the crowd and up at Martha. 'Maybe *you'd* do better looking after your *own* family, instead of plastering yourself in the paper at every opportunity.' She paused before moving closer, her eyes narrowing with suspicion: 'You're a DFL, aren't you?'

The collective gaze of the crowd now shifted to Martha, who remained silent.

The man in the sun visor responded instead: 'Yeah, she's a DFL all right. And where does she live now? Close to the development, that's where. She's just worried it's going to spoil her special view!'

A communal groan of disappointment spread among the onlookers. Martha stared at a sea of unhappy faces but seemed to take this as her cue to turn quickly back to face the man. 'Yes,' she said firmly, 'I am a DFL. But I've lived here for almost fifteen years and I love this town every bit as much as you do.'

Pearl sensed the crowd wasn't wholly convinced. Their earlier confidence had been shaken. But in the pause that followed, another voice suddenly piped up.

'She's telling the truth.'

A tall figure moved purposefully to stand not before Martha but in the middle of those assembled. In his early thirties, he wore a white collarless shirt with a bright red bandanna tied around his neck and a leather hat pulled forward on his head. Mud-streaked jeans were tucked into worn boots. Raising a grimy hand, he took off his hat and pushed his long dark hair back from his face, revealing soulful eyes and dark good looks. He took a moment to calm himself before continuing.

'D'you seriously believe that Invicta Land really cares about you or your housing shortages?' With no reply he went on: 'Take a look at the prices they expect to get for those new homes. How much "affordable" housing is there actually going to be? And if the local council really wants to solve the housing problem, surely they could start by doing up all the homes that have been left empty at the local army barracks. There are *plenty* of other places to build cheap houses without bulldozing the few green spaces in this town – but none of those are being used. Ask yourselves why not.' He paused. No one spoke. The man went on, 'I'll tell you – because developers *prefer* building on greenfield sites and local councils like keeping developers happy. Green spaces are cheap to build on and

17

companies like Invicta know they can get top prices in those areas. So don't be naïve about this.'

He paused for a moment and looked up at Martha Laker. She pointed at him. 'He's right,' she said finally. 'Invicta Land thinks we're all fools. They'd have us believe they've dealt us a comprehensive defeat today – but that couldn't be further from the truth. I say to you all: our battle is not finished – it's only just beginning. And we *will* carry on. With your help, we'll fight together to stop this blot on our beloved landscape. Once and for all.'

In the next instant, Martha's voice became engulfed in loud applause. Whistles blew, people cheered and Gloria Greenwood, still standing beside Pearl, nudged her as she commented: 'I'll say one thing about that woman: she doesn't give up without a fight. Aren't you glad she's on our side?'

As Gloria moved off to congratulate the handsome man in the red bandanna for his contribution, Pearl found herself nodding. 'Yes,' she said softly to herself, aware that her own son was one of many young people from local families who might never be able to afford to rent or buy a small flat for himself in his home town of Whitstable. The thought that someone like Martha Laker and the Whitstable Preservation Society might continue working on behalf of Charlie and everyone else in the same position was certainly something to be applauded, but as the crowd began to disperse and the woman in the pink jacket disappeared, Pearl saw that one person was still firmly unimpressed. The man in the white visor remained rooted to the spot – scowling. A moment later, his hand reached into his pocket for his mobile phone and he turned abruptly on his heels. Pearl watched his figure receding into the distance along the beach – and decided to follow.

Once on the promenade, Pearl found herself surrounded by a raucous group of Spanish teenagers. They blocked her path before finally parting to allow her to pass, by which time the man in the visor had seemingly vanished. Ahead, Pearl viewed only wooden trestle tables on the beach at which couples were sitting, sampling oysters on the half shell, while young children played on the shingle beach. The man in the visor was nowhere to be seen, until, glancing towards the sunken car park at old Keam's Yard, Pearl suddenly caught sight of the visor – this time in the hand of the man who was standing by a top-of-the-range silver Lexus. Its rear passenger door opened and the man got inside, turning his head towards someone already seated there.

Pearl followed on quickly, about to descend a few wooden steps leading into the car park, only to find herself confronted by a young mum, struggling to heave a toddler and pushchair up to the beach. 'Couldn't give me a hand, could you?' The young woman wiped a weary hand through a damp fringe and Pearl took charge of the pushchair. Glancing across the low sea wall towards the car cark, Pearl saw the rear lights of the Lexus flashing on as the engine started up. The man in the back seat was turning to fasten his seat belt. As he did so Pearl caught sight of a woman beside him . . . a pink jacket . . . a blonde ponytail . . .

'Thanks for your help!'

The young mum had spoken up before leaning forward to take the brake off her pushchair, and with her son now safely settled back into it, she offered Pearl the warmest of smiles. But a sudden cool breeze, blowing in with a fresh tide, sent a chill through Pearl – as did the sight of the silver Lexus slowly gliding out of the car park.

CHAPTER THREE

Throughout the twenty years of running her restaurant, Pearl had become adept at looking beyond her customers' appreciation of The Whitstable Pearl's menu, and as she went about her busy day she found herself peering straight into the lives of those who came into her establishment, carefully noting how the loud sizzle of chilli prawns might highlight an awkward silence between the couple who had ordered them, or how the overuse of mobile phones during a meal could provide a welcome distraction for those preferring not to engage with one another. Similarly, a stray look or a stolen glance would not go unnoticed and Pearl could easily recognise whether this signalled a negative response or, more often, a moment of fateful attraction which could develop after a few more glasses of Pearl's fine wines.

It was true that Pearl Nolan was a 'people person' and would always do her best to ensure her customers enjoyed their time in The Whitstable Pearl, but in the early days, the restaurant had presented a huge challenge for a young single mother with only the support of her immediate family. Now, over twenty years on, and with Pearl in her early forties, the business ticked over nicely with the help of a few trusted members of staff. As she entered her kitchen, following the rally on the beach, she found everyone fully occupied. Kitchen hand Ahmed was helping the chef, Dean, to garnish a dish of red mullet in *escabeche*, while young waitress Ruby was out on the restaurant floor and Dolly, whose culinary skills left much to be desired, was busy in the safe but nonetheless essential duty of quartering lemons to accompany oysters on the half shell. Her face lit up as soon as she saw Pearl.

'There you are!' she exclaimed.

Instantly, Pearl saw that her mother had changed her hair colour – yet again. Her fringe had been magenta before Pearl's trip to Bruges, but now it was a stunning aquatic green, which gave Dolly the look of an ageing mermaid. She instantly abandoned her lemons and leaned forward to kiss her daughter before wiping her hands on her apron and firmly clutching Pearl by the shoulders, so that she could take a good look at her. After a moment, she gave a satisfied nod. 'Good,' she said. 'You're looking nice and relaxed.'

'That's because I am.' Pearl smiled, slipping out of her jacket and hanging it up by the back door. 'It was a lovely break.'

Dolly rolled up the sleeves of the crimson blouse she was wearing and began rinsing her hands at the sink. 'I don't doubt it,' she said. 'Bruges is a wonderful old city but time away anywhere would have done you the world of good. You know what they say: a change is as good as a rest.' She turned off the tap, dried her hands and unrolled her sleeves. 'How did McGuire enjoy it?'

'We both had a great time,' Pearl said, reservedly, aware that a rapprochement between her mother and McGuire was only very recent, and therefore remained rather fragile. Dolly held an antipathy towards the police in general, not least because, in spite of her age, she remained a teenage rebel at heart and liked to rail against authority. In particular, however, she feared that Pearl's relationship with a police detective like McGuire was likely to involve her daughter in more cases – and, more importantly, put her in jeopardy – as had happened in the recent past. The fact that McGuire had demonstrated his own desire to put a distance between Pearl and his work had allowed Dolly to make an unholy alliance with him – though how long this would last had yet to be seen. Certainly, Dolly and McGuire seemed to have their work cut out in keeping Pearl away from local crime – especially since Nolan's Detective Agency had been in operation.

Dolly watched her daughter securing her long dark curls high on her head – a ritual that took place before every restaurant service. Pearl was as tall and willowy as her mother was short and stout, and the pinning up of Pearl's hair served to emphasise her slender neck and natural grace.

After checking Dean's menu and complimenting her chef on his red mullet dish of the day, Pearl turned to her mother and asked: 'What do you know about Martha Laker?'

Dolly was suitably surprised by the non sequitur but Pearl nodded back to the door and explained: 'She was on the beach at a rally this morning.'

'Rally?' Dolly frowned.

Pearl nodded. 'Did you know the Save Our Downs campaign has lost its case?'

Dolly's face set. 'Damn it,' she cursed. 'I was hoping the judge would see sense and find for the campaign.' She appeared crestfallen at the news and Pearl felt the need to console her.

'Well,' she said, 'all's not lost because it seems Martha and the Whitstable Preservation Society are going to fight on.'

'Good for them!' said Dolly. 'If Invicta Land is ever allowed to build so close to our downs there'll be no green space left in this town before long, you mark my words.'

Pearl checked their bookings for the day while asking: 'You really think it can be stopped?'

'If anyone can do it – it'll be Martha,' said Dolly, convinced.

'And why do you think that?'

'Because the woman never gives up, that's why. She's persevering, indomitable . . . and remember how hard she fought to save those old oak trees the supermarket wanted to take down? Every single one now has a preservation order on it – and rightly so. We've such a small swathe of trees across the town – and hardly any rural space – Martha Laker's just what we need.'

'A DFL,' said Pearl. Dolly looked admonishingly at her daughter but Pearl continued: 'Well, it's rather ironic, isn't it? An outsider taking up the cause?'

Dolly wrestled with this thought then conceded: 'Maybe. But a drowning man doesn't look too closely at the hand that saves him. Besides, Martha isn't exactly a blow-in. She's lived here long enough to love our town – and to fight for it – when needed.' She smiled now.

'So,' said Pearl, 'you like her?'

Dolly considered the question for a moment then admitted: 'I can't say I know her very well but what I do know I like – and I respect her. She's honest, plain-speaking, bolshie, committed—' She broke off as she saw Pearl's smile. 'What's so funny?'

Pearl was about to point out that Dolly was listing the very qualities she could have used to describe herself, when at that moment the kitchen door swung open to reveal Pearl's young waitress Ruby with a look of dread on her pretty face.

'What is it?' asked Pearl.

'Councillor Radcliffe,' said the girl ominously. 'He's just arrived with a couple of guests.'

'Has he booked?' asked Dolly.

Ruby shook her head.

'Then tell him we're full!'

'Tell him no such thing,' said Pearl calmly.

Dolly's face set. 'We don't need his custom. He's a pompous old—'

'Let me deal with it,' Pearl insisted. Moving quickly to

Ruby, the two women disappeared together through the swing doors.

Once in the restaurant, Ruby pointed out three men standing near the door. Two were sharp-suited business-men, one of whom was instantly recognisable to Pearl as a local property magnate, Gordon Weller; the other – a younger man, with short black hair and an avian look about him – was unknown to Pearl. Both men appeared to be at the mercy of local councillor Peter Radcliffe, who was addressing them loudly – and at length.

Pearl turned to her waitress. 'All right, Ruby,' she said. 'Leave this to me.'

As she moved off towards the men, Radcliffe caught her gaze. 'Ah, at last!' he exclaimed. 'I'm looking for a table.'

'For three?' Pearl raised some menus in her hand, trying to ignore the ridiculous toupee Radcliffe always wore, which had earned him the nickname 'Ratty' among his constituents.

He nodded, then paused before suggesting: 'How about the window seat?'

Pearl hesitated for a moment before: 'Fine.'

At this, Radcliffe preened and, with an expansive gesture, indicated the table to his guests. 'Take a seat, gentlemen,' he proclaimed, as if the restaurant was his own. Weller, a stocky man in his early fifties, who looked like he had enjoyed a lifetime of business lunches, took his seat first while the younger man continued to appraise

Pearl. Radcliffe pointed to her. 'May I introduce Pearl Nolan – owner of The Whitstable Pearl.'

The older man nodded. 'Gordon Weller,' he announced.

Pearl offered a polite smile to him then turned her attention to the younger man who took a seat beside Weller as Radcliffe introduced him. 'And this is Jason Ritchie.' Radcliffe took pride in adding: 'Co-director, with Gordon here, of Invicta Land. Jason's currently living in the renovated windmill close to the site.'

'Black Mill?' asked Pearl. The young businessman nodded and offered his hand to Pearl who shook it, before glancing back guiltily towards the kitchen. As she did so, she saw Dolly glaring her disapproval from the swing doors. Her mother shook her head ruefully and then disappeared back inside the kitchen.

Radcliffe offered Pearl a proud smirk 'So, these are two very important gentlemen,' he announced. 'Both of whom would like to try your famous oysters.' He held Pearl's gaze for a moment before adjusting his toupee, which looked like something Pearl's cats might have fought over.

Jason Ritchie flashed a charming smile at Pearl but she quickly produced her notepad as a distraction.

'Anything else?'

'I think three glasses of champagne might be in order,' said Gordon Weller.

'And why not?' Radcliffe smiled. 'There's certainly cause for celebration today. In fact, it's a shame I didn't bring some of my best cigars for later. You like a fine Havana, don't you, Gordon?'

'Not any more,' said the developer. 'I managed to give them up – along with the cigarettes. In the end, it was them or me,' he admitted.

Pearl saw Dolly, again at the swing doors, this time beckoning her urgently back to the kitchen. 'I'll be right back,' she said, turning with her order.

As she entered the kitchen, Dolly instantly reproached her. 'Pearl, how could you!' she hissed.

Ignoring her mother's look, Pearl handed the oyster order to Dean, hoping for kitchen efficiency to silence any further complaints. But as she approached the fridge to grab a bottle of champagne, Dolly followed, continuing in a loud whisper: 'Has that trip away softened you up?'

Pearl failed to reply and gave her full attention to pouring three flutes of champagne. Dolly moved in closer, adding: 'Allowing Ratty into this place is bad enough, but you could at least have put them on a less conspicuous table. The whole town will be able to see they're here.'

'So?' asked Pearl, setting her champagne flutes on a tray.

Dolly huffed. '"So" you're likely to get a reputation for collaborating with the enemy. Is that what you want?'

Pearl waited until Dean had finished assembling a platter of the finest Pacific rock oysters, all neatly arranged around a bowl of Mignonette sauce, before she finally responded: 'Sometimes it pays to remain neutral.'

Dolly's brow furrowed. 'And since when has profit been more important to you than principle?'

'I didn't mean financial payment.'

'Then what *did* you mean?' asked Dolly, confused.

'I meant in general.' She reached out her hand for the quartered lemons. Dolly obliged by shoving the plate on to her, while commenting: 'Still time to lace them with rat poison.'

Pearl glanced sharply at her. 'Don't you think we've had enough murders in this town?'

'Where some people are concerned, we could do with a few more.' Dolly looked at Pearl, unrepentant.

'That's not something to joke about.'

'And who said I'm joking?'

Pearl gave up on arguing with her mother and picked up her tray, heading out of the kitchen and back into the restaurant where she found a few young couples now seated around her seafood bar. Ruby, taking their orders, flashed a smile as Pearl moved on to the window table, where she settled the order in front of Radcliffe and his guests.

'Magnificent!' Ratty declared, staring down at the platter of oysters before selecting the largest for himself. 'Tuck in, boys.'

With an extravagant gesture, he tipped the oyster into his mouth and gave a single wet crunch before downing some champagne. 'Care to join us, Pearl?' he asked.

She shook her head. 'Thanks, but I'm afraid I have a restaurant to run.'

'Surely you can find a few moments to toast some good news for your town?' asked Weller, choosing an oyster for himself.

'You mean the court ruling?' Pearl asked.

'What else?' said Radcliffe brightly, offering a simpering smile for his guests. 'Nothing much slips past Pearl Nolan,' he explained. 'Not only does she own this fine establishment, she also runs a little detective agency, so there's not much that escapes her. Always got your nose close to the ground, haven't you, Pearl?'

He looked at her now, waiting for a response, but Pearl had taken exception to his pejorative description of her as a local busybody – and failed to give one.

It was left to Ritchie to ask: 'I . . . suppose having a restaurant like this does put you at the heart of the community?'

Radcliffe beamed once more and sipped his champagne. 'Rather like being a councillor,' he commented before downing another oyster.

Ritchie ignored him, still looking to Pearl for a reply. Finally, she gave it. 'I trained as a police officer,' she explained. 'It was a long time ago but nevertheless the experience still comes in useful.'

'As does your . . . friendship . . . with that local detective sergeant, I shouldn't wonder,' said Radcliffe, his smirk back in place.

'He's a detective chief inspector,' Pearl said, 'and you'll probably find it no secret that the fight against the Invicta Land development goes on?'

Radcliffe hesitated, champagne flute in hand. Pearl continued. 'Oh, sorry. Didn't you know? Martha Laker said as much in a rally on the beach this morning. In fact, she gave an impassioned speech and made it clear she intends to oppose it.'

'I'm sure she did,' said Radcliffe, unimpressed, before downing his glass of champagne. 'The woman's a loon.'

'A rather determined loon,' said Pearl.

Radcliffe opened his mouth to protest but it was Jason Ritchie who spoke. 'You're right,' he said to Pearl. 'If Martha Laker wasn't so opposed to this scheme, she'd be someone I wouldn't mind having on our team.' Radcliffe's head snapped sharply towards him but Ritchie continued. 'She's as passionate about the environment as we are about this development. It's a shame she's on the wrong side, because she's just the sort of person I'd like to work alongside at Invicta Land.'

'Perish the thought,' said Radcliffe. 'She's an inveterate self-publicist.'

'Well, publicity's important,' said Weller, finally offering his own view. His gaze met Ritchie's as he continued: 'We all need good press and she's managed that well in the past.'

Ritchie nodded. 'Yes, she's made quite a name for herself. So we could certainly take a lesson or two from her on that.'

Councillor Radcliffe frowned, confused. 'But—'

Ritchie broke in. 'It's an old cliché: developers are evil and only interested in profit. While people continue to believe that, it allows campaign groups to occupy the moral high ground and give the impression they're always seeking to preserve what's good.'

'A simpleton's view,' said Radcliffe dismissively.

'Simplistic,' said Ritchie. 'But while we're ranged on

different sides like this, it makes it harder for local people to see the truth.'

'Which is?' asked Pearl, impressed by the young developer's grasp of the situation.

'People will always need homes,' said Ritchie, 'and if a development is completed sensitively, and with the consent of local people, it can bring more benefits than disadvantages to the community.' He toyed with his glass and eyed Pearl. 'Progress doesn't have to be a dirty word.'

Throughout this exchange Weller had seemed thoughtful as he tapped his index finger against his glass but now he nodded and pointed to his partner as he decided: 'Jason's right. I remember this town some forty years ago. No one could deny it was totally run-down and dependent on its fishing industry. There were dilapidated properties wherever you looked. Even the castle was in a poor state. But look at it today – renovated with a Lottery grant, the gardens restored and all the old local dwellings gentrified? Even the smelly old fishing huts have been done up and rented out to holidaymakers. There's a burgeoning local economy – from which you're also now benefiting.' He eyed Pearl knowingly, then glanced towards her seafood bar. It was clear that the couples seated there were not locals but DFLs – that much was apparent from their accents, their bleached-teeth smiles and salon tans.

Pearl considered disputing Weller's point, then decided against explaining that there was one important drawback to Whitstable's new-found popularity: its proximity to London compromised the single thing that contributed most to its popularity – namely, its individuality. The High Street was full of quirky independent shops but they were becoming increasingly threatened by the ability of incoming chain stores to meet freeholders' rent increases. A few local campaigns had boosted the determination of local traders to fend off high rent hikes for the time being, but every local shop owner feared the day their rent might become unaffordable – the day on which they would have to vacate their premises and allow the town to become like any other 'clone' high street in the country. Pearl knew this to be true, but there was little point trying to explain it to Radcliffe and a pair of property developers, who she suspected viewed Whitstable merely as a ripe location from which to profit, not a beguiling seaside town in which to build a life. It was true Gordon Weller had been born locally but he had long since moved out to an imposing property in the neighbouring leafy parish of Chestfield – which remained safe from development, for the most part, because at least a third of the village consisted of totally unspoilt woodland.

Pearl was just about to excuse herself from the conversation when the trill of her mobile phone sounded with perfect timing. 'Enjoy your oysters, gentlemen,' she said, moving off to take the call. Checking her phone, she saw the caller was Charlie.

'Hi, Mum. How was your weekend?' Pearl's son sounded bright and animated on the line.

'Great,' replied Pearl economically, then: 'I'm at the restaurant right now.' She knew that, once reminded,

Charlie would appreciate how little time she had to chat, but still he went on: 'Has Gran told you?'

'Told me?' Pearl suddenly remembered Dolly's text from this morning and glanced back towards the kitchen, wondering how Radcliffe and the fight against a local development could possibly have eclipsed news of a favour needed by her son.

'Charlie, I'm sorry. It's full on here but she did mention you needed some help with something?'

'That's right. It's my flat.'

'What about it?'

'There's something structurally wrong with the building.'

'What?' asked Pearl, alarmed.

'Don't worry,' Charlie replied quickly, 'it's not about to fall down or anything, but it needs to be fixed straight away. The council have made an enforcement order so we've all had a notice from the landlord this morning.' He paused. 'Is it okay if I come home for a week or two?'

CHAPTER FOUR

Mike McGuire raised his face to a high-pressure shower head and allowed needle-sharp hot water to wash away the tensions of the day. His first shift back at work since the trip to Bruges with Pearl had included a session with his boss, Superintendent Maurice Welch, and throughout the tedium of Welch's lecture on the need for improved crime detection rates, McGuire had suffered a deteriorating ache in his cervical vertebrae – appropriate, considering Welch was undoubtedly McGuire's biggest pain in the neck.

The feeling was mutual. Although Welch had approved McGuire's initial secondment to Canterbury CID, he hadn't expected that the former Met officer would choose to join the Canterbury force permanently. Welch resented McGuire's experience and efficiency, both of which put his superior to shame and highlighted the fact that the superintendent was merely a big fish in an extremely small pond. If Welch could find a reason to move the DFL on, he would; he had even resorted to drafting in the services of an attractive DS as a 'honey trap' – though the plan had resulted in failure, with beautiful DS Terri Bosley subsequently moving to the Met herself. McGuire should have returned to London long before now, but one thing still kept him in Canterbury: the city's proximity to Pearl Nolan, just eight miles down the road in Whitstable. There was irony in the fact that McGuire's initial move to Canterbury had been made to help him move on from a previous relationship – but now he found himself involved in another.

Mike McGuire still couldn't be quite sure of Pearl's feelings, but what he did know was that one thing alone had kept his spirits raised today: the thought of sitting across the table from her, for a candlelit dinner booked at JoJo's restaurant on the grassy slopes of Whitstable's neighbouring town of Tankerton. The restaurant was a popular place, with a stunning panoramic view of the coastline straight out to the horizon where, by day, bleached windfarm sails turned on the breeze, and, by night, they studded the dark sky with their own mechanical stars. JoJo's had also been the setting for their first ever dinner date – and so it seemed to McGuire to be the perfect location for a special meal on their return from Bruges, somewhere to reinforce their resolution never to allow work to come between them. He had even managed to book the same table they had shared before, and he now smiled at the thought, remembering how Pearl's old suitor, her fruit and veg supplier Marty Smith, had spied them through the restaurant's plate-glass window as he had wheeled an order into JoJo's kitchen

– shocked to see the woman of his dreams on a date with another man.

McGuire turned off the shower and stepped from the cubicle. He wrapped a towel around his waist, grabbing another to dry his blond hair, and padded into the bedroom of his riverside Canterbury apartment. After getting into a clean pair of jeans he pushed open his window and stared down at the fast-flowing current of the Great Stour River that lay below it. On the opposite bank, the alfresco dining area of an Italian pizzeria looked inviting, its tables spread with red and white gingham cloths, around which couples sat, enjoying glasses of red wine in the warm evening sun. The vine-covered trellis above them extended towards a jetty from which tourists could take boat trips to visit the fourteenth-century Dominican priories on the banks of the river, finally ending up in a peaceful garden area that had been the site of the old Abbot's Mill in the city. One day, thought McGuire, he would take the trip with Pearl and become a tourist himself, if he could only avoid scrutiny from Welch. As a local private detective, Pearl had given McGuire a wealth of useful background information, as well as evidence for his cases – two things he valued in the light of recent staffing cuts. But his association with Pearl also presented him with a dilemma because McGuire had never formally registered her as an 'informant'. By doing so, he knew their relationship would have to be monitored – and he didn't much relish the idea of Welch making capital out of that. Besides,

McGuire's increasing attachment to Pearl was as much of a conundrum to him as she was herself – and he knew that was half the attraction. He didn't need to be a detective to realise that their recent trip to Bruges had brought them closer. Nevertheless, there always seemed to be plenty to keep them apart – principally, murder. But if he could just get Pearl to stick to their agreement not to allow work to come between them, McGuire felt he could keep things on an even keel – long enough, at least, to see if he could really make things work.

An even keel. He smiled at the nautical metaphor. He was a London man who had fallen for the daughter of an oyster fisherman. He knew nothing about the Kent coastline or the surrounding countryside, but with every passing day he felt the city seeping out of his system – and memories fading of a life lived before . . .

He moved away from the window, opened his wardrobe and slipped into a clean white shirt before checking his appearance in the mirror. He had acquired a tan from the trip to Bruges and his blond hair had bleached up in the sun. Wandering back into the bathroom he splashed some citrus aftershave on his jaw and slipped a heavy diver's watch on to his wrist. Noting the time, he saw he had fifty minutes before he was due at Seaspray Cottage; the route through the picturesque area of Blean would take only twenty. McGuire wasn't much for scenery but it made a nice change to be driving on roads on which fellow motorists often gave way – even when he wasn't in a police car. His mobile phone rang. Heading into the living room, his spirits rose as he wondered if it might be Pearl – but soon fell as he clocked the caller ID . . .

Some ten minutes later at Seaspray Cottage, Pearl almost missed the sound of her own phone ringing above the loud music that was sounding from Charlie's bedroom. She glanced at a clock on the wall, registering how little time she had to get ready for her date, then picked up the receiver to answer the call from McGuire, trying not to sound too stressed.

'I'm almost ready,' she lied.

McGuire's voice sounded like a bell tolling. 'I'm sorry, Pearl,' he began. 'I'm not going to be able to make it.'

Feeling physically winded by this news, Pearl slumped into an armchair. 'Why not?'

'Because—' McGuire had barely uttered another word when Pearl suddenly spoke over him.

'Hold on,' she said quickly. As she left the line, McGuire heard loud music sounding through his mobile and tapped impatiently along to it as he waited for Pearl to return.

Meanwhile, at the other end of the line, Pearl crossed the room to close her living-room door against the guitar solo still sounding from Charlie's bedroom. It was one of his own compositions, and a favourite of Pearl's, but right now she wished her son was playing unplugged and not through an amp. When she spoke again into the phone to McGuire, it was in a loud whisper. 'I've had to bring him home.'

'Him?'

'Charlie.'

'Is . . . something wrong?'

'No.' Then: 'Yes.' Pearl corrected herself and explained. 'Look, Charlie's fine but his flat needs urgent work. Something to do with the roof ties? It's an old building and he's had to move out while it's all being repaired. We've only just got home. It took for ever to load up my car with his stuff.' Pearl glanced across at the numerous bags and backpacks that had been dumped around the living room of Seaspray Cottage and admitted: 'I think he might be here for a while.' She heaved a sigh then asked: 'So, what's happened? Why can't you make it tonight?'

McGuire braced himself before explaining. 'CPS have just confirmed I'm needed in court tomorrow.'

'Tomorrow?' echoed Pearl.

'Yeah,' McGuire sounded defeated. 'I just had calls from Witness Care and the OIC – the Officer in the Case at court? I have to go through everything with him tonight, but first I have to get to the station. I've left my tablet there, on which my Policy File is stored – it's where I've logged every decision in this case. I'm really sorry, Pearl,' he said sincerely. 'I've worked on a hundred cases since this one, but it's domestic abuse and I owe it to the victim to familiarise myself with it again.'

At the other end of the line Pearl tried to make sense of this. 'I see. But . . . how come you've had such short notice?'

'Court's a circus,' said McGuire. 'Barristers don't exactly give special consideration to police officers.' He pushed his hand through his hair. 'I promise I'll make it up to you.'

'Of course you will,' said Pearl finally, raising a smile. 'I'll make sure of that.'

The blaring music suddenly came to an abrupt end and a heavy footfall down the stairs prefaced Charlie's appearance in the room. He was slipping into a clean T-shirt and checking his pockets for his mobile phone and keys.

'Going out?' Pearl asked.

'Neppy,' Charlie replied sparely. 'Just for a bit. There's a band on tonight.'

'Right.'

'Fat Angel.'

'Sorry?'

'That's the band's name. Fancy coming?'

Pearl shook her head. 'No, I . . .' She indicated the phone in her hand.

'Oh, sorry!' said Charlie quickly. He pointed towards the back door. 'I'll shoot off.' He had just begun to move off and Pearl was about to resume her conversation with McGuire, when he turned back and offered a tight smile. 'Look,' Charlie whispered, 'don't let me get in the way here, will you? I mean, I . . . do appreciate I'm crashing your world.'

As Pearl looked up at him, she realised with some irony that while she had missed having her son around at home, he had returned just as she had been looking forward to spending some quality time with McGuire – not that there seemed much chance of that with his current responsibilities.

'It's okay,' she said. 'Have a good time.'

Charlie leaned in and gave her a peck on the cheek before heading for the garden door, whistling as he went.

'Pearl?'

At the sound of McGuire's disembodied voice, Pearl glanced down at the receiver in her hand and replied quickly: 'Sorry, that was—'

'Charlie?'

'He's just gone out.'

'So you're going to be on your own?' asked McGuire guiltily.

'Don't worry about it,' she said bravely, glancing around at Charlie's bags littering her living room. 'I've got plenty to do. I'll call JoJo's and cancel the table. You get back to work.'

'Pearl?'

'Yes?'

Her voice was expectant and for a moment McGuire hesitated. Another officer in his position might well try winging the case tomorrow – but McGuire couldn't bring himself to do so. Instead he said: 'I'll call as soon as I can.'

'Good luck in court.'

'Thanks.'

McGuire summoned a smile then heard a click on the line. Realising Pearl had gone, he tossed his mobile on to the table, his smile slowly fading as he recognised his plans for the evening were, to use another nautical term, well and truly scuppered.

*

Back at Seaspray Cottage, Pearl took a deep breath as she resolved to try to tidy her living room. She was heading for one of Charlie's many bags when a phone rang – not the bell on her landline or the trill of her smartphone but the tone for the mobile she used exclusively for Nolan's Detective Agency. Before she had time to say a word, a man's voice came quickly on the line.

'Pearl Nolan?'

'Speaking.'

'I'd like an urgent appointment.'

'How urgent?'

'Right now?'

She frowned. The voice was familiar but Pearl couldn't quite place it. 'Who's speaking?'

'Take a look out of your back window.'

Pearl did so, and saw a man standing on the promenade at her garden gate. He offered a knowing smile. It was Jason Ritchie.

Five minutes later, the young developer was seated in Pearl's beach-hut office, casually dressed and idly toying with a large native oyster shell which she used as a paperweight. As Ritchie turned it over in his hand, Pearl imagined he was used to far more sophisticated desk accessories but nevertheless he commented, 'Cool,' before setting the shell down again.

'So, you wanted to discuss something?'

Ritchie sat back in his chair and took his time before replying. 'You may already know that your local council granted planning permission for the Invicta development two years ago. But the formal notice was never issued.'

'Because of the legal challenge, you mean?'

Ritchie nodded. 'Exactly.'

'Go on.'

'Gordon and I have done as much as we can in the interim – especially to . . . enhance the scheme's "green credentials"? We'll be presenting those ideas to the council soon, along with some proposals to mitigate any possible air pollution caused by extra traffic generated from a new housing development. In short,' he continued, 'we've done our level best to make this development work for everyone. Nevertheless, as you mentioned in your restaurant today, it seems Mrs Laker and her associates will continue to appeal. Ultimately, that will be a waste of time – for her as well as us.'

'How can you be so sure of that?' asked Pearl, unconvinced.

'Because a judge has already rejected all the arguments put forward – and Gordon and I are determined to see this project through. This is an important development,' said Ritchie. 'It will provide affordable housing for young people and families in this area.'

'*If* they can afford it,' Pearl countered. She paused for a moment before explaining: 'Let me tell you: my son lives in Canterbury. But I doubt that he'll ever be able to buy there and he won't be able to afford property on your development either. You know as well as I do, your buyers will come from London – just as they have here in

Whitstable – snapping up property for holiday homes. And as to your "green credentials", I'm sure you're referring to the usual hoops concerning air quality and infrastructure that you'd have to jump through in any case?'

'That's a matter of opinion,' said Ritchie.

'Or a matter of fact,' said Pearl, holding his gaze.

Ritchie shook his head and continued with a softer tone and a harder message: 'Look, whatever happens, this development *will* go ahead. We have the council on side – even the government's on side – they're under pressure to encourage more house building – and that's precisely what we're doing: building homes.'

'On green space,' said Pearl. 'You can't blame people for wanting to hold on to what little we have.'

'I don't. But the fact of the matter is we *own* the twelve acres known as Laker's Field. Would you prefer it if we just sat on it and waited for its value to increase? There's a name for that: "land banking". No one likes development companies that don't do what they say on the tin – develop. But you can't have it both ways. So what do local people want most around here? A bit of grass and woodland to walk the dog on a sunny afternoon? Or a home – for a lifetime; an asset that can be passed down through their family?' He paused, then continued: 'Sometimes it's difficult for people to view an issue properly – especially when someone's standing in the way.'

Pearl knew what he was referring to. 'The Whitstable Preservation Society is respected by local people,' she told him firmly.

'So I hear,' agreed Ritchie. 'And I am doing my home-work. I always do. Because I like to see things from everyone's perspective.'

Pearl frowned at this. 'Why?'

Ritchie looked at her. It was clear he had been brought up short by her question so Pearl clarified for him: 'You claim this development will be built whether local people want it or not. So why bother trying to see their point of view?'

Ritchie looked away then back at her. 'Because,' he began, 'believe it or not, I'm proud of what I do. And I'm proud of what we build. Invicta is a respectable company, doing good work—'

'Making good profits,' said Pearl quickly.

'And what's wrong with that?' asked Ritchie defensively. 'We create homes . . . jobs . . . and we pay our fair share of taxes. Check out our company accounts. There's no off-shore tax avoidance. Everything's above board.'

'Then why are you here?' asked Pearl. She leaned back in her chair. Ritchie fixed her with his gaze as he replied: 'I'm here because I want to win a clean fight. On the arguments – nothing more. The people in your town deserve that.'

Pearl shook her head. 'I don't understand.'

'You have a great little business of your own,' he said. 'The Whitstable Pearl? Good food, nice clientele – a warm welcome for local residents and business people – *and* DFLs like me.' He paused then tilted his head, birdlike, to one side. 'You had a chance to turn me . . . us . . . away this lunchtime – but you didn't. I've seen for myself:

46

Whitstable's a quirky little place – quaint and attractive to visitors? An anachronism when you look at a lot of seaside towns these days. But I reckon you're smart enough to know that your town needs something more than what already attracts so many visitors here: a high street full of independent shops, a clean beach and an oyster festival once a year?' He shook his head. 'No. Whitstable needs to embrace something else if it's going to survive.'

'Like?'

Ritchie shrugged before replying. 'Progress,' he said simply. 'You can't stand in its way. Things will move forward whether you like it or not. So either you move with them or you'll be left behind. Sink or swim. But it strikes me you're a survivor.'

Pearl considered him. 'You still haven't told me why you're here.'

'Let's just say I'm prepared to reward you for keeping me in the loop – helping me with some background knowledge. My . . . "homework"?'

'You mean . . . you want me to spy for you?'

Ritchie laughed. 'Now that would be plain stupid of me. If push came to shove, I think I know which side you'd be on.' He paused again. 'Nevertheless, someone as smart as you . . . could become a go-between.'

'For you – *against* the campaign?'

'For the sake of this town. Look at things closely and you'll see that this . . . "campaign" is actually nothing more than a few individuals with their own axes to grind. Some are just defending their own interests.'

'Martha Laker?'

'You said it – not me.'

Pearl realised that the heady cedarwood fragrance of Ritchie's aftershave was beginning to dominate the room. In need of some air, she got up and moved to the window, pushing it open as she commented: 'She's a thorn in your side.'

'Yes,' said Ritchie starkly. 'But she's really no different from me. A DFL. The tragedy for your town would be if local people failed to realise what Gordon and I are trying to do here – he's a local man – and together we're trying to build something of value for everyone. What's Martha Laker going to do? Conserve? No. She just wants to preserve what she's got – at everyone else's expense.'

He waited for Pearl's response. On her silence, he continued. 'She's using everyone, reducing the debate to a simple battle between local people and greedy developers; trying to persuade others to fight *her* battle.'

Pearl considered this, then returned to her seat. 'If you're right, she's doing a good job of it. Or you wouldn't be here trying to persuade me otherwise.'

'I'm here,' said Ritchie quickly, 'because I can see you're not like the sheep that follow Martha Laker. I can see you like to make your own decisions.' He picked up the native oyster shell in his hand and toyed with it again as he looked Pearl in the eye. 'You're not like a lot of people around here – small-minded, provincial.' He held her look but Pearl knew she had heard enough.

Leaning forward she took the shell from his hand. 'I'm a native,' she said firmly, 'just like this.' She raised the shell in her hand, and held Ritchie's gaze. 'This is *my* town. *My* community. *My* home. And I promise you I'll fight just as hard as the next person for all that.'

In the moments that followed, nothing could be heard but the sound of waves breaking on the shore outside. The first notes of music began drifting across from the Old Neptune pub and Ritchie took them as his cue to get up. 'And I thought you were a professional.'

Pearl frowned at this. 'What?'

'Detective,' he said casually. 'You said yourself you'd had some police training? But maybe these days you're happier serving oysters.'

He began to move to the door, then hesitated and looked back. Noting Pearl's expression, he knew he had struck a nerve. 'Or . . . maybe I'm right,' he said. 'Maybe you would really like to do something useful for this town?' He reached into his jacket pocket for something, then continued: 'If you're as smart as I think, you'll take this and we'll talk again. Think about it.' He paused for a moment, then tossed something on to Pearl's desk before turning for the door. This time, he failed to look back.

Once he had gone, Pearl got up and moved to the window, watching as Ritchie headed for the promenade. Returning to her desk, she picked up what he had left behind: a slip of paper folded around a business card. Unfolding it, she saw it was a cheque, made out to Nolan's Detective Agency, for a healthy four-figure sum that would more than cover a deposit and a few months' rent on a new flat for Charlie in Canterbury – and one that didn't require urgent building work.

Ritchie's words echoed for Pearl. If she was professional enough she might very well take up his offer and try to act as go-between in any possible negotiations between DFLs and Whitstable natives. Having listened to everything he had said, she now wondered whether perhaps she could even manage to find a compromise that suited everyone. She frowned, deep in thought, as she questioned herself: what Ritchie had said was credible but could he really be trusted? For that matter, could Martha Laker be trusted? Pearl looked again towards her window and this time saw only a fleet of small white sailboats scudding past like butterflies on the breeze. She made a decision. Grabbing her jacket, she quickly left the beach hut.

A few moments later, Pearl was on the promenade, looking in either direction for signs of Ritchie. In the distance, she finally caught sight of him: he had just reached a terrace of new-build holiday homes that overlooked the beach near to the Old Neptune. She continued on quickly, keeping her eyes on Ritchie as he mounted the stone steps that crossed the sea wall on to the street at Neptune Gap. Locals and DFLs alike were seated around trestle tables on the beach outside the pub, waiting to join in the evening ritual of witnessing the sun dropping into the sea behind the Isle of Sheppey. But Ritchie didn't linger. Instead, he was heading to a vehicle parked up outside the pub near the landlord's jeep. Opening the driver's door he got inside, slipped on some stylish Ray-Ban sunglasses and gunned the car's engine before setting off towards Island Wall – in a smart, silver Lexus.

CHAPTER FIVE

Early the following morning, Pearl's Fiat joined the steady flow of traffic heading out of town via Borstal Hill. Before reaching its crest Pearl took a sharp left turn and parked at the end of a dirt road. Sitting quietly for a few moments, she glanced across at a handful of family homes set back on one side of the same road. Shiny cars. Neat front lawns. Lives lived behind vertical blinds and net curtains. On the other side of the road, a tall privet hedge marked the boundary of a residential property, which, like many others in the area, had once been a local farm.

Pearl got out of her car and walked on towards a country lane ahead. It was well trodden, but narrowed by sycamores and an abundance of cow parsley topped with delicate white flowers, amongst which butterflies danced in the early-morning sun. Dolly refused to allow cow parsley into the house, citing its less common name of 'mother die'. Looking at the plant, Pearl now wondered if this superstition had grown up due to its resemblance to poisonous hemlock. As she walked on along the lane, it was easy to forget she was still in Whitstable and not deep in the heart of the countryside, with birdsong and the lazy drone of bees silencing the rush-hour traffic.

A hundred metres on, and the lane finally opened up into an expanse that was known as Laker's Field, after the old farmhouse to which it had once belonged. Twelve acres of hay meadow stretched out in front of Pearl, bathed gold in the morning sun, and bordered in the distance by the deep emerald fringe of Benacre Wood. Pearl allowed herself to take a deep breath while she considered the view before her. At one time, the property known as Laker's Farm had enjoyed the same view, with the sails of its old windmill creaking on the breeze. But two decades ago, the mill had begun to disintegrate and what remained of its original structure had been incorporated into the farmhouse itself to become, in due course, Martha Laker's new home. Pearl turned away from the field to view Martha's property. The substantial renovation had been sensitively done, using lime plaster on the exterior, across which ivy had been allowed to climb. A wall of vegetation seemed not only to protect the privacy of the residence but also allowed it to blend seamlessly into the landscape. The front entrance was indicated only by a narrow rustic path which disappeared into tall shrubs on either side. As Pearl struck out on it, the heady smell of apple blossom and jasmine filled the warm air.

It had been some time since Pearl had visited this area, though as a child she had sometimes played on the grassy expanse of nearby Duncan Down, sledging down its slopes in the winter and playing hide-and-seek in an area known as Trench Wood. But principally, and perhaps because Pearl's father, Tommy Nolan, had been an oyster fisherman, Pearl's own playing field had been Whitstable's pebbled beach – and the sea had become the one place where she felt most at home. Reflecting on this, she suddenly heard a rustle in the undergrowth ahead and stopped in her tracks. The sound was soon followed by the appearance of a large black dog bounding towards her. On seeing Pearl, the creature halted, leaned back on its haunches and threw up its head, its growl becoming a low bark, loud enough to raise an alarm. The animal appeared to be a sturdy Labrador but at close quarters its dark eyes seemed drooping and slightly bloodshot, which suggested to Pearl that the dog might in fact be part hound. She spoke in a quiet, calm tone while reaching into her jacket pocket.

'Here,' she whispered. The animal stopped barking but continued its low growl. Staring at her in mistrust, the creature's dark eyes moved to Pearl's hand as she loosened a sweet from the packet she had found in her pocket. She offered it. The dog inched forward, summoned by curiosity, eyes still trained upon her while it sniffed the fruit jelly in her palm. With a sudden swift twirl of a wet tongue, Pearl's offering was gratefully accepted. She breathed a sigh of relief, but in the next instant felt the sudden weight of a heavy hand clamping down on her shoulder. Turning quickly, she found herself staring up at a man standing behind her.

'What're you doing?' he asked, suspicious, as he noted the dog swallowing. The man looked familiar to Pearl – as did the red bandanna around his neck and the leather hat he wore – but Pearl's eyes shifted to the hefty axe he carried. It was made of a light wood with a carved handle. Sunlight glinted on the polished blade, which bore a decorative engraved pattern. Before she had a chance to speak, another voice sounded.

'Who's there?'

Footsteps on the path sent the dog bounding directly to Martha Laker's side. She quickly leaned down to pet the animal then frowned at what she saw.

'Ben?'

The man nodded to Martha as he explained: 'I heard the dog barking. Found someone on the path here.'

He continued to scrutinise Pearl, who paused for a moment before moving forward to introduce herself. 'I'm Pearl Nolan.'

'I know,' said Martha Laker brightly. 'The Whitstable Pearl?' She gave a half-smile then beckoned. 'Come through.'

Holding the dog's collar, Martha gestured for Pearl to follow and as they rounded a corner, the path opened up to reveal the front lawn of Martha's home. She released the dog, which immediately headed back to sit obediently at the man's side.

'So,' said Martha, 'I gather you two have just met?'

'Informally,' said Pearl, eyeing the dark-haired man in the red bandanna.

'This is Ben Tyler – my neighbour,' Martha explained. 'Ben lives close to Benacre Wood.'

'I didn't know there were any houses there?' said Pearl, turning to Tyler.

'It's a shepherd's hut,' he explained.

'And in case you're wondering,' said Martha, 'Ben has full permission from the landowner to be there.' At this, Tyler seemed to relax a little. He now gave a charming smile and took off his hat to run long slender fingers through his dark hair. There was no doubt in Pearl's mind that this was the same man who had spoken up on Martha's behalf on the beach yesterday. Returning his smile, she waited as Ben finally nodded politely, his expression softening as he turned to Martha.

'You said you needed this,' he said, offering her the axe. 'Want me to chop the wood for you?' He pointed towards a stack of heavy logs near Martha's front door but she shook her head.

'I can manage.' Reaching for the axe which Ben handed to her, she studied it, impressed. 'Your handiwork?' she asked.

Ben gave a nod. 'Carved the handle from some ash that came down in Benacre Wood.'

Pearl noted how the dog continued to stare up at Tyler, panting, almost laughing.

Martha noticed too and smiled before asking Ben: 'How d'you fancy taking Scooby for a wander?'

At this, Tyler simply nodded. 'Come on, boy.' The dog sprang up excitedly and followed on beside him.

Martha watched them go, calling after Ben: 'And thanks for this!' She brandished the axe, waiting until man and dog had finally disappeared before turning back to Pearl. 'He looks happy now,' she said, though Pearl couldn't be sure if she was referring to Ben or the dog – until she added: 'I swear Scooby loves Ben more than me.'

'Some people have a way with animals.'

'That's true,' Martha agreed. 'Do you have a dog?'

Pearl shook her head. 'Two cats.'

As Martha nodded, Pearl considered she might have been reflecting on the common trope of the single woman living with only a 'familiar' for company – and felt the need to explain: 'I took them on after their owner died.'

'Good for you.' Martha moved to the log pile and began rolling back the sleeves of her white shirt. 'D'you mind if I carry on? The wood burner's low on fuel.'

Pearl shook her head and took some time before broaching something. 'I heard you speak on the beach yesterday.'

'I know,' said Martha. 'I saw you in the crowd.'

'Ben was there too.'

At this, Martha hesitated, axe in hand. 'That's right.' She looked back at Pearl. 'He understands what we're trying to do here.'

'Saving Laker's Field from development?'

'The land no longer belongs to my family,' Martha explained, before wielding the axe high above her shoulder and bringing it down on a trunk of sycamore. She went on:

'I inherited the farmhouse but the acreage had been sold on the death of my uncle, Richard Laker.'

Pearl glanced up at the house. 'Hard to believe it was once a modest farmhouse.'

Martha looked sharply at her and asked: 'Is that a criticism?'

'Not at all,' said Pearl quickly, 'just an observation. It looks like a wonderful home.'

'You're right.' Martha's gaze followed Pearl's. 'I'd never set foot in Whitstable before, but once I came here to the farm I ploughed every penny I had into the place in order to save the original building from demolition. The farm had belonged to members of my family since 1760. Extraordinary,' she went on, laying a hand gently on the wall of her property. 'They were living here and working this land even before the French Revolution.' She reflected on this for a moment, then picked up the axe again. 'The windmill was too far gone to save and . . . what use is a mill without corn or wheat? I inherited a ruin – but now I live here.' A silence fell before Martha struck out again with the axe.

Pearl looked up towards a Juliet balcony in front of tall French windows. 'Your bedroom?'

Martha nodded and wiped a strand of hair from her brow.

'That must be a wonderful view across the field towards Benacre,' said Pearl.

At this, Martha looked slowly back. 'You think I'm fighting to save a view?' she asked. 'I am,' she admitted.

'But even if this development was located far beyond Laker's Field and Benacre Wood, I would still oppose it. You heard what I said at the rally yesterday – every word of which is true.' She fixed Pearl with a stare but in the next instant, a mobile phone sounded and Martha dropped the axe and reached inside the pocket of her jeans. Taking out a smartphone, she checked the caller ID and apologised quickly to Pearl: 'Sorry, I have to take this.' Giving her attention to the call, she answered: 'Hi, Chris, what can you tell me?' A pause then: 'That's good.' She nodded and listened further before frowning at something. 'No. We don't need permission. It's taking place on the Crown of the Down. And I told you before, it's a celebration – a pageant *not* a protest.' She nodded again. 'That's right.' Another pause. 'Of course,' she said brightly. 'And bring a photographer.' She smiled now. 'Yes. You can be sure I'll give a statement – and so will Fred Clark.' Another pause before: 'See you then.'

Martha ended the call and for a few moments seemed lost in a world of her own before remembering Pearl. She slipped the phone back into her pocket and explained: 'News editor of the *Chronicle*.'

Pearl nodded and allowed Martha to continue: 'To be honest, we've had trouble persuading the paper to put our side of the argument but there are some things they can't fail to cover.'

'A "pageant"?' asked Pearl.

'Tomorrow,' said Martha. 'On the downs. We're organising a special event to celebrate our local green space.

The land – and its history – what it means to local people.'
She paused for a moment before explaining further. 'It's
short notice so the *Chronicle*'s agreed to put up an online
story later today. That should serve to spread the word – a
rallying call.'

'For?'

'For everyone who cares, of course,' said Martha. 'And
I'm hoping that includes you.' She fixed her gaze on Pearl.
'Why else are you here?'

Pearl hesitated before offering a reply, wondering what
Martha Laker would say if she knew about Jason Ritchie's
visit and the offer he had made. But before she could reply,
a young woman approached from the path, carrying a large
wooden trug, laden with wild sage, clary and columbine.
'Martha, look what I just—' She broke off abruptly at the
sight of Pearl, and looked to Martha for an explanation.

'This is Pearl Nolan,' Martha said. 'From the restaurant
in the High Street?'

Close up, Pearl noticed how the woman's long fair
braids, slim frame and delicate features, dotted with
cinnamon freckles, made her appear far younger than her
real age – which Pearl now put at around thirty. Her baby-
blue eyes betrayed confusion but Martha smiled kindly
and said: 'It's okay.' Taking the wooden trug she drew
the woman in closer – then kissed her tenderly on the lips
before looking proudly back at Pearl. 'This is my partner,
Jane Orritt. We live here together.'

At this, Jane looked equally proud, then stared questioningly at Pearl as she asked: 'Are you . . . here to help?'

At that moment, a flock of starlings suddenly took to the air, swooping and swerving, dipping and shape-shifting before disappearing into the blue sky. Pearl suddenly remembered how, as a child, she had watched such murmurations before the birds roosted – beautiful patterns created by creatures acting together in unison. Pearl's father Tommy had explained to her how they did so for safety, just like the shoaling of fish. *There's always safety in numbers.* With that thought in mind, Pearl glanced back at Martha Laker and the expectant look on the face of her partner, Jane. She finally made her decision: 'Yes,' said Pearl. 'I'd like to help.'

Later, in the kitchen of The Whitstable Pearl, Dolly looked up thoughtfully from the prawn sandwiches she was preparing and echoed something Pearl had just told her: 'A pageant?'

'That's right,' said Pearl, 'with a medieval theme. It's being held from midday tomorrow on the Crown of the Down. It was the old pitch-pot beacon there that gave Martha the idea.'

Dolly raised her eyebrows. 'It's not "old" – it's a replica,' she said. 'It's only been there since—'

'I know,' Pearl said quickly, 'but it still harks back to other times – when beacons were lit to warn of invaders?'

Dolly nodded slowly. 'I see. So it fits with the whole idea of us . . . holding back Invicta Land?' She frowned for a moment before reminding Pearl: 'Though Invicta means "undefeated" in Latin.'

'I know that too,' said Pearl, 'but that's what the campaigners hope to remain.' She paused before confiding: 'I'm going to close the restaurant tomorrow. We'll put a sign on the door, directing customers to the downs – and we'll serve food from there – a special menu to fit with the theme.'

Dolly's face broke into a smile. 'Good for you!' she exclaimed, wiping her hands on her apron. 'What can I do?'

Pearl wasn't at all convinced that Dolly's culinary skills would be an asset to the event, so instead she suggested: 'Create some costumes with Charlie.'

'Costumes?'

'It's fancy dress.'

'How wonderful!' Dolly smiled, pointing a finger at her daughter. 'I'm glad you've finally come to your senses to support Martha.'

'And her partner, Jane,' Pearl added.

'Business partner?' asked Dolly, finishing the last of her sandwiches.

'Life partner.'

At this, Dolly looked up. 'Oh? I didn't know Martha was bisexual.'

'Is she?' asked Pearl.

'Well,' said Dolly, 'she was married at some point, and has a child, I believe. Probably grown up now . . .' She mused for a moment then looked irritated with herself. 'Not that it matters, of course. I really shouldn't go labelling people.'

Pearl frowned. 'What d'you mean?'

'About their sexuality, of course,' Dolly replied. 'After all, it's just like a piece of string – we're all at different ends of it, and maybe Martha's now more comfortable in this new relationship.' She looked up, lost in thought for a moment, then said: 'You know, the real surprise for me is that she's teamed up with Fred Clark on this campaign.'

'And why's that?' asked Pearl.

'Well, because he's so unlike Martha,' said Dolly thoughtfully. 'He usually does everything by the book. He's the type who'll try negotiating with councillors rather than protesting at County Hall. He was a civil servant – a conservative in both senses of the word. He's pro-establishment and obsessed with the past. You know the type – all for tradition? Personality wise, he and Martha are chalk and cheese.'

'Which is . . .' said Pearl, 'maybe why they complement one another?'

'Perhaps,' Dolly conceded.

'And perhaps why,' Pearl added, as a thought suddenly came to her, 'it would be difficult for Invicta Land to make an ally of either of them – if they're both on the same side?'

'Yes,' said Dolly. 'Clever move on Fred's part. If it *was* his move, I mean.'

Dolly saw Pearl's confused look and explained: 'He's a chess buff.'

'Is he?' Pearl's question invited more details but Dolly had taken on a dreamy smile as if she was thinking of something else. 'You know, I can remember being wildly in love with a girl at school.'

'Really?' asked Pearl, shocked by her mother's non sequitur.

'Yes,' said Dolly. 'I was quite sure I'd never find a man to compete. But then I met your father.' She smiled again. 'True love.' She paused and gave a small sigh before going on. 'Maybe Martha's found the same with . . .' Her lost look told Pearl she was in need of a name.

'Jane Orritt,' said Pearl. 'And yes,' she continued, reflecting for a moment, 'it certainly did look like true love.'

CHAPTER SIX

Pearl's fruit and vegetable supplier, Marty Smith, had dark good looks and a toned body gained from lifting weights at the gym and heavy crates in his shop. He also kept fit with a two-man kayak on the estuary, though he preferred the term 'tandem', as he was keen to find a female partner to fill a space in his craft – and in his life. Marty was an honest man who rose early and worked late, having single-handedly transformed his father's greengrocer's shop, Granny Smith's, into an upmarket store, Cornucopia. He now owned a large house in the neighbouring town of Tankerton and drove a convertible sports car that turned heads as it sped through the High Street. By most people's standards, Marty was an eligible bachelor, but over the years Pearl had failed to find him any more than just a casual friend and supplier. Marty, however, had never given up hope of capturing Pearl's heart and as he watched her in her restaurant kitchen, setting out items of food on platters, his gaze remained fixed on her – rather than on the carefully stacked tarts she had just created.

'Well?' she asked. 'What do you think?'

Feeling like a voyeur, Marty stammered a response. 'Oh . . . gorgeous.'

Pearl considered the food on her platter. 'Appetising?'

'Yeah,' said Marty. 'That too.' His eyes remained glued to Pearl. She was standing in front of him with the late-afternoon sunlight streaming through the window and passing through the sky-blue vintage dress she wore that was covered in tiny white seagulls. Marty was able to trace the dark outline of Pearl's long shapely legs leading up to her slim body. Her hair was pinned up with a pretty silver comb, exposing her slender neck. Marty almost sighed to himself as he followed its contours.

'Are you sure?' she asked, turning sharply.

Marty nodded. 'Oh, yes,' he said. 'Certain.'

Pearl frowned. 'Do you know what they are?'

At this, Marty looked blank.

'I just told you,' she reminded him. '*Tart de Brymlent*.' She picked up a sheet of paper and handed it to him. Marty glanced down at it as she explained: 'That's a medieval recipe for a fish and fruit pie. It was usually made for Lent, when no meat was meant to be eaten, but I happened to have a good supply of salmon and hake, and I got the rest of the ingredients from you, remember? Figs, raisins, apples, pears, prunes, dates . . . ' She smiled at him now.

Standing so close to her, Marty felt his heart was about to leap out of his chest. Incapable of speech, he managed only to nod slowly – like the village idiot he felt himself to be in that moment. Pearl took the recipe from his hand. 'What are you providing?'

'Hmm?' Marty asked, still dazed.

'For the pageant.'

'Oh . . .' He sprang back to life. 'I'll . . . come up with something special.'

Pearl put her tarts in the fridge and Marty went on: 'They want some overripe fruit for the stocks, so I'm letting them have a batch of old apricots and berries.'

'Stocks?' asked Pearl.

'Yeah,' said Marty. 'Haven't you been up there yet? The Museum Trustees have lent the organisers some old stocks for the day. You know, the medieval torture? Actually,' he went on, 'strictly speaking, they're not stocks, it's a pillory, because stocks are for putting feet in, but a pillory's for the hands and head.'

Pearl took this in as she wiped her hands on her apron. 'I didn't know that.'

'Didn't you?' asked Marty, pleased with himself. 'Well, it's just a bit of fun – we don't want any casualties, do we?'

As Pearl closed her fridge door and began washing her hands at the sink, Marty followed her there. He was still wearing a green Cornucopia T-shirt and baseball cap, both of which matched the colour of his eyes. He thought for a moment then slipped the cap from his head, wiping it across his hot brow, before clearing his throat to broach something. 'So I . . . hear you went away last weekend?'

Pearl finished at the sink and turned to see how close he was behind her. She quickly sidestepped him and moved to dry her hands, before unpacking a crate he had just brought. Though Marty paid good money to three efficient delivery boys, he always made Pearl's deliveries personally.

'Everything here?' she began, keen to change the subject as she checked the items in Marty's crate.

'Of course,' he said, observing Pearl as she unpacked several Kos lettuces, some baby cucumbers and a batch of samphire. He handed her a receipt book and, as Pearl signed, she felt his eyes upon her. 'So,' he began again, 'did you have a nice time – wherever it was you went?'

Pearl left a pause before replying. 'Bruges.'

'Eh?'

'Bruges,' she repeated. 'It's in Belgium. A lovely old medieval city.' She handed back the receipt book and took out the hair comb that had been keeping her curls in place.

Marty watched her dark hair tumble to her shoulders. 'Why d'you choose there?'

'I didn't,' she said. 'It was a surprise.'

The smile on Marty's face suddenly froze as he suspected his worst fears had just been realised. Pearl had not gone away alone – but with McGuire.

'Right,' he said. 'Well, I suppose if it had been down to you, you'd have gone for something a bit more . . . upmarket?'

Pearl failed to respond but took off her apron and moved to where her jacket hung near the kitchen door. Marty followed her again and leaned against the wall as he watched her slip into it. 'Did I tell you I'm all booked up for Dubai in September?' he said proudly.

'No.' Pearl flipped her hair from under her jacket collar.

'Yeah,' he continued. 'Nothing "medieval" about that trip. Five-star skyscraper hotel; twenty-four-hour shopping; cordon blue restaurants.' He winked.

'I'm sure,' said Pearl politely, refusing to rise to his bait.

As she picked up her bag, Marty realised he had only a limited time to act. 'Look, it's going to be a nice evening,' he said quickly, nodding his head towards the kitchen window. 'Fancy a quick drink?'

'Marty, I—'

'Oh come on, you've been working all day – and on the old fish pies. Let's go down to the beach – to the Neppy? I've got the kayak there. We could go and chill on the waves?' He began miming with an invisible paddle, and Pearl's heart sank at the hopeful look in his green eyes.

'I can't,' she said quickly, feeling it was best to dash Marty's hopes quickly rather than slowly; like ripping off a plaster, it would be less painful after the initial shock. 'I've got Charlie at home at the moment.'

Marty frowned. 'Charlie?'

'Yeah, he's got a few problems at his flat in Canterbury and it's nice to be able to spend some quality time together. You know how much I've missed seeing him.'

Marty nodded slowly. 'Yeah,' he said, also knowing how much he had missed seeing Pearl since McGuire had come into her life. He tried one last time. 'Well, why don't you *both* come and I'll treat you to some dinner?'

With one shake of her head, Pearl extinguished Marty's last hope. 'Not tonight, Marty. Tomorrow's going to be a long day.'

At this, Marty finally nodded wearily. 'Yeah, I s'pose you're right. We've all got to do our bit . . .' He gave her a knowing look as he went on: 'Against DFLs coming here and trying to take over?'

Pearl knew Marty's reference was a jibe at McGuire, but she refused to rise to it. Marty continued, seeking to drive home his point: 'No one understands this town like we do, eh? Locals. Like you and me?'

'And everyone else who'll be coming along tomorrow,' Pearl said. 'The campaign *is* led by a DFL, remember?'

'Oh, the Laker woman, you mean?'

Seeing Marty's confusion, Pearl asked: 'Did you know she inherited the farm from some distant relative? Before that, she'd never even set foot in Whitstable.'

Marty computed this and shrugged. 'Well,' he said, 'family's family, right? And that's still Laker's Field.'

'But maybe not for much longer,' said Pearl. '*If* the developers get their way.'

'Don't worry,' said Marty, determined. 'They won't. It's what tomorrow's all about, isn't it? Showing what a community can do if we all pull together?'

Pearl nodded slowly. 'Yes,' she said, 'that's *exactly* what it's about.'

Marty smiled at this, pleased they had at last found something to agree on. 'Then tomorrow is another day,' he said. Slapping his baseball cap back on to his head, he held on to that thought and the knowledge that he didn't have too long to wait before seeing Pearl again. 'Tomorrow.' he said again, before finally exiting.

A short while later, having left the evening shift to Chef Dean, Pearl headed home along the beach. The air was briny from the incoming tide and, as she passed the Horsebridge Cultural Centre on a road that had once been the route for horses ferrying cargoes of oysters from ship to shore, Pearl considered the many changes that had taken place in her town over the centuries – and within her own lifetime. Developments had sprung up everywhere – even facing the beach. Rooftops seemed higher, sea views were fewer. The horizon now included the wind farm, and yet, the green space known as Duncan Down remained unscathed at the top of the hill, managed by a group of volunteers and protected by its Village Green status. How long that would remain so for the land that bordered it, including Laker's Field, was anyone's guess, especially considering Invicta Land's ambitions.

Listening to Jason Ritchie in her office last night, Pearl realised he had been trying to convince her that his intentions were altruistic. But he was a good businessman and it was clear he had made an astute assessment of Pearl and her status within the town. One thing he hadn't bargained for was her intelligence. She paused for a moment and sat down on the old sea wall. Taking her mobile from her pocket, she found the young developer's number from the logged call to her. She had been too busy to call him today but now she marshalled her thoughts and dialled his number, listening to the ringtone as she waited for the call to connect. Ritchie's voice soon sounded on the line, but only to explain via a recorded message that he was currently unavailable. Pearl waited for a tone, then decided to ring off. Anything she had left to say to Jason Ritchie could wait – for now.

A short while later, Pearl entered her sea-facing garden and rounded her beach hut to catch sight of a seated figure, bathed in the evening sunlight. For a moment she imagined she might be looking at a ghost as she registered a stout woman in a long scarlet dress wearing a broad hat on her head from which medieval 'cover chiefs' descended to frame her cheeks. The 'ghost' then came to life as Dolly turned to Pearl and raised the wine glass in her hand. 'Well?' she said. 'Aren't you going to say hello to the Widow of Bath?'

Pearl came forward as Dolly explained, 'With Canterbury just down the road, I thought it was only right to pay homage to Geoffrey Chaucer.' She glanced towards the open kitchen door as a court jester appeared with a bottle of wine and some glasses in his hand. Seeing Pearl, Charlie dipped his tricorn hat. Bells rang from each of its corners. 'Every pageant needs a jester,' he said and smiled.

Pearl was impressed. 'This is amazing . . .' But she trailed off as a figure stepped out of her beach hut.

'Hope you didn't mind . . .' said Ruby, wearing a serving wench's gown with a low-cut neckline and a girdle laced tightly around her tiny waist. 'I just used your office as a changing room.' She curtsied and Pearl shook her head in astonishment. 'How on earth did you manage to get all this together in such a short time?'

'Oh, but there's more!' said Dolly. 'Here, take this and head upstairs.' She poured a large glass of wine and handed it to Pearl, nodding her head towards the kitchen door. 'Go on,' she said. 'I can't wait to see what you think.'

On their knowing smiles, Pearl quickly disappeared inside.

At the top of the stairs, Pearl took a sip of her wine and opened her bedroom door. On the coverlet of her bed she found a long emerald-green gown with a scalloped neckline and a thin gold chain that hung from the hips all the way to the floor. Beside it was a *hennin*, the conical headdress and veil once worn by aristocratic women in the Middle Ages. It was covered in red satin with a billow of green chiffon issuing from its point. After slipping it on to her head, Pearl held the dress up against herself and checked her appearance in the mirror. She couldn't help thinking back to Bruges – to the hotel room in the fairy-tale castle on the river – and McGuire . . .

Setting the dress and *hennin* carefully down again, she now took another sip of wine and picked up her phone to dial a number.

After a few rings, McGuire answered.

'How's the court case going?' Pearl asked.

'Adjourned,' he explained. 'But there's still a good chance we'll get the right verdict.'

'Good.' Pearl spoke quickly now: 'And what're the chances of you getting over to Whitstable tomorrow afternoon?'

'For?'

'A pageant.'

On the other end of the line, McGuire frowned. He had just emerged from a lift and was facing a labyrinth of corridors in Canterbury Police Station. After a long day, he thought he might be imagining things.

'Pageant?' he queried.

'It'll be fun,' Pearl went on. 'A celebration. Up on the downs. Medieval.'

'Medieval—'

'And for a good cause,' she said quickly, not allowing him a chance to speak. 'Besides,' she went on, 'I want to see you.'

McGuire smiled at this, hoping he wasn't imagining things after all. 'Me too.'

A young DC suddenly passed him in the corridor and McGuire lowered his voice to a whisper. 'I think I can get away for a few hours,' he said softly.

'Great,' smiled Pearl, before remembering. 'Oh, and . . . it's fancy dress?'

McGuire considered this. 'No problem,' he said, unfazed. 'I'll come as a policeman.'

CHAPTER SEVEN

The Crown of the Down was a high clearing on a section of downs that was now protected by Village Green status. It was also a spectacular vantage point from which to view Whitstable's coastline and, to the west, the silhouette of the Isle of Sheppey snaking out towards the horizon. Down through the centuries, Kent's shoreline had been studded with pitch-pot beacons that had been lit to warn of impending invasion by sea, and while Dolly had been correct in saying that the beacon presiding over the downs was a modern-day replica, it nevertheless made for a natural centrepiece for the Save our Downs medieval pageant.

Martha's rallying cry had resulted in a fair number of people arriving in full medieval costume, including students from the local circus school who provided a colourful performance: juggling, tumbling and stilt-walking. A group of musicians played a lively old English folk song. Dressed as Robin Hood, the singer was keeping time on a *bodrhán* while his Merry Men accompanied him on flute, lute and fiddle. Stalls had been set up, together with a large tent marked *Victuals and Ale*, and a great trade was being done by The Whitstable Pearl stall on which Charlie was shucking oysters, Ruby taking payment and Dolly, as the Widow of Bath, making short work of Pearl's tarts. Already on her third, she mumbled to Pearl, 'I have to say, these are absolutely irresistible.'

'So I see.' Pearl sighed knowingly, realising she would soon have to find something for Dolly to do or risk her special *tarts de Brymlent* running out before everyone had arrived.

'Can I try one?' The voice behind Pearl sounded muffled. On turning, Pearl saw the reason why. A tall figure was dressed in a jousting outfit, face obscured by a metal knight's helmet.

Lifting the visor, Dolly smiled and said: 'Good morrow, Marty!'

Pearl offered him one of her tarts but as Marty went to reach for it, he paused as he remembered he was wearing heavy gauntlets. He gave a helpless look. 'Don't suppose you could oblige?'

Pearl helped Marty with the tart. As it met his lips he took a large bite, then munched appreciatively. 'Mmmm. Nice combination,' he said. 'Your fish. My fruit?' He winked, then made the mistake of nodding, which caused his visor to slam shut.

Pearl frowned, concerned. 'Aren't you hot in there?'

'Yes,' Marty admitted, pushing his visor back up with

his gauntlet. 'Lucky I didn't opt for the full body armour. How they used to fight in this lot, I'll never know.' He clanked uncomfortably and after the visor slammed shut once more, he decided to take off the helmet.

'That's better.' He sighed with relief. 'Can I leave this with you, Charlie?'

'Sure.' Pearl's son took the helmet and deposited it behind the stall before suggesting: 'Looks like you might have room for one of these now?' He offered a platter of oysters to Marty, who raised his hand, then stared down again at his heavy gauntlet.

'Here,' said Pearl, tipping an oyster into Marty's mouth. He closed his eyes, smacked his lips and sighed once more. 'Heaven.'

'And we've plenty more here.' Ruby smiled, indicating the bivalves stacked on beds of ice.

'What did you contribute?' asked Pearl.

Marty nodded across to his own stall on which staff members, dressed in their signature green T-shirts, were setting up a magnificent cornucopia of colourful fruit. 'What do you think?' he asked.

'You've done this event proud,' said Pearl.

At this, Marty beamed at her, adding: 'I'm also donating coconuts for the shy.' He waited for a further compliment but Pearl's attention had been stolen by the sight of Martha Laker, dressed as a medieval Queen of Spades, with Jane, beside her, as Queen of Hearts – both sporting respective emblems on their bodices. Martha smiled and approached.

'Do I spy another member of our royal family?' she

asked, eyeing the emerald-green gown and Pearl's *hennin* firmly planted on her head. 'You look every inch a fairy-tale princess. Don't you think so, Jane?' The Queen of Hearts beside her nodded her agreement.

'The costume was chosen for me,' Pearl explained, gathering the long chiffon train that flowed from the headdress and looking at her mother, who said: 'Well done for managing such a great turnout.'

'It's a community endeavour,' Martha insisted.

'Yes,' said Pearl, remembering, 'but your publicity clearly worked.'

Martha looked around at the crowds. 'We're expecting far more.'

'Publicity?' asked Pearl. 'Or people?'

'Both,' said Jane.

Martha nodded, 'I must say, I was grateful for Chris's story.'

'Chris?' asked Pearl, before remembering the phone call she'd overheard at Laker's Farm. 'You mean the reporter you were briefing yesterday?'

Martha nodded and indicated a young man in his mid-twenties who, with an older couple, was chatting to the Reverend Prudence Lawson of Whitstable's St Alfred's Church. Rev Pru, as she was more commonly known, was a pretty, energetic woman with a penchant for miniskirts, but today she was fully attired for the occasion in an ornate surplice that suited the medieval theme.

'That's the Latimer family with Rev Pru,' said Jane. 'Our local media hierarchy.'

Martha fixed her gaze on the trio but it was Dolly who explained for Pearl's benefit: 'Bill Latimer's the owner of the *Kent Chronicle* newspaper, and his wife . . . Oh, what's her name?'

'Olivia,' said Martha. 'And Chris is their son.'

She continued to eye them while Dolly went on: 'Of course, you're right. Olivia was a ballet dancer. Professional. Until she had a bad car accident. She was in hospital for months and there were rumours she might never walk again – let alone dance. She was in a wheelchair for a very long time.'

'Yes,' said Martha, 'but I suppose ballet gives you a great discipline. She certainly found the determination to pull through.'

'True,' said Dolly, 'though she was never able to get back to her career. Shame.' She paused as she remembered something. 'I once saw her dance Odile in *Swan Lake*, at the Marlowe in Canterbury. Years ago now, of course, but she was superb. Maybe it was just too hard for her to consider taking a lesser role than prima ballerina.'

'So . . . she gave up dancing?' asked Pearl.

'Yes,' said Dolly. 'Must have been a wrench but she found other things in life to focus on.'

'Art,' said Martha. 'She's a very good portrait painter.'

'And a very good mother,' said Dolly. 'I remember Chris Latimer was at boarding school at one time but he came home once his mum gained more mobility. She's devoted to him.'

Pearl looked across at the couple, who were conspicuous for their lack of medieval costume. Bill Latimer was an attractive man, tall and slim in a lightweight linen suit, though he appeared slightly stooped as though having spent a lifetime hunched at a desk. His wife was a fragile beauty with fine dark features, a delicate mouth and eyes hidden by large framed sunglasses.

'There's a certain sadness about her, don't you think?' said Dolly. 'I wonder if she ever recovered properly from that accident.' She took another of Pearl's tarts.

Jane frowned, troubled. 'I wish she'd come and see me.'

As Pearl turned to her, Martha explained proudly: 'Jane's a homoeopath. Fully registered. She has a good reputation for putting all her patients back on form.'

Martha smiled at her partner but Jane said: 'I've told you before; it's not me. It's the homoeopathy.'

'I don't doubt it,' piped up Dolly. 'I've been using homoeopathic remedies for years.'

'Oh, come on,' said Marty, as though his leg was being pulled. 'Everyone knows that's a load of quackery.'

'Typical doubting Thomas!' said Dolly, but Jane tried to gently defuse the situation.

'It's okay,' she said. 'A lot of people think the same, but I can assure you I wouldn't be practising if I did. I'm afraid the scientific community struggles to understand how highly diluted substances can possibly affect anyone's constitution. Nevertheless, lots of GPs are also trained homoeopaths, and its central concept whereby a substance may be harmful in large doses, but beneficial in small amounts, is well documented in biology – and also toxicology.'

'Treating like with like,' Dolly announced to Marty – as though to a child.

Jane nodded. 'You'll find this in conventional medicine too, with allergens like pollen being given to hay fever patients, for example, to desensitise them.'

Marty still looked sceptical. 'Mind over matter,' he said. 'Placebo effect.' He smiled at Pearl, proud of himself for remembering this.

'In that case,' said Jane, 'why would homoeopathic remedies work for very young children and animals?'

Marty looked suitably stumped as he searched unsuccessfully for a reply. A different voice finally offered one: 'I can assure you, there are many racehorse trainers who rely on homoeopathy for the well-being of their race stock.'

Turning, they saw Bill Latimer smiling behind them. 'I did a feature on that once for the *Chronicle*,' he explained. 'Fascinating stuff.' He gave a wave and a smile to his wife and son who were still standing with Rev Pru by the beacon, then he glanced quickly around at the crowds. 'Looks like you've managed to pull off another successful event,' he said to Martha.

'And I'm hoping you'll be covering it,' she said. 'It would be rather hard for you to ignore?'

'Not me,' said Bill. 'The *Chronicle*. We're not exactly synonymous. I've told you, Chris has all but taken over the paper now.'

Martha glanced across at the reporter, who was still talking to his mother, and said, 'He was meant to bring along a photographer.' Edgy, she looked around in an effort to find one.

'That'll be me,' Bill explained. He produced a camera from his pocket. 'The paper doesn't run to such things these days.'

'Well, at least you're still in business,' said Dolly brightly, brushing crumbs from her gown.

'Only just,' said Bill. 'We're under a lot of pressure.'

'From online newspapers?' Pearl asked, offering him a complimentary oyster. 'There seem to be so many of them these days.'

'That's true,' said Bill. 'We're online too, of course, but many of our competitors don't have to pay for offices as we do.' He chose an oyster for himself, tipped it into his mouth, swallowed and smiled at Pearl. 'Delicious. But then I should expect nothing less. I've read so many reviews of The Whitstable Pearl, I must come in some time with my wife.' He stared across towards the beacon, where Rev Pru was now talking to Chris Latimer; Olivia's gaze was fixed on Bill. She gave him a smile.

'You'll be very welcome,' said Pearl, but before she could add another word, a young man's arrival caused Martha to exclaim: 'Simon!'

Pulling the young man closer, Martha held him tightly as she asked: 'Have you just got here?'

An older man appeared and answered for him: 'Yes. We got settled into the cottage first.' The man was in his late forties, with an athletic build and close-cropped hair that helped to mask the fact it was receding.

He leaned forward and gave Martha a chaste kiss on either cheek.

'This is Adam Stone,' she said. 'And our son, Simon.'

The tall young man gave a friendly smile but his father managed only a polite nod, which failed to conceal the stress he was clearly feeling in that moment. His whole expression was taut, while in contrast, Simon seemed as relaxed as his mother, whom he resembled, with an unruly mane of dark hair falling almost to his shoulders. Martha stared up at her son with obvious love as she said: 'It's so good to have you back.' She was still gazing at Simon when she seemed to remember Adam, and felt the need to clarify: 'In England, I mean, and for the event today.' For the benefit of everyone else, she explained: 'Simon lives in France with his dad.' Her arm tightly encircled her son's shoulder and for a moment, to Pearl, they looked like twins. 'I'm very proud of him,' she went on. 'Especially of his activism.'

Charlie overheard this. 'Activism?' he echoed, curious.

'I'm involved in a few campaigns,' Simon explained, 'highlighting climate change.'

Charlie smiled approvingly. 'In France?'

Simon nodded but it was his father who replied: 'We live in Toulouse.'

'My son was arrested recently in Paris,' Martha said proudly.

'But not for long,' his father added.

Simon explained: 'The authorities were keen for us not to gain any capital from it.'

'They never are,' said Jane, offering an innocent smile. 'How long are you back for?'

'I'm not sure—' Simon began, breaking off as his words clashed with those of his father who said simultaneously: 'Not long.'

Simon remained silent while Adam reminded him, 'You've still got your place at uni.'

'I know,' said Simon, clearly torn. 'But I told you, I may take another year off to do some voluntary work.'

'Here?' asked Pearl.

Simon nodded. 'I've been helping some of the environmental groups: Greenpeace and Friends of the Earth.'

'Well done you!' said Dolly.

'What're you planning to study?' asked Charlie.

Before Simon could explain, his father replied for him again: 'Si's got a place at the Faculty of Medicine at the Sorbonne.' Turning to his son, he added: 'But they won't hold it for you for ever.'

As Martha continued to gaze proudly at her son, Simon returned her smile. 'I really need to decide where I'm going to be based.' He looked between his parents and Pearl guessed this decision involved more of a difficult choice between parents than countries.

Adam knew it too and closed down the conversation by suggesting: 'Why don't we get something to eat?'

'Good idea,' said Dolly. 'Oysters, anyone?' She offered a platter – and a choice of her own: 'Or there's Pearl's medieval tarts?'

Adam opted for an oyster while Simon tried a tart,

taking a bite before signalling his approval. After taking payment, Pearl waited for Adam's response to her oysters.

Finally it came: 'That's as good as any in Brittany,' he declared.

Dolly raised a warning finger. 'Careful,' she said. 'We're very proud of our local oysters.'

'Yes,' Pearl agreed, 'we're a small town but we have a lot to be proud of.'

'And that,' said Jane, 'is something on which we can all agree.' She looked between Adam and Martha, clearly hopeful that some diplomacy on her part might create a détente – for now.

A few minutes later, the music that had been sailing on the breeze for some time suddenly came to an end. Chris Latimer from the *Chronicle* came across, checking his watch, as he announced to Martha: 'Almost twelve o'clock. Time for you to light the beacon.'

Martha glanced around the crowd, frustrated. 'Has anyone seen Fred Clark? He should have been here long before this.'

Bill Latimer looked around. 'Not exactly Fred's sort of thing, is it?' he said, vaguely amused.

Martha eyed him coldly. 'He agreed to take part,' she informed him. 'And he has an important role to play in this – as we all do.' As she held Bill's look, the smile on his face seemed to melt beneath the fire in her stare. At that moment, a number of people emerged from the beer tent, including some press photographers with cameras slung about their necks. Martha's dog, Scooby, suddenly took off towards the entrance to nearby Trench Wood, only to reappear again, this time walking obediently at Ben Tyler's side.

'Martha?' called Chris Latimer, beckoning her to join him near the beacon. Troubled, she looked back at Jane, who nodded. Taking this as a sign they could wait no longer, Martha put down the cup in her hand and headed purposefully across the grass to the beacon.

As she took up her position, a young circus performer came forward and offered her a flaming torch at the end of a long pole. Voices were silenced. Finally Martha spoke. 'Thank you all for coming,' she began. 'For celebrating, together, this area of land – our Crown of the Down – which is now protected by Village Green status. It is precious land for the use of all, and protected from development for generations to come. That status wasn't just awarded. It was acquired – fought for – by people who cared enough to want to save this green space for future generations. Throughout history, people have always fought for what they value. Rarely is anything given – it has to be earned – and defended with determination, commitment and strength of purpose. We recently suffered a setback to our campaign but we continue with our own fight because we know it is worthwhile. In the next few weeks we will need to come together once more to show our own sense of purpose. We will use everything available to us to get our message across to others to join us. So I'm pleased to see our local media are here today to help spread our message. You know as well as I do that the people of our town deserve not only free access to this land here but to Laker's Field also – and to the truth. So if you don't tell it – *I* will.' She fixed the crowd with a steely glare. Camera shutters clicked and a TV news crew jostled into place.

A voice piped up. 'That's it, you tell 'em, Martha!'

Another: 'Martha, Queen of the Downs!'

Martha's expression softened with this support. 'I was hoping that Frederick Clark from the Whitstable Preservation Society would be here to light this beacon for us today but . . .' She looked around, disappointed, before continuing: 'We will remain united in fighting Invicta Land and—' She broke off suddenly as she saw onlookers were beginning to make way for someone. Glinting in the sunlight, a gold crown was bobbing above heads, moving towards the beacon where those assembled finally separated, revealing the crowned figure to be Frederick Clark.

A broad smile spread across Martha's face. 'At last,' she said, relieved. 'Where would a queen be without a king – and where would our campaign be without . . . Frederick Clark!'

A loud cheer went up. Frederick looked at Martha, then at all those gathered. An awkward expression on his face suddenly transformed into one of purpose. He took the flame offered by Martha and spoke in a commanding voice: 'Thank you all for coming today. I am, as many of you know, a man of tradition. And the tradition of signalling, by using a fire lit upon a hill, is an ancient one. In the Bible, in the Book of Jeremiah, we can read that a "sign of fire" was a warning of evil to come. The prophet, Isaiah, spelled out the disasters, ending with the words: "till ye be left as a beacon upon the top of a mountain".' Frederick stared out towards the coastline as he went on: 'Not since 1066 has an invading force crossed the water to land upon our shores. Tradition has served us well. Tradition is important. It will be our guide.' After another pause, he raised the flaming pole above his head and then used it to light the beacon.

A cheer went up and Frederick called out in a loud voice: 'Save our downs!'

The chant came back from all those assembled: 'Save our downs!'

The band struck up once more and the circus performers resumed their tumbling and acrobatics. Pearl was reflecting on what she had just witnessed when a voice suddenly asked: 'Fancy some mead?'

She turned to see Marty with two large beakers in his hands.

'I . . . don't think so,' she said. 'It's only just gone midday.'

'Yes,' said Marty, 'so the sun's past the yardarm.' He gave a lopsided grin and looked down at the beakers in his hands. 'Well, if you don't like mead, I can always get you something else?' He indicated the *Victuals and Ale* tent. 'Come on,' he said, nudging Pearl, a little too roughly for her liking.

He took another sip of his drink but his grin began to fade as he realised Pearl was no longer paying attention. Instead, she was looking straight ahead – at Mike McGuire.

CHAPTER EIGHT

As Pearl took off across the green towards Mike McGuire, Dolly witnessed Marty Smith's face collapse like a punctured balloon.

'Here,' she said, offering him the consolation prize of another oyster. But Marty declined with a sharp shake of his head and downed both beakers of mead in his hands before slamming them down on to The Whitstable Pearl's counter and heading off back to the *Victuals and Ale* tent – alone.

As Pearl reached McGuire, the detective smiled, taking note of the costume she was wearing and the breeze catching the chiffon train that fell from the point of the *hennin*.

'I'm letting the side down,' he said. He was wearing an open-necked shirt and jeans – a jacket thrown across his shoulder.

'Don't worry,' said Pearl. 'You're not the only one who's failed to dress for the occasion.' She nodded towards Chris

Latimer talking to his mother, Olivia, while her husband took photos of Martha and Frederick by the pitch-pot beacon. Bill gestured for Martha to move off nearer to some trees – positioning her against a woodland backdrop – and Pearl turned back to McGuire to ask: 'Have you just come off duty?'

McGuire nodded. In fact, after a fair amount of persuasion he had managed to swap shifts with a fellow officer, but said only: 'Free all afternoon. So, what's the plan?'

Pearl checked to make sure that Charlie, Ruby and Dolly were all busy at The Whitstable Pearl's stall, then took hold of McGuire's arm. 'Let's start,' she said, 'with a walk in the woods.' She smiled mischievously.

Moments later Pearl and McGuire had left behind the crowds as they took a path through the trees. When she was sure they were finally alone, Pearl slipped off her headdress and turned to face McGuire. He pulled her towards him and held her close before kissing her. The sounds of the old English folk music playing at the pageant slowly faded into the distance, to be replaced with birdsong and the drone of bees.

As they finally broke away, McGuire scanned Pearl's face, and she asked: 'Worth the wait?'

He returned her smile, pushed her dark curls back from her face and noted she was wearing the natural pearl earrings he had once bought her as a gift. He leaned forward and gently kissed her neck.

'I'm sorry about the other night,' he whispered. 'After everything we said—'

Pearl put a finger to his lips. 'It's okay. I understand.'

His eyes searched hers. 'Do you?'

She nodded. 'There are always going to be times when things get in the way – your job, my family. That's Life.' She smiled then went on. 'It's seldom perfect. But I do want us to spend more time together – and we will. That's why I invited you here today. I don't have to be on the stall all day so we could . . .' She raised her eyebrows.

McGuire looked at her. 'Here?'

Pearl smiled. 'Just a little further on, there's a small . . . secluded . . . patch of meadow. Unless, that is,' she hesitated, 'you suffer from hay fever?'

McGuire took her hand. 'Come on.'

They headed further across the downs as McGuire asked: 'So what's today all about? This pageant?'

'Community spirit,' said Pearl proudly. 'Local people sticking together to fight a housing development.'

'I see,' said McGuire sparely.

Pearl looked at him, curious. 'What do you see?'

McGuire gave an innocent shrug. 'I don't know enough about it,' he said diplomatically. Pearl took this for evasiveness. 'You've come across this kind of protest before?'

McGuire eyed her and said knowingly: 'Eco toffs?'

Pearl frowned at this, but McGuire went on. 'Look, if you really want to know, I once had to police a protest in London. It involved kids occupying trees.'

'And?'

'And it turned out they were putting themselves on the line – risking arrest and prosecution – all for a bunch of champagne swampies who lived nearby.'

Pearl looked appalled. 'Champagne—'

'NIMBYs,' said McGuire, speaking over her. 'Not In My Back Yard.'

'That's not what's going on here,' said Pearl firmly.

'No?' McGuire didn't look too convinced.

'No.' Pearl repeated.

'Okay,' said McGuire with a shrug. 'But everyone knows we need more housing and no one wants it if it means sacrificing some green space on their doorstep. That's NIMBY-ism.'

Pearl stopped suddenly in her tracks. 'All right,' she said crisply. 'Go on. Dole out the usual insults and discredit everyone's efforts!'

McGuire was taken aback by her keen sense of offence. He opened his mouth to speak. 'Pearl—'

But she cut in quickly: 'What's so wrong with being a NIMBY?' she asked. 'If we all took an interest in what happens in our "back yards" we might just be able to say "no" to much more.'

McGuire noted her passion and put his hands up in surrender, trying to make amends. 'Okay. I'm sorry,' he said gently.

'For?'

'Upsetting you.'

'I'm not upset.' Pearl took a deep breath, looked away,

and then back at him as she tried to make sense of her feelings. 'I'm disappointed,' she said finally. 'I thought you'd understand. But it seems I was wrong.' She started to move off. McGuire went after her.

'Pearl.'

She halted suddenly but not on McGuire's instruction. He noted her reaction. 'What is it?'

Putting a finger to her lips, Pearl silenced him, whispering: 'Did you just hear something?'

'Like what?'

Pearl said nothing but tilted her head as she tried to focus on a certain sound. But whatever it was that had caught her attention seemed to have vanished.

'I could have sworn I heard voices,' she explained. 'Maybe I was mistaken.'

McGuire now listened – then shrugged. 'It was probably just the wind in the trees.'

Pearl nodded. 'Yes,' she agreed. 'But . . . I'm sure I—' She broke off abruptly at the sound of a woman's muffled scream. Exchanging looks, she and McGuire moved quickly on in its direction, reaching the entrance to the secluded patch of meadow just as another smaller scream subsided. McGuire stepped forward but Pearl laid a hand on his arm. Gesturing for him to stay back, she pointed to something through the wall of trees that lined the meadow's entrance. A familiar leather hat lay upon long grass, almost hidden by wildflowers.

'Tyler . . .' she whispered.

'What?' asked McGuire.

'Ben Tyler,' Pearl explained. 'I met him yesterday.' Peering closer through the trees, Pearl and McGuire watched as Martha Laker's neighbour raised his body from a carpet of long grass scattered with blood-red poppies and oxeye daisies. His chest was bare, brown and glistening with sweat. He leaned up on his elbow and a smile spread across his handsome face as he slipped a long blade of grass into the corner of his mouth. Lying close beside him, a woman now got up and slipped the strap of her sun-top over her shoulder before she returned Tyler's smile and kissed him – long and hard.

'I don't believe it . . .' said Pearl under her breath.

'Believe what?' said McGuire, becoming increasingly confused.

'That's Gloria Greenwood,' said Pearl. 'She runs Pets' Parlour in the High Street. I saw her only the other day—' She broke off and gave a small shrug. 'But then, I suppose Ben does have a way about him.'

McGuire shot her a look. 'What kind of a "way"?'

'A certain animal magnetism,' said Pearl, musing. 'He's a country man. Martha's dog adores him.'

'And who's Martha?'

'Martha Laker, leader of the Save Our Downs campaign.' Looking back at McGuire, Pearl made a decision. 'Come on,' she said, 'let's go back and I'll introduce you to her. She might just be able to enlighten you about a few things.'

McGuire's knowledge of rural idylls ran only to a few short strolls in city parks, but he was more than willing to lose himself in a meadow on the downs – with Pearl. He glanced back towards the woodland and tried to get Pearl back on track. 'But . . . I thought we were going to—'

'We were,' said Pearl. 'But not now – not unless you want Ben and Gloria to think we're spying on them?'

McGuire heaved a sigh, gave up and reluctantly followed Pearl back the way they had come. After all, the day was still young.

Five minutes later, on seeing Pearl and McGuire returning to the pageant, Marty Smith downed the drink in his hand and gave a dark, brooding look before disappearing back into the beer tent. Martha was right: scores of people had arrived for the event – just as she had predicted – but they also included Councillor Peter Radcliffe and his wife Hilary. Pearl tried to avoid the councillor's gaze but there was no escaping him.

'Ah, princess for the day, are we?' Radcliffe smiled smugly, noting Pearl's gown and headdress.

'And you?' asked Pearl, noticing that he hadn't bothered to come in costume at all – although Hilary Radcliffe was dressed as a female musketeer in thigh-high black boots, a low-cut mini-dress emblazoned with a fleur-de-lis and a wide-brimmed hat, complete with white plume.

Radcliffe looked proudly at his wife and explained: 'Hilary's got into the spirit of things, but I thought it would be rather unseemly for a councillor to be caught in fancy dress.' His gaze shifted to McGuire. 'I see you think the same way, Inspector?'

'Chief Inspector,' said McGuire.

'Oh, that's right,' said Radcliffe. 'Credit where credit's due. Here on duty, are we?'

'No,' said McGuire starkly.

'Good,' Radcliffe replied. 'There's no need to police the event. It's not as if we're expecting any trouble today. After all, it's just a "celebration".'

At that moment, the music came to a sudden end as two suited figures appeared, mounting the slope to the Crown of the Down.

'Oh no,' said Pearl under her breath, as she recognised Gordon Weller and Jason Ritchie. 'What are *they* doing here?'

'I invited them,' Radcliffe announced proudly. 'This is, after all, an inclusive event.' He looked between Pearl and McGuire – his gaze lingering on the police detective as he said pointedly, 'DFLs welcome, I see.' He gave one of his simpering smiles. 'Allow me to introduce you, Chief Inspector; this is Gordon Weller and Jason Ritchie of Invicta Land – the development company responsible for bringing new homes to our town.'

Jason took the first move and stepped forward to offer his hand to McGuire – but it was another voice that spoke.

'You're not welcome here,' said Marty Smith gruffly.

Turning, Pearl saw Marty standing with yet another full beaker of mead in his hand.

'No . . .' she said under her breath.

But Weller seemed unperturbed. 'I think you'll find we're as entitled to be here as anyone,' he said. 'This is public land – with Village Green status.'

A murmur went around the crowd. This time, Jason spoke – and for everyone's benefit. 'Look,' he began, 'we don't want to spoil anyone's entertainment today, but we'd appreciate it if you could give me a few moments to explain—'

'Didn't you hear?' Marty broke in, stepping forward unsteadily. 'I said—'

'Okay,' said McGuire, making a quick assessment of the situation. 'Calm down.'

McGuire's words only served to further rile Marty, whose eyes narrowed as he went on: 'And who are *you* to tell me what to do? You've no right to be here either.' He looked between McGuire and the developers. 'Or did they book you for a bit of police protection?'

A murmur went round. 'Now, look—' said McGuire.

But this time it was Pearl who broke in. 'He has every right to be here.'

'Oh yeah?' said Marty.

'Yes,' Pearl insisted. 'I invited him.'

Marty's face creased like a toddler about to throw a tantrum.

'Go and cool off,' Pearl ordered him. In the next instant, she grabbed the beaker from his hand and for a brief moment, Marty looked as though he was about to do as he'd been told. He stepped away, only to turn back quickly on his heels and take a powerful swing at McGuire. Still unsteady on his feet, his fist met with Ritchie's jaw instead, and the young developer staggered back under the force. A sudden loud cheer went up.

Radcliffe pointed at Marty but his words were directed to McGuire: 'Arrest that man! '

'He didn't mean it,' Pearl protested.

'Oh yes I did!' yelled Marty. The crowd cheered again and Marty turned to them, emboldened by their support.

'Take it easy,' said McGuire calmly, as he reached out to take Marty's arm.

'Get your hands off me!' Marty shouted.

'Let me deal with this,' said Pearl, stepping in.

But Radcliffe railed. 'No! There's a senior police officer here and that was assault.'

Dolly stepped in now with a view of her own: 'The developer got in the way.'

Pearl ignored Dolly's comment and explained to Radcliffe: 'DCI McGuire is off duty.'

'I don't care,' said Radcliffe. 'I want that man arrested. Now!'

He pointed at Marty but it was Ritchie who stepped forward. 'It's okay,' he said, rubbing his jaw. 'No harm done.'

As Ritchie brushed down his jacket, Pearl saw Marty looking broodily at McGuire. She turned to the police detective and whispered: 'Look, maybe you being here is only making things worse?'

McGuire looked at Pearl askance. He'd only just arrived but already things were going badly wrong. Before Pearl could explain further, Marty announced: 'She's right. You're not needed here. You're an outsider. So get lost!'

At the sound of more encouragement from the crowd,

Marty now turned his attention to the developers. 'And as for *you* . . .'

He raised his hand and started to move forward but McGuire warned him: 'Take one more step and you'll be under arrest.'

A hush went around the crowd.

'McGuire—' warned Pearl.

But Radcliffe broke in. 'Go on, Inspector. Do your duty. Arrest that man!'

'Just let him try,' said Marty, eyeballing McGuire before he turned to the developers and waved a shaky finger at them, like a conductor's baton. 'I warned you both. But if you won't listen, there's only one place for you.'

'Oh yes?' said Weller, seemingly unconcerned. As a large stocky man, he began shaping up to Marty. 'Surprise me,' he said finally.

At this, a tense stand-off followed, before, in one sharp move, Marty suddenly leapt upon Weller, grabbing him by his jacket collar and attempting to drag him away.

'Oh no,' wailed Pearl. 'Marty, let him go!'

But Marty ignored her and with an arm curled around Weller's neck, he continued to struggle the developer across to the pillory where the older man protested, fighting for breath. 'Take your hands off me . . .'

Cameras began to click. Pearl moved towards the brawling pair but McGuire was quicker. Grabbing hold of Marty's arms, he managed to free Weller while forcing Marty's hands around his back.

'What are you doing?' screamed Pearl, seeing Marty

clearly bemused by his own arrest. McGuire ignored her as he began to caution Marty, advising him that anything he said could be taken down as evidence and used against him. In the next moment a local TV news crew arrived and followed McGuire as he began to push Marty down-hill, away from the Crown of the Down. Everyone's gaze seemed to shift towards Pearl, including that of Dolly, Charlie and Ruby at the stall – and Martha Laker and Jane Orritt at the beacon – while at the edge of Trench Wood, Ben Tyler looked on, with a flushed Gloria Greenwood at his side.

CHAPTER NINE

A few hours after the fracas at the pageant, Pearl was on her laptop in her living room at Seaspray Cottage, transfixed by an online news story from the local *Chronicle* that included a series of photos taken by Bill Latimer. They showed Marty swinging a punch at Jason Ritchie and dragging Gordon Weller across to the pillory before finally being hauled away himself by McGuire. The headline and story read:

'Peaceful' pageant ends in violence

by News Editor Chris Latimer

Thursday 18 June 2020

Promoted as a 'peaceful protest and celebration of local green space', a fancy-dress pageant, jointly organised by the Save Our Downs campaign and the Whitstable Preservation Society, resulted in violence and the arrest of a local man.

The event took place on the site of the Crown of the Down, close to an area of land on which a contentious housing development is proposed by the company Invicta Land, which seeks to build homes on the area known as Laker's Field.

At today's pageant, Gordon Weller, 51, a co-director of Invicta Land, was assaulted by Whitstable trader Marty Smith, 40, owner of Cornucopia fruit and vegetable store in Whitstable High Street.

Mr Weller told the Chronicle, 'I was greatly shocked by the unprovoked attack and I'm sure I could well have sustained serious injury if it hadn't been for the swift and effective action of Canterbury police detective, DCI McGuire, who was present at the event and intervened to make an arrest.'

Martha Laker, spokesperson for the Save Our Downs campaign, was unavailable for comment.

Pearl's jaw dropped open on reading this, but Dolly's voice commented through the phone clutched to her ear: 'I really don't know what else you expected, Pearl. Inviting the police along like that?'

Pearl's heart sank on hearing her mother refer to McGuire this way.

'McGuire's a good friend.'

'Is he?' Dolly queried knowingly. 'If he was, maybe he wouldn't have trooped one of our own off to the cop shop like that.'

'Marty was asking for trouble,' said Pearl. 'He'd had far too much to drink and—'

'Admittedly,' Dolly cut in, 'the man can't hold his mead, but feelings are running high about this development—'

'Which is why Peter Radcliffe should never have brought the developers to the pageant!'

'You're right,' agreed Dolly. 'But I warned you not to roll out the welcome mat to them at the restaurant. That was bound to send out the wrong message.'

'Oh, so it's all *my* fault?' Pearl asked, exasperated.

'I'm just saying it's best not to try to appease the likes of Ratty and his cronies. Send them a firm message, right from the start, then everyone knows where they stand.'

Pearl considered this as her hand moved to her bag and took out the cheque folded around Jason Ritchie's business card. 'Yes,' she said softly, 'I should have done that.'

'What did you say?' asked Dolly, noting the shift in Pearl's tone.

'I said, perhaps you're right,' Pearl replied, before she asked apprehensively: 'And what did Charlie have to say?'

'Nothing much,' Dolly lied, knowing full well Charlie's feelings on the matter were in line with her own. Instead, she merely added: 'After we'd cleared up the stall, he and Martha's son, Simon, went off into town for a beer. It's a nice evening, after all, and Charlie had worked hard all day.'

'Yes, he had,' said Pearl, disappointment clearly showing in her voice about the way the day had gone for her.

Dolly felt the need to lift her spirits. 'Look, don't worry,' she said. 'I'm sure McGuire won't be able to hold Marty for much longer – not unless he wants to create a martyr in this town. Have you heard anything?'

Pearl shook her head wearily. 'No. But I expect Marty may be left to sleep it off for the night at the police station.'

Dolly considered this. 'Well,' she began, 'my advice to you would be to stay out of all this and let things die down, or you'll only be caught in the middle. And you're *not* in the middle; you know which side you're on, Pearl. Just like the oyster, you're a Whitstable native. Nothing will change that. Now get an early night and let's talk again tomorrow.'

In the next moment, the line went dead and Pearl found herself looking down at Ritchie's cheque and the business card, both of which bore the name Invicta Land. She took her mobile from her pocket and dialled the developer's number. It rang a few times before his voice came on the line. As soon as she heard it, she spoke quickly: 'Jason, this is Pearl Nolan . . .'

But as Ritchie's voice continued on, Pearl realised she was listening to a voicemail message, explaining that as he was busy right now, callers should leave a message. *Busy doing what?* Pearl decided to ring off while she tried to imagine what the developer might be engaged in at that very moment. Perhaps he was in a business meeting with Gordon Weller or enjoying a good meal at an expensive restaurant, celebrating the fact that the pageant had produced such good publicity for them both, with the police having to arrest a drunken supporter of the local campaign.

Slipping her phone into her pocket, Pearl stared down again at the cheque then quickly ripped it into tiny pieces and cast them on to the logs that lay in her Victorian fireplace – wishing the fire was lit so she could watch the pieces burn. It now seemed all too clear that Jason Ritchie had tried to manipulate her, to persuade her that she might have a role to play in serving the best interests of her town, when all the while he had simply been inveigling her into acting for Invicta Land – 'taking sides', as Dolly had so bluntly put it. As a businessman, he had surely recognised that the restaurant and its owner acted as a fulcrum between locals and outsiders, and he had tried to use this to his advantage.

She shook her head, angry with herself for having so nearly been charmed by Ritchie, then she looked up at her own reflection in the mirror above the fireplace, noticing something that brought her up short. She was wearing only one of the pearl earrings that had been given to her as a present by McGuire . . .

It was almost 9.30 that evening when, having thoroughly but fruitlessly searched Seaspray Cottage, Pearl set off in her Fiat for Borstal Hill. Parking up on land near to Stanley Road, she took a heavy Maglite torch from her glove compartment and headed on through the entrance to Duncan Down. As she struck out towards the Crown of the Down, an image remained lodged in her mind of the fracas that had taken place earlier that day when she had tried to physically separate Marty from the developers. It now seemed perfectly possible that she might have lost the earring at exactly that time, and, with a bit of luck, before the site was fully cleared of stalls and tents, she might yet have a chance of finding it. Left until tomorrow, she felt sure she would never see it again.

A sliver of moonlight rose above the trees. Leaves of silver birches shivered in the breeze and the night had a sharp edge to it. A primordial fear of dark woodland seemed to remind her of all the dark fairy tales that had fuelled her childhood nightmares – stories in which characters strayed beyond the safety of their homes and into forests where dangerous things could happen and monsters lurked at every turn. The lessons Pearl had learned from those stories was that strange people lived in the woods: fairies, witches, ogres, spirits – and, she thought now, Ben Tyler. She cast her mind back to finding him earlier that day in the meadow with Gloria Greenwood. A surprise. Or was it? He was an attractive man. A mysterious figure – maybe even a romantic hero to some – like Heathcliff in *Wuthering Heights* – or perhaps, Mellors, the gardener, to Gloria Greenwood's Lady Chatterley . . .

As she trekked on using the path before her, the words of a Kipling poem learned at school echoed in her memory:

> *They shut the road through the woods,*
> *Seventy years ago.*
> *Weather and rain have undone it again,*
> *And now you would never know*
> *There was once a road through the woods*
> *Before they planted the trees.*
> *It is underneath the coppice and heath,*
> *And the thin anemones . . .*

No matter how hard she tried, Pearl could remember no more. But the words of the poem reminded her how quickly nature could reclaim ancient pathways and hide all traces left by man – though vestiges would always remain – as they did in Trench Wood, which she was passing at that very moment. Pearl directed the Maglite's beam on to land where angle irons and old metal marked the lines of narrow slit trenches, once dug to protect Home Guard observers from air attack during the last World War. She was reminded of Frederick Clark's speech earlier that day. *No invaders since 1066*. But he had also mentioned biblical warnings of 'evil to come'... A rustle of the leaves in the trees distracted her. The sudden hoot of a tawny owl. A flash of amber eyes upon the path as a dog fox stood its ground, eyeing Pearl – a threat to its own territory – before it loped off into the undergrowth.

Pearl also moved on, aware that she had returned from Bruges with so many positive expectations of a busy summer at The Whitstable Pearl – and a closer relationship with McGuire – perhaps even an interesting case to fully tax her powers of detection. But within the space of only forty-eight hours she had managed to alienate members of her family and McGuire, and had almost compromised her own integrity by even considering a retainer from an enemy of the town. On top of that, she had managed to lose one of her most treasured pieces of jewellery. She chided herself. But it wasn't too late to put any of it right, including finding her earring.

A few moments later, the land opened up before her on to the Crown of the Down. Pearl took in the sight of the tall silhouette of the beacon against a starry sky. In the far distance, the sea lay like a shimmering strip of cloth upon which the navigation lights of freighters and fishing boats blinked red and green. She moved on quickly to the piece of ground on which Marty had lashed out at McGuire – and landed a punch instead on Jason Ritchie. Setting her torch on the ground, she got down on her hands and knees and began a fingertip search of the grass. Thinking back to the contretemps that afternoon, she could now understand that Marty's attack on the developers had been more than a simple act of machismo executed for McGuire's benefit. Marty's truculence had also ensured that everyone had witnessed the police detective protecting the interests of Invicta Land and, by doing so, he had implicated Pearl because of her relationship with McGuire.

Sifting cold blades of grass between her fingers, she found nothing but a few discarded sweet wrappers – and insects scurrying quickly away from her touch. As she directed the torch's beam to light another area, she realised she was as angry with McGuire as she was with Marty, for he had risen to the bait. McGuire was trained to deal with such incidents and had today's melee involved anyone other than Marty, Pearl felt sure things might not have escalated and resulted in an arrest. McGuire had surely been more interested in demonstrating his power, rather than defusing the rantings of a drunken man.

Lashing out, as Marty had done, had also reflected badly on the campaign and its leader, Martha, who had always insisted that the most powerful element of peaceful protest was peace itself. Considering all this, Pearl sighed to herself and gave up searching for what she felt could well be likened to the proverbial needle in a haystack. She wasn't one to give up easily, but at that moment she saw that the beam from her torch was fading along with its battery. Everything seemed to be conspiring against her.

Struggling to her feet, she was just brushing down her jeans when she heard something in the nearby trees. Her heart began to pound as she called out, 'Who's there?'

With no response, she clutched the heavy Maglite to her chest like a weapon. But in the next instant, a dark form was suddenly upon her. Before she had gained a chance to strike out, a wet snout nuzzled her hand.

'Don't mind the dog!' a man's voice called. 'He knows you now so he won't harm you.' Out of the shadows, Ben Tyler came striding forward. He slipped his leather hat from his head and looked around as he asked, 'What're you doing here at this time of night?'

'I could ask you the same?' said Pearl, relieved.

Martha Laker's dog bounded away from them both and into the shadows, as Ben came forward to explain. 'I like to walk after dark,' he said. 'Martha always lets the dog come with me. She's busy. I'm doing her a favour.' He was still eyeing her questioningly – or maybe distrustfully after what had happened with McGuire this afternoon.

Finally Pearl admitted, 'I lost something today. Something special. A piece of jewellery. I thought there was a chance I could find it here but—' Before she could continue, her mobile phone sounded. Checking the caller ID, she saw it was McGuire, and excused herself to Tyler so she could take the call. McGuire's voice sounded: 'Where are you?'

'On the downs,' she said quickly. 'And you?'

'Outside your cottage,' he explained. 'We should talk.'

'I know,' she replied in frustration. 'I'll be back soon

but—' She broke off as her next words were drowned out by Martha's dog howling and barking. Several feet away, in the darkness, Scooby appeared to be in distress as he bayed at a dark structure.

'Hold on,' said Pearl to McGuire on the line. Moving with Tyler across to the dog, Pearl shone the Maglite. Its weak beam found the pillory – and a figure trapped within it. A dummy, thought Pearl, as the head was lowered and the hands hung loose on either side. Ben Tyler issued an order and the dog stopped barking. Instead, the animal now began to whimper as Tyler reached forward.

McGuire's voice sounded from Pearl's mobile. 'Are you still there?'

Pearl was speechless. The weak beam of the torch in her hand was illuminating lifeless features. Gordon Weller's eyes were glassy, his skin pallid, mouth open – as though he was about to speak – but it was Pearl who finally did so.

'You'd better come,' she said to McGuire on her mobile. 'Right away.'

CHAPTER TEN

It was two hours before Pearl was released from Canterbury Police Station. She had given a full statement to a young DC on McGuire's team, but for reasons of protocol not to McGuire himself, as he and Pearl were known to one another. Tyler and Pearl had been separated before questioning so there could be no chance of them, as witnesses, influencing their individual recollections of the discovery of the body. The crime scene had been secured and Weller's body had been photographed and videoed while CSI officers worked within a tent on the Crown of the Down to protect any possible clues or forensic evidence. Pearl knew, from her police training, that this early period of an investigation was crucial, and that McGuire would have his hands full with the case.

It seemed impossible to believe that a pageant staged to save the local downs could have resulted in such a horrific conclusion – but Weller was dead and his body had been found in highly suspicious circumstances. The man had made himself unpopular in Whitstable but nevertheless a murder in the town was always viewed as an attack on the whole community. Weller may have been a partner in Invicta Land – but he had also been a local man. If an autopsy determined his death to have been the result of murder, Marty Smith had surely implicated himself by launching an attack that day on the property developer, in full view of everyone. McGuire had duly arrested him at the pageant, but Pearl now hoped that Marty had been detained in custody long enough to put him out of the frame of a possible murder investigation. A fresh day would bring an opportunity for Pearl to learn more from McGuire about the progress of the investigation, but for now, in spite of all their resolutions, Pearl and McGuire were separated once more – this time by her discovery of a dead body on the downs.

On being driven back to Seaspray Cottage, Pearl found Charlie waiting up for her. He had tidied up the cottage as an act of consideration for how she might feel on returning home after finding Weller's body. He hugged her, then his eyes scanned her face, as he asked: 'Can I get you anything? Are you hungry . . .?'

'I'm fine,' Pearl lied. 'But I could do with a glass of wine?'

Charlie nodded and hurried off to the kitchen, returning with a glass of chilled Sauvignon for his mother and a beer for himself. He watched Pearl sip her drink.

'Thank God there was someone with you when you found the body,' he said, sitting down on the sofa.

'Yes,' Pearl agreed. 'Ben Tyler was out walking Martha Laker's dog. At least, that's what I think he was doing.' She sat down beside her son and took another sip of her wine as she considered Tyler's timely appearance on the scene.

'And what were you doing there?'

'Trying to find something.'

Charlie frowned. 'Like what?'

'It doesn't matter.' Too tired to go into details about the importance of her lost earring, she managed a weak smile for him.

'Well,' said Charlie, 'I doubt if McGuire'll have you down as a suspect.' He paused for a moment, then: 'I expect a man like Weller must have had plenty of enemies.' He sipped his beer.

Pearl looked at him. 'Because of the development, you mean?'

'Yeah. But he was a rich businessman, right? He could've been involved in all sorts of shady deals.' He gave a shrug. 'You know what I mean.' He got up as if to escape his mother's scrutiny.

'No,' said Pearl, 'I'm not sure I do. In fact, I'm not even sure yet if Gordon Weller was murdered.'

Charlie turned quickly to face her. 'Oh, come on. If it wasn't murder, why has McGuire rearrested Marty?'

Pearl was taken aback. 'What do you mean?'

At his mother's shocked reaction, Charlie went on: 'Marty was released this afternoon after that bust-up at the pageant, but then the cops took him in again this evening.'

'How do you know all this?' asked Pearl, suspicious.

'The whole town knows,' he said. 'Marty's neighbours saw two police cars arrive at his place and then the police bundled him away. It's no secret.'

'Thanks to Martha Laker, no doubt,' said Pearl resentfully.

Charlie frowned at this but Pearl went on, more positively this time. 'Look, I'm sure he's just been taken in for routine questioning. And that's only to be expected after what happened this afternoon.' She sipped her wine but could see Charlie wasn't satisfied.

'Are you sure?' asked Charlie. 'Or are the police trying to find a way to pin this on him?'

Pearl looked up to see her son looking distrustfully at her. A thought came to her: 'Have you been talking to your gran about this?'

'Of course,' said Charlie. 'She's an expert on police tactics.'

Pearl got to her feet and said with exasperation, 'Charlie, you should know by now not to listen to everything she has to say about the police.'

'Because of McGuire?' he said challengingly. On his mother's silence, Charlie went on: 'Marty's no killer – and you know that. He was only saying what everyone around here thinks.'

'Not "everyone",' said Pearl. 'I'm sure there are some who support this development. And Marty assaulted Gordon Weller today, remember? Weller's body was in the same pillory Marty had been trying to force him into only this afternoon.' She paused. 'So McGuire's just doing his job – what any good police officer would do in his position.'

'Including you?'

'Of course.'

'Except you're not a police officer,' Charlie reminded her. 'You're my mother.' He paused then took a deep breath and set down his beer. 'I'm sorry, Mum, but if you don't mind, I really need to go to bed.' He looked at her, fretful, not wanting to argue further.

Feeling exactly the same, Pearl nodded. 'Go on,' she said softly.

Charlie came across and kissed her, then left the room. Pearl heard his footsteps on the stairs and waited for the sound of his bedroom door closing before she wandered to the window and looked out, trying to make sense of her feelings.

The sight of the retreating tide seemed to underscore a sense of abandonment for her. Increasingly, she was feeling uncomfortably camped between two sides of an important dispute. The issue of the development on the downs was clearly demonstrating to Pearl that she could appease Dolly and Charlie only by displeasing McGuire. Now that murder had intervened, she could see even less chance of building bridges.

Looking away from the view from her window, she picked up her smartphone – not to make a call but to reflect on more carefree times. She brought up a store of images: photographs taken during her recent break with McGuire. There were far more than she remembered, each capturing a moment she now cherished. She saw herself standing on a balcony overlooking the pretty waterfront terrace of a canal-side hotel; McGuire smiling at her in the sunshine at the bustling Sunday-morning market of the Veemarkt Square; a selfie of Pearl and McGuire kissing against a backdrop of four old windmills that stood on the grass-covered original city wall; an early-morning shot of Pearl sleeping peacefully in the huge four-poster bed in their hotel room; a breathtaking view across the whole city of Bruges and its surroundings, taken after Pearl and McGuire had climbed 366 steps to the top of the Belfry of Bruges. It had been no easy task for Pearl to mount the narrow steep staircase of the leaning bell tower, not because of a lack of fitness, as the restaurant ensured she was constantly kept on her toes, but because of her fear of heights. She had always steered clear of fairground attractions like the Big Wheel and Helter Skelter and tried, at all times, to avoid being near vertiginous drops, but McGuire had persuaded her that clambering to the top of the 83-metre-high building would be worthwhile – and she had trusted him. What had made the challenge manageable for Pearl was that the hike up the stone steps, with only a rope rail for support, was regularly interrupted by floors on which a welcome rest could be taken. Finally, having reached the summit, a 360-degree view of the city and a kiss from McGuire had made her head spin – the moment captured for ever by a fellow tourist using Pearl's camera.

Her gaze now lingered on this shot: McGuire's arm firmly supporting her, encircling her shoulder, keeping her safe, above the medieval city spread out below . . . It was shortly after this photograph had been taken that she and McGuire had declared their commitment not to let work come between them – a promise so easily made at the time. At such a distance from all their usual responsibilities, in that fairy-tale setting, it had seemed entirely possible that any future conflict could be avoided by simply finding more time for one another. Once home, that was proving to be far more challenging.

Pearl's world was full of commitments – to her customers at the restaurant, to her clients at the agency, but also to her family and her community. Now, it seemed all too clear that the promise had been easier for McGuire to make because his existing commitments were simply to his job – and to Pearl. From the very beginning of their relationship, McGuire had made no secret of the fact that he believed they would encounter far fewer problems if Pearl remained a restaurateur – with no ambitions to compete with his own job. McGuire was the police professional – Pearl was a frustrated amateur – and yet it had been Pearl's dogged perseverance, her local knowledge and her sheer gut instinct that had produced a positive result in every case on which she and McGuire had collaborated. It was a risky collaboration due to the tensions with McGuire's superior, Welch, but nevertheless, it was equally true that McGuire had gained professional kudos from the results of Pearl's own skills and efforts.

Having now become a joint witness in what appeared to be a new murder case, Pearl was not about to withdraw from a further challenge connected to a burning local issue – the development on the downs. She hoped McGuire would see things from her point of view and draw on her help again, allowing them to work in partnership rather than to be constantly ranged in competition . . .

Just as she was considering this, the smartphone in her hands sounded. Answering the call, she fully expected it to be McGuire and was surprised when another man's voice sounded quickly on the line.

'Pearl Nolan?'

'Who's this?'

'Chris Latimer. The *Chronicle*. Look, I know it's late but I wondered if you might have anything you'd like to say about finding Gordon Weller's body?'

Pearl frowned. 'How did you get my number?'

Chris ignored her question and went on: 'I understand there was a traveller with you.'

'Traveller?' asked Pearl.

'Yes, he's living in a shepherd's hut close to the downs. Did you know he was responsible for the death of another man?'

'I'm sorry?' asked Pearl, dazed by this news.

'Ben Tyler. He was tried for manslaughter two years ago. I understand he was with you when you came across Gordon Weller's body – trapped in that pillory? Must have been quite a shock for you.'

'I . . .' Pearl's voice trailed off, her mind racing until she managed to gather her thoughts. 'I can't talk about this,' she said finally.

'I understand,' said Chris. 'It must have been quite an ordeal,' he went on, 'even for someone like you – a private detective? So . . . there's nothing you want to add to the story?'

'What story?' asked Pearl, becoming increasingly fractious.

'The one that's going live any moment.'

Pearl took a second to absorb this, then glanced at her laptop and said only: 'I'm sorry.' Putting down the receiver, she moved quickly to her laptop and opened its lid. Switching it on, she waited impatiently for the screen to light. Once it had done so, she punched a few key words into her search engine. *Death . . . Downs . . .* then: *Whitstable.* A link appeared from the *Chronicle*'s online newspaper. A news story – joining others from local TV news channels – all on the same subject.

Invicta Developer Found Dead on the Downs

by News Editor Chris Latimer

Thursday 18 June 2020

The body of local property developer Gordon Weller, 51, has been found dead in Whitstable on an area of land known as the Crown of the Down.

Earlier today a pageant took place on the same site, organised by two campaign groups opposed to a contentious development involving Mr Weller's company, Invicta Land.

The pageant ended in violence when Mr Weller was assaulted and a local man was subsequently arrested. Mr Weller's body was discovered later this evening.

DCI Mike McGuire of Canterbury CID issued the following statement: 'Police were called at 9.47 p.m. on Thursday 18 June 2020 and attended an area of the downs in Whitstable following the discovery of a body by members of the public.

'A male, identified as Gordon Weller, was pronounced dead at the scene. Pending further reports, Mr Weller's death is being treated as unexplained. Canterbury Police appeal for any information from the public.'

Pearl turned away from the screen. Chris Latimer had moved quickly to get his story and in a few hours the contents of McGuire's media statement would surely be the talk of the town. Pearl could only wonder if his appeal was about to bear fruit.

CHAPTER ELEVEN

The next morning Pearl woke after a fitful sleep. Glancing at her smartphone, she saw it showed no new messages. On getting up, she put on her red silk dressing gown and stepped out on to the landing to see Charlie's bedroom door was ajar. Looking in on him, she found her son still fast asleep so she quickly headed back into her room, pausing as she saw a long green dress, with a scalloped neckline, hanging on her wardrobe door with the *hennin* – a reminder of an event that had ended so differently from the way she had hoped. Quickly throwing on some clothes, she tiptoed past Charlie's room and headed straight downstairs and on to the beach, where she hoped that the clear coastline would offer her some space to think.

When Pearl arrived on West Beach, the sun had yet to burn through the clouds. Seabirds were feeding – turnstones and gulls scavenging amid the seaweed that had been abandoned by the outgoing tide. Pearl had walked as far as the Peace Bench when her attention was drawn to a car pulling up on Neptune Gap – not a silver Lexus this time, but a police car. The driver's door opened and a man stepped out, pausing for a moment as he caught sight of an unmistakable silhouette . . .

McGuire saw Pearl standing near the shoreline, her long hair caught by the offshore breeze, and though he knew he had a full agenda that morning, which included an important briefing with Welch, he also knew he desperately needed to speak to her. He headed across the beach just as Pearl looked down, noting one particular carved message on the bench – 'Wage Peace'.

McGuire spoke first. 'I'm sorry I couldn't call,' he said sincerely.

Pearl turned to him and nodded. McGuire continued: 'I haven't been able to get away until now.'

'I read the story in the press,' she said. 'Have you had any help from the public?'

McGuire shook his head. 'No one seems to have seen anything – apart from you and Ben Tyler.'

'What's happened to Marty?' she asked quickly.

At her hopeful look, McGuire felt conflicted. 'I . . . had to bring him in again for questioning – under arrest – and properly cautioned.' He waited for Pearl's response and saw her moonstone-grey eyes sadden. 'Pearl—'

'It's okay,' she said quickly. 'I understand. But there are plenty in this town who won't.' She looked at McGuire but didn't have the heart to tell him this included Charlie. Instead, she slumped down on the bench. McGuire eyed her with concern, recognising that this was one of the few times he had ever seen her look defeated. He sat down beside her and put his arm around her.

'Are you okay?'

She nodded quickly, rallying as she asked: 'What have you managed to find out?'

McGuire shook his head. 'Not much. Yet. Still waiting for autopsy reports but one thing's certain – there's no way Weller put himself in those stocks.'

'Pillory,' said Pearl.

'What?'

'Stocks are for feet. Pillories are for the hands and head.' She paused, remembering that it was Marty who had explained this to her, then she went on quickly, trying to make use of what she knew would be limited time together: 'And what about Tyler?' she asked. 'I got a call last night from a journalist at the *Chronicle*. He said Ben Tyler had been responsible for killing someone – a while ago – and he'd been charged with manslaughter?'

'That's true,' said McGuire. 'A fight. Bare-knuckle boxing match at a horse fair in Ireland. Tyler dealt his opponent a knockout punch. The guy never came round.'

Pearl looked away as she took this in. McGuire went on. 'But he swears he had nothing to do with Weller's death and his statement corroborates your own.'

Pearl met his gaze. 'So what now?'

McGuire shrugged. 'The usual,' he said. 'CSI are on the case. We've set up an incident room. My team are conducting interviews and checking out alibis. I'll be talking to everyone that knew Weller or was involved with him . . .'

'Including Martha Laker?'

McGuire gave a defensive nod. 'Of course,' he said. 'In fact, I'm on my way there right now but—' He broke off, then spoke more softly. 'I needed to see you first.'

For a moment Pearl lost herself in his blue eyes. She smiled sadly, comforted by his admission, but the smile froze on her lips as she saw McGuire reaching into his pocket to take out a small plastic bag. Inside it was a pearl earring. Pearl looked at him. 'That's what I was looking for last night,' she said. 'On the downs. I told the DC who interviewed me.' She reached out to take the bag from McGuire but he pulled it back.

'I can't let you have it, Pearl,' he said quickly. 'It's evidence.'

'Evidence of what?' she asked, affronted. 'I didn't lie in my statement but I could hardly go into detail, could I? Explain that you gave it to me?' Her eyes searched his for understanding then she began again, this time trying to explain clearly and precisely. 'Look, I realised I had lost an earring and went up to the downs to search for it.'

'In the dark?'

'I took a torch.'

'And met with Tyler.'

'We didn't meet – he happened to be out.'

'On the downs – at night.'

'He was walking Martha's dog. I told you yesterday, he's a country man.'

'A traveller,' said McGuire.

'Whatever.' Pearl was becoming increasingly irritated by McGuire's tone. 'But I didn't think it was strange for him to be out like that.'

'Stumbling across a dead body with you?'

'What are you trying to say?' she asked suddenly.

'What I've said before, Pearl – murder seems to stalk you.'

She paused, took a deep breath and gathered her thoughts. 'Maybe it does,' she conceded, then: 'Could Weller's death have been the result of a . . . prank gone wrong?'

'By your friend Marty Smith?'

'He's not my friend. He's one of my suppliers. And there was no need for you to arrest him at the pageant.'

'Please don't tell me how to do my job—'

'But you weren't there on duty – you were my guest.'

'And Smith was out of order.'

'I know. But the way you handled things only made matters worse.'

'For who?'

'For everyone!'

McGuire said nothing but turned away from her. Pearl gave a heavy sigh and tried to explain. 'I'm sorry, but if you're going to get to the bottom of Weller's death, you'll need two crucial things: information and cooperation. And that means getting the local community back on side.'

'You?' asked McGuire.

Pearl shook her head slowly. 'No, not just me. Yesterday at the pageant, you lost trust in front of everyone.' She looked away as she remembered Charlie's reaction last night. 'And so have I,' she said, realising this.

'Then maybe you shouldn't have got involved,' McGuire said softly.

'How could I not?' she asked. 'This is *my* town.'

McGuire looked at her. 'Of course it is,' he said, his voice dropping to a whisper. 'The Whitstable Pearl.' In the silence that followed, a smile suddenly played on his lips. He leaned forward and kissed her gently, testing her reaction. Pearl reached for him and allowed him to hold her close, feeling her own frustration finally draining away. Breaking apart, her expression clouded as she caught sight of something beyond McGuire's shoulder. Charlie was standing at his bedroom window. His eyes met Pearl's before he let the curtain fall and turned away.

McGuire looked back, in an effort to take Pearl's view. 'What is it?' he asked.

But Charlie had disappeared from the window and Pearl shook her head slowly. 'Nothing.' she lied. 'Go on. You'd better talk to Martha.'

Less than an hour later, Pearl drew up in her car on Miller's Court, named after Black Mill, an old smock windmill that had been built in the early nineteenth century but which had long ago become a private residence – and was now the impressive home Jason Ritchie was currently renting. Getting out of her car, Pearl gazed up at the imposing structure; as a schoolchild she had learned that the mill, originally painted white, had once acted as a navigational aid for sailors until its weatherboard exterior had been tarred, giving it its new name. At one time it had belonged to Laurence Irving, the artist grandson of the actor Henry Irving, who had converted part of it into a studio. Later, with the extension of new living quarters, it had become a motel and restaurant. Over the years, Pearl had seen photos of its interior on various estate agents' websites, whenever the property had come up for sale, and though it no longer fulfilled its original function, Black Mill still possessed all its original major machinery, as well as a fantail, a device looking much like a miniature windmill, mounted at right angles to its 'sails', or 'sweeps' as they were always known in Kent. From an old school project, Pearl knew that the white fantail turned the revolving cap on the upper section of the windmill in order to bring it around into the wind so the sweeps would turn – though a massive brake wheel in the cap now ensured they remained stationary.

Looking around, Pearl noted there was no silver Lexus in the driveway so she took out her mobile to dial Ritchie's number, still looking up at Black Mill as she waited for her call to connect. Finally she heard Ritchie's voicemail, again inviting her to leave a message.

Frustrated, she ended the call and turned quickly – only to find herself coming face to face with Chris Latimer. He shrugged his shoulders and said: 'If you're looking for Jason Ritchie, he seems to have gone to ground.' He gave a wry smile. 'Perhaps that's not surprising in the circumstances.' He paused for a moment then stepped forward. 'I don't believe we've been properly introduced yet.' He offered his hand and Pearl took it. Latimer smiled and went on. 'Sorry to have called so late last night but I'm sure you understand. I have a job to do. As have you – or I'm guessing you wouldn't be here right now. Two strings to your bow, right? Restaurant owner and local detective? The two rather complement one other.'

'I'm not sure I know what you mean?' asked Pearl innocently.

'Oh, I'm sure you do,' said Chris. 'I once did a stint waiting tables. Amazing what you get to overhear in restaurants.' He smiled again, knowingly this time. 'Why were you on the downs last night? Did you get a tip-off?'

Pearl shook her head. 'No,' she said firmly. 'Finding Weller's body had nothing at all to do with the reason I was there.'

She began to move off but Chris quickly followed her. 'Which was?' He smiled again. 'Come on, there's no such thing as coincidence. You know that as well as I do.'

Pearl turned again to face him. 'Do I?'

He smiled at her evasiveness. 'I promise I won't tell.'

'Except in an exclusive in the *Chronicle*?'

'Well, we can't offer much money these days but nevertheless the paper still has a public duty to get news out to local people. Our motto is—'

'*Praesertim Vero*,' said Pearl quickly. 'It's been on your front page for a very long time.'

'And proudly so. "Truth above all."' He went on, more earnestly now: 'The Chronicle Group has been in our family since nineteen twenty-eight. My father's run it, my grandfather and my great-grandfather too. And yes, there've been a lot of changes in that time, but we've always tried to serve the community.'

'Lucratively so?'

Chris gave a shrug and admitted, 'Until now. In the last fifteen years over two hundred local newspapers have disappeared in this country, and more than half the towns in the UK have no local newspaper at all. I think that's a great shame – and not just because I rely on one for my living.'

'Really?' asked Pearl, unconvinced.

'Really,' said Chris with conviction. 'A good local paper holds up a mirror to its own community, encourages accountability, exposes corruption . . . and wrongdoings of all kinds—'

'And supports local campaigns?' Pearl interrupted.

'For sure.'

'I sensed from Martha's speech at the pageant she's a little disappointed with the press coverage.'

Chris shrugged. 'Yeah, well, nothing's ever quite enough for some people. We do try to give a balanced view on most issues.'

'You mean you like to sit on the fence to please both parties?'

Chris frowned. 'Look, a campaign has to *earn* support – be *worth* supporting. I think we both know that this development is going to happen whether we like it or not.'

Pearl appraised him before asking: '*Do* you like it?'

Chris looked away for a moment then turned back to

Pearl with a stark admission: 'No. As a matter of fact, I've got a lot of sympathy with the cause. I don't want to see the area ruined.' He looked up at Black Mill. 'And to be honest, I can understand how Martha feels. By rights, she should have inherited a mill as impressive as this. Instead, she was left a run-down old farmhouse which she's done a fair job of restoring.' He paused. 'Soon, it'll overlook a bunch of char-acterless "new builds" – as will everything else around here.'

'While the developer rents Black Mill,' said Pearl. Her eyes moved from the mill to Latimer. She saw he looked genuinely troubled. 'Doesn't seem right, does it?' she asked.

Chris regained his composure. He shook his head but said: 'It doesn't really matter what I think. I did my bit for Martha – advertised her pageant. Now, I'm trying to get to the bottom of a murder.'

'And so am I,' said Pearl, adding, 'though neither of us knows, for sure, if it *was* murder.'

'Oh, come on,' said Latimer. 'Weller didn't put himself in that contraption on the downs, and whoever *did* put him there must have done it when he was still conscious. You know yourself, a dead body is a dead weight. And Weller was a big man – not just in status. I imagine he must have weighed two hundred and forty pounds?'

'Maybe,' said Pearl. 'But "imagining" won't get us very far. What we need are facts.' She paused then asked: 'Have you managed to speak to Ritchie yet?'

Chris shook his head. 'The only help I've had so far has been given to me by the Senior Investigating Officer on the case.'

'DCI Mike McGuire.'

Chris gave a nod. 'But, as I'm sure you know, he has a responsibility to ensure that responses to media inquiries about police activity should be open, honest and transparent.' Pearl took this in as Chris went on: 'And *my* responsibility is to get the news out.'

'News?' asked Pearl. 'Or the truth?'

'To me, they're one and the same,' said Chris, 'but if McGuire does what he's meant to do as SIO, he'll make my job a whole lot easier.'

Pearl considered her conversation with McGuire that morning, then looked away. Latimer took her pensiveness for guilt. 'Look, if you've something to hide . . .'

'About?' Pearl said sharply.

'A relationship?' He waited for her response. Pearl struggled for a moment, aware that McGuire's superintendent would throw the book at him for any undisclosed relationship with a witness or informant such as Pearl. Chris Latimer went on: 'I don't need to print that,' he said, 'but I would like to know why you were both up on the downs last night?'

Pearl opened her mouth to speak then closed it again. 'You mean, me and—'

'Ben Tyler,' Latimer said quickly.

Feeling a wave of relief wash over her, Pearl smiled.

'What is it?' Latimer asked, confused.

'You . . . think Ben Tyler and I are . . . ?' She trailed off, amused at the thought.

'Aren't you?'

'No. We just happened to be in the same area at the same time. I only met him a few days ago . . .'

'Then consider yourself lucky.'

'I'm sorry?'

'I've done some digging around,' said Latimer, 'and . . . well, let's just say, since Tyler set up camp in that shepherd's hut, there are more women walking their dogs on the downs than ever before.' He gave her a knowing look and Pearl's thoughts drifted back to discovering Tyler in the meadow with Gloria Greenwood. But she said only: 'He was on his own last night. Apart from Scooby.'

Chris frowned at this. Pearl explained: 'Martha Laker's dog.'

From Latimer's expression she could tell he was weighing up the possibility of another liaison – this time between Tyler and Martha – but he quickly dismissed the thought as he commented: 'I guess Martha's one woman who *won't* come under Tyler's spell.' Looking at Pearl, he went on, 'Still, it was lucky for you that he showed up when he did.' He eyed her. 'Finding Weller's body together gives you both a mutual alibi, doesn't it?' Reaching into his wallet for something he then handed a business card to Pearl. 'Maybe we can help each other. Always better to work together than alone.'

'Confucius?' said Pearl wryly.

'Bill Latimer. My dad. He's a great one for cooperation.'

With that, he gave a final smile then turned quickly and walked off the forecourt of Black Mill towards a red Toyota. As he opened the driver's door, he tipped a brief salute to Pearl before getting into the car and tearing away down Borstal Hill.

Half an hour later, in a corridor of Canterbury Police Station, DCI Mike McGuire was struggling out of his jacket while trying to keep his mobile phone clasped to his ear. The station windows had recently been double-glazed and he felt like he was in a sauna. He finally tossed his jacket over his shoulder, and replied to his caller. 'Yeah, he's right. Weller was a heavy man. One person could never have transported his body to the downs.'

On the end of the line, Pearl asked: 'But someone could've driven him there when he was still alive?'

'Unlikely,' said McGuire. He paused to stare out of the window and viewed the usual parade of traffic snaking its way along the stretch of road known as Longport beneath the ancient city walls. He went on: 'Weller's Daimler was found by my team parked on South View Road, just off Borstal Hill. It was seen there by local residents just after nine p.m. CCTV in the High Street clocked it ten minutes before. Looks like he'd headed to the downs alone.'

'To meet someone?'

'We don't know that yet.'

'Well, have you checked his phone calls?'

At that moment, one of McGuire's DCs passed him in the corridor. He paused to watch him go, then continued in a quieter tone: 'We haven't yet found Weller's phone but we're going through his accounts and checking with the company.'

'How about Jason Ritchie?'

'Haven't caught up with him – yet.'

Pearl took this in. 'Neither has Chris Latimer from the local paper,' she said thoughtfully. 'It shouldn't be that difficult to find him, surely? He's a businessman. He needs to be contactable. And his partner in Invicta Land has just been found dead—'

'So,' said McGuire, 'maybe he's on a business trip. We'll find him,' he added confidently.

'What about time of death?'

'Still waiting for the autopsy but most likely it occurred between nine-ten and—'

'Nine-forty,' said Pearl, breaking in. 'Just before I arrived . . .'

'With Tyler,' McGuire reminded her.

'Did you take his statement last night?'

'Yep.'

'And questioned him since?'

'Just about to.'

'What about forensics?'

'Nothing found of any consequence – apart from your earring. Remember, there were two hundred or more people trampling across that whole area yesterday. And there's no CCTV on the downs.'

Pearl considered this. 'Latimer seems grateful for your statement.'

McGuire sighed. 'That's all he's had, Pearl. I'm simply asking for information from the public.'

'And me?'

'We've been here before. If you know anything, or if you discover anything, work with me – not against me.'

After a pause, Pearl nodded. 'Okay,' she said, 'I will. Now what did Martha Laker have to say?'

'Not a lot. She was home alone last night . . . Well, with her partner.'

'Another mutual alibi,' mused Pearl.

'Just like you and Tyler.'

'But I don't need an alibi,' said Pearl. 'I know I didn't kill Weller. So you can cross me off your list.'

'Marty Smith's still on it,' McGuire informed her.

'You're wasting your time,' said Pearl. 'Marty wouldn't kill Weller—'

'Maybe he didn't intend to,' said McGuire, breaking in. 'I'll know more once the autopsy results are through, but until then, he's still a prime suspect – with no alibi for the time of death.'

Pearl took this in before asking: 'What about Weller's family?'

'None to speak of,' said McGuire. 'He was married as a young man. It didn't last long and they divorced thirty years ago. Seems he was a loner who lived for his work.'

'Like someone else I know,' said Pearl playfully.

McGuire saw Welch heading towards him. 'I've got to go.'

'I know,' said Pearl. The phone went dead in her hand.

Much later that same afternoon, Pearl managed to get away from the restaurant and walked the length of Borstal Hill to South View Road. Instead of heading along the path to Martha's house, she turned and carried on across Laker's Field in the direction of Benacre Wood. Entering the shelter of the dense trees, Pearl remembered how every spring this only surviving section of local ancient woodland would be completely carpeted in delicate English bluebells. Early flowering provided nectar for bees, hoverflies and butterflies, but it also made full use of whatever sunlight reached the woodland floor before the canopy of trees cast its shade. She found herself trying once again to remember the old Kipling poem from her childhood:

> *There was once a road through the woods*
> *Before they planted the trees.*
> *It is underneath the coppice and heath,*
> *And the thin anemones . . .*

Concentrating hard, she began to summon the next line . . .

> *Only the keeper sees*
> *That, where the—*

The next words disappeared from her mind as a kestrel suddenly flew up before her, flapping wings frantically before using the momentum to glide smoothly through the tall trees. Pearl watched the bird disappear before she walked on, heading not towards the heart of the wood but to some open land that lay just beyond it. Emerging from the wood, she finally found what she had been looking for. A shepherd's hut parked up in a field – not the kind of quaint timber centrepiece that had been springing up recently in gardens around Whitstable, but a solid, hand-crafted wagon with corrugated iron walls, heavy cast-iron wheels, decorative ironmongery around its windows and a curved roof topped with sedum on which wildflowers were growing. Six feet from its stable door, Pearl spied an extinguished log fire and a small axe lying on its side near a pile of wood. Suddenly, she was reminded that Benacre Wood itself was shaped like an axe, the 'head' lying close to a dual carriageway known locally as the Old Thanet Way, while the 'handle' ran the length of a wildflower meadow near to a clearing where standing stones had been erected to mark the ancient nature of the landscape.

Looking back in the direction in which she had come, Pearl computed that it would take just a few minutes to walk from this shepherd's hut to the Crown of the Down. It was wholly possible that Tyler could have murdered Gordon Weller and been on his way back to Martha Laker's home, with her dog, when he heard Pearl arrive on the downs – or perhaps saw the weak beam from her Maglite torch shining near the pillory . . .

'What're you doing here?' A woman's voice suddenly broke into Pearl's thoughts. Turning, she saw Martha Laker approaching. 'Spying for the police?'

Pearl ignored her question and looked beyond Martha to see if she was alone.

'Is Jane with you?'

Martha shook her head. 'With patients – at her surgery. You still haven't answered my question.'

Pearl offered a knowing smile. 'Why are you so suspicious about seeing me here? And why would I be "spying" for the police?'

'Good people from the campaign are being targeted, that's why. Ben gave a statement to the police last night – as did you – but you haven't been taken in again for questioning – and he has. That suggests there's one rule for you and another for—'

'Ben's new to the area,' said Pearl, cutting in. 'It's often easier for a witness to be questioned at the station.'

'Ben's a traveller,' said Martha starkly. 'But he also happens to be a loyal supporter of our cause – as is Marty Smith – who's also being harassed by the local police.'

Pearl spoke up quickly. 'I'm not here to defend police procedure . . .'

'Then why *are* you here?'

'Because I found Gordon Weller's body.'

'And you think his murder was down to one of us in the campaign?' Martha's eyes remained narrowed with distrust.

'I'm here to help,' said Pearl in frustration.

'Help who?' Martha demanded. 'Us? Or the police?' She paused for a moment then went on: 'For your information, I'm more than happy to tell you right now that, I, for one, won't mourn the death of Gordon Weller. He may have been a local man but he joined forces with Ritchie to profit from this development, as if he didn't have enough money. But then for some, no amount of money, *or* power, is ever enough.' Martha's anger was palpable, tension written on her face.

'And you don't think *you* have power?' asked Pearl. Martha looked up sharply. Pearl continued: 'It's not a dirty word for you, is it? You've used your own power over local people – powers of persuasion? You've persuaded them to come on side.'

Martha shook her head. 'No,' she said firmly. 'No, I just gave them a voice. The power is theirs to make their own choice – as Weller made his.'

She began to turn away but Pearl went on, 'And because he made the wrong choice, he had to die?'

Martha turned back, looking unconcerned. 'That's not for me to say. I've been honest and I've told you: I shan't shed any tears for him. I have none to shed for the likes of Gordon Weller.'

A moment hung between them before a black flash bounded past them from the direction of Benacre Wood. Martha's dog was suddenly between them, turning excitedly in a circle, tongue lolling at the sight of someone else approaching. On seeing Pearl, Ben Tyler halted in his tracks then came slowly forward, while Martha asked: 'Is everything . . . all right?'

After a pause, Tyler nodded. 'Yes,' he said. 'The police had a few more questions for me but . . .' He paused for a moment, eyes on Pearl. 'I told them all I know.'

At this, Martha looked relieved. 'Good.' She hugged Tyler warmly – a little too warmly, thought Pearl – then she put her arm through his and they walked off towards the shepherd's hut, the dog following on behind.

*

Pearl headed back down Borstal Hill and walked through the High Street straight on to the beach. Immediately, she felt a sense of relief – and belonging – especially when she saw a fleet of local fishing boats working in the bay. As a child, she had come to the beach on summer afternoons such as this, heading directly from school to the harbour to meet her father, Tommy, returning from a fishing trip on the lowering tide. She would wait impatiently for him to moor his boat, and for the touch of his strong, nut-brown hands to frame her cheeks before he kissed her – treasuring her – his very own Pearl. For hours she would sit with him down on the quay, checking his catch for small starfish which, given half a chance, would cloak themselves around the oysters' shells and suck the life from the oyster inside. Some said the disturbance of the seabed from the laying of cables to the wind farm had resulted in an increase in starfish that would prove to be the end of Whitstable's native oysters – but Tommy Nolan, dead for more than ten years, had no cause to worry about that.

Pearl had just enough time to check her mobile – no one had called – before her battery finally faded. She considered for a moment that she could either return home and recharge it or remain out of contact – at this point in time, the latter option felt preferable. Glancing over at her small dinghy moored on the beach, she made a sudden decision and headed across to it. Taking off her black canvas pumps she threw them into the boat and dragged it down to the shoreline.

Five minutes later, Pearl was at sea – with no need of an outboard as her white sails were set against a northerly breeze. Staring back towards land, she knew that from this vantage point everything looked totally different – including the sea itself, a sheet of bright turquoise beneath uninterrupted blue skies. The view mirrored Pearl's own clarity of thought – something she had been searching for but had failed to find on the downs, where her thoughts had remained as tangled as the undergrowth in Benacre Wood. But the sea held no fear for Pearl and in spite of its power, which her father had taught her never to underestimate, she felt safer here on the estuary waters than she did up on the downs.

She trimmed her sails, relieved to be back in control, then took a deep breath of sea air and remembered Charlie's words to her when she returned from the police station: *A man like Weller must have had plenty of enemies*. Pearl had instantly taken exception to this, as if Charlie was offering up an excuse for the man's murder, but now she saw that her son had been simply stating the obvious: with money came power and with power came enemies – and perhaps even Weller's new business partner, Jason Ritchie, could be counted as such. As Chris Latimer had said, Ritchie appeared to have gone to ground. But why? Was he merely trying to escape awkward questions from the press and police? Or could he really have killed his own business partner, fled the murder scene and disappeared? If so, McGuire had the resources to catch up with him. Until then, Pearl decided, she would make things easier for herself, stop asking questions she couldn't answer and, also stop tacking against the northerly wind and take a much easier course by running with it, down the coast to West Beach. Tonight, she would do what she did well: cook a wonderful meal for Charlie and spend some quality time with him . . .

An hour later, the sun was low in the sky when Pearl finally padded, barefoot, back to Seaspray Cottage, her black canvas shoes in her hand. Entering by the garden gate she walked the length of her garden, breathing in the heady fragrance of honeysuckle and lavender. She had used the short voyage back to decide what she would cook this evening: one of Charlie's favourites – paella. Once inside the kitchen, she called out, 'I'm home!'

Silence.

Tossing her keys on to the kitchen table she entered the dining room and called upstairs, 'Charlie?'

It took only seconds to climb the narrow staircase to her son's room and discover he definitely wasn't home. His room was empty, but a few drawers were open and some folded T-shirts lay abandoned on the bed, giving Pearl the impression that he may have been packing. She was just trying to make sense of this when the landline phone sounded. Quickly grabbing the receiver, Pearl found Dolly on the line. 'I couldn't reach you on your mobile.'

'Battery's dead,' said Pearl. 'Have you seen Charlie?'

'Yes. That's why I'm ringing.' Dolly paused, and Pearl felt anxiety rising in her chest.

'What is it?' she asked.

'Promise you won't get angry?'

'What's happened? Where is he?'

'Charlie's okay,' said Dolly quickly, 'but . . .' She paused again before explaining: 'He's joined the protest camp.'

'He's what?' asked Pearl incredulously.

'He's not alone, Pearl. There's quite a few of them. All well prepared too. Up on the downs.'

Pearl frowned at the thought. 'But . . . they can't be. It's a crime scene—'

'Not at Snowdrop Valley,' said Dolly. 'It's away from the Crown of the Down and has Village Green status, so it's public land. They're legally entitled to exercise their democratic right to protest there. The police can't touch them.'

Dolly's words echoed for Pearl as she looked down to see she was holding one of Charlie's T-shirts tightly against her chest.

CHAPTER TWELVE

Snowdrop Valley lay on the south-western side of the downs, close to the original source of the Gorrell Stream, which took its name from the blood-red 'gory' colour of the water created by the outflow from old iron works. A memorial bench stood in nearby Oak Meadow dedicated to a former resident, Anne Wilks, a redoubtable woman and tireless campaigner who had lived in Whitstable for eighty-two years until her death and who had fought to keep public paths and rights of way open as well as preventing building on the beach. Pearl read the bench's inscription – *Si Monumentum Requiris Circumspice* – and recognised it as the epitaph of Sir Christopher Wren, architect of St Paul's Cathedral: 'If you seek my monument look around you.' She took in the calm picturesque natural setting and realised that Snowdrop Valley had no doubt been chosen by Martha out of respect for this sentiment.

It also reminded Pearl of the 'peace bench' on the beach and the rousing speech Martha had given there only days ago on a sunny morning. It had been a day that had begun so promisingly, waking up to a breakfast prepared and served by McGuire before they had reaffirmed a commitment to find more time for one another. Since then, everything had undergone a seismic shift – firstly with Charlie's return home, and now his disappearance to the protest camp.

Snowdrop Valley was viewed by most as a peaceful haven – away from the tourists and DFLs who gawked in shop windows or ambled along the High Street at their usual snail's pace, clogging up Harbour Street's pavements for the residents and traders who struggled to go about their business at a more urgent tempo. Local people conducted themselves with all the usual haste of modern life but still in the hope that, one day, they might become strangers in another town, finding unfamiliar streets along which they too could amble and dawdle.

It was at that moment that Pearl recognised herself to be an outsider in strange territory. Her own haven was the coast; the sea was in her DNA, gifted to her by her father, and his before him, from a bloodline of fishermen whose own harvests were not gathered from the land but from the seabed itself. The estuary waters coursed through Pearl's veins – ebbing and flowing with the beat of her heart – but it was not so for Charlie, who had come to feel at home in a university city filled with tourists, bars, chain stores and restaurants. For Charlie, Canterbury offered a welcome contrast to all he had ever known in Whitstable and, in due course, he had become a city boy, though he clearly cared enough to camp out in this rural spot in order to protect it.

'Curiosity got the better of you?' A familiar voice rang out behind her. Turning, Pearl saw that Marty was calling to her from a distance, down in the valley. For a moment she was taken aback to see him without his usual green T-shirt and baseball cap. Instead, his chest was bare and his blue jeans were rolled up to his calves. He waited for Pearl's response.

'Where's Charlie?' she asked.

'Here,' said Marty. 'With the rest of us. We've got quite a crowd now,' he called proudly.

'And who's taking care of your shop?'

'No one. I've closed up for the time being.'

Pearl frowned at this. 'But . . . you never close,' she said. 'You're open seven days a week. Bank holidays, too.'

'Yeah, well, some things are more important than work.' He shrugged. 'Besides, I was getting pestered by that reporter from the *Chronicle* – the one who was here for the pageant.'

'Chris Latimer?'

Marty gave a nod. 'My solicitor told me not to comment – especially to the press. And Martha says the media's not to be trusted.'

'I don't know why she should say that,' said Pearl, slightly confused. 'They've supported her in the past.'

'Not to be trusted.' Marty repeated like an automaton. 'Fred said the same.'

'Frederick Clark, you mean?'

Marty nodded again. 'The media's only out for themselves – and a story. Give them a quote, they'll garble it and move on to something else.'

Pearl paused to consider the new Marty. Under her gaze he gave a half-smile and flexed a pectoral.

'So, you have a solicitor now,' said Pearl.

Marty nodded. 'Barrett and Chambers in the High Street. They're offering free advice to the campaign – and to me. They said I shouldn't talk to the police without legal representation and if I need someone higher up the chain they can get me a barrister's opinion.' He paused, then added: 'I'm not going to let your friend push a murder rap on to me.'

'And why would he want to do that?'

'Oh come on, Pearl, why do you think?'

'Tell me.'

Marty hesitated. 'Maybe you should ask him,' he said knowingly. 'And while you're at it, you might point out that I'm just a local man trying to defend a piece of land. I'm not a scapegoat.'

'No,' said Pearl. 'You made yourself a prime suspect, considering what you tried to do to Gordon Weller two days ago.'

Marty scowled at this. 'He asked for it!'

'And did he ask to be murdered too?'

Before Marty could respond, Pearl saw Charlie appear, further down in the valley. 'Mum? Is that you?'

Pearl noted his guilty look and moved down to him.

'So, Gran told you,' Charlie asked, 'about me being here?'

Pearl nodded but remained silent.

'And ... you do understand?' Another pause before Pearl nodded again. 'Yes.' At this, Charlie finally gave a smile and turned sideways, indicating for her to join him. Looking back once at Marty, Pearl followed her son down into the valley.

A few moments later, as Pearl continued to trail after Charlie, she remembered that in February, this same area was always flooded with snowdrops – but now it was carpeted with sleeping bags – having become home to at least a hundred or so protesters who had set up camp beneath the trees. Women were preparing food while a group of men were carefully observing Ben Tyler as he used a large knife to craft a gnarled piece of wood into a staff. Tribal drums, sounded by a group of teenagers, were silenced as Pearl appeared. Heads turned, eyes followed her as she made her way through the camp. Martha Laker's face broke into a smile and she got to her feet, wiping her hands down her jeans as she left her partner, Jane, stirring a pot of soup cooking on a log fire.

'So,' she exclaimed. 'Have you come to join us?'

'I've come to see my son,' Pearl explained.

Martha looked between Pearl and Charlie. 'Of course.' She smiled once more and explained: 'Charlie's been setting up camp here with Si.' She glanced across to where Simon was helping to erect some tents. He offered Pearl a polite nod.

Looking around, Pearl noticed Jane was now grinding

something in a mortar and pestle – perhaps peppercorns for the soup, thought Pearl, as she asked: 'How long do you intend staying here?'

'As long as it takes,' said Jane brightly.

Martha laid a hand on Charlie's shoulder, causing Pearl to feel uncomfortable. The gesture could have been seen perhaps as a sign of camaraderie and shared commitment, or a display of gratitude and affection, but Pearl's concern in that moment was that her son had come under Martha's spell and was about to become another pawn in her game.

'You really think you can change things just by being here?' she asked.

Martha's smile was still painted on her face. 'Peaceful protest can be a most powerful weapon,' she said. '*Never doubt that a small group of thoughtful, committed citizens can change the world; indeed, it's the only thing that ever has.*' She paused. 'Not my words – but they're well worth noting,' she added, raising her voice so that everyone paid attention.

She cast a look around as Pearl commented, 'I thought you wanted to save Laker's Field from development – not change the world.'

'It amounts to the same thing,' said Martha. 'Do nothing and there'll never be change. But everything we do – or we don't do – makes a difference.' She held Pearl's gaze and continued: 'We need to win this campaign. So we need to be adaptable, to change tactics when required and to unnerve our opponent. Campaigning is rather like a game of chess.' She paused, tilting her head to one side, and asked: 'Do you play?'

'Not since school.'

'Then maybe you should take it up again,' said Martha. 'It's a beautiful game that requires logic, creativity but also intuition – and, occasionally, a sacrifice – though ultimately it's possible to gain more than you lose. It's not always necessary to hold on to every piece, what's important is using what you have to greatest effect – and achieving a final victory.'

'Checkmate,' said Pearl.

'Exactly.' Martha smiled. 'Some say the origin of the term is "*sheikh mat*" – Arabic for the king is dead?' She continued: 'But the purpose of the game is actually to render the king helpless – so that he submits.' She eyed Pearl until she finally became aware of Frederick Clark standing by an oak tree. He appeared pensive and nodded his head sharply for her to join him. Martha betrayed some irritation and tried to ignore him but he called out to her.

'Martha?'

'What is it?' she asked brusquely.

'I need to talk to you,' he said. 'Straight away.'

Heads turned at his tone. Martha looked exasperated. 'Excuse me,' she said to Pearl before she headed across to him. Pearl saw that Charlie was staring after Martha.

'Isn't she amazing?' he said. 'She has so much energy – she hasn't stopped since we got here.'

'And did she ask you to come?' asked Pearl.

Charlie shook his head. 'No. Si did,' he replied. 'He just explained that they needed as many people as possible here.' He looked at Pearl. 'I tried to call you to let you know, but your phone was off and . . .'

'You thought you'd let your gran explain instead?'

Charlie shrugged, aware that this had been a convenient cop-out at the time.

Pearl gazed across to Simon, who had now finished erecting the second tent. 'And what does Simon's father have to say about him being here?'

Charlie frowned but gave a confident look as he said, 'He'll come round.'

'Will he?' asked Pearl, unconvinced.

'Look,' Charlie lowered his voice, 'it's difficult between Si's dad and Martha. They don't get on.'

'And maybe it's more complicated than that,' Pearl suggested. 'Maybe Simon's father doesn't want him living here – in England.'

'I can understand that,' said Charlie. 'He brought Si up.'

'Yes—' said Pearl, breaking off as she looked across to where Simon was standing, wearing rough clothes with his long dark hair unkempt and a day's stubble on his chin. She turned back to Charlie. 'And maybe Simon's father would prefer it if he was concentrating on his studies rather than playing survival skills in this wood.'

Her comment found its mark with her son, but before Charlie could frame a response, Marty reappeared, carrying a heavy pile of wood in his arms. He moved across and dumped it ostentatiously on the ground before taking up an axe and, with great effect, raised it high above his shoulder before letting it fall on some timber. Having cleaved a log in two with one fell blow, he now tossed the smaller logs to one side and smiled for Pearl's benefit before repeating the action.

'Good to see you here, Pearl.' It was Frederick Clark who had spoken. He approached, explaining: 'I've just let Martha know there's a TV news crew on its way. She and I are going to have to prepare a statement.' He took off a pair of tortoiseshell glasses and slipped them on to his head. 'Are you joining us?' he asked expectantly.

'I'm afraid not,' said Pearl. 'This is just a flying visit.'

Frederick looked disappointed at this – though Charlie seemed unsurprised. 'I have to get back to the restaurant,' she explained.

'Of course,' said Frederick. Pearl looked between her son and the pot of soup boiling on the wood fire – then she made a decision. 'I . . . could bring some food later for the camp?'

'That would be very gratefully received.' Frederick smiled.

'Yeah,' said Charlie, lowering his voice to a whisper as he explained, 'Jane's vegan soup is fine for one meal but . . . we could really do with some of your cooking here.' He leaned in quickly, winked and gave Pearl a peck on her cheek before heading off towards Simon.

Pearl watched him go and Frederick waited for a moment before confiding: 'I have to say, the news of Gordon Weller's death has been a great shock.' Pearl glanced back at him and he added: 'To us all, of course.'

He looked sufficiently pained for Pearl to ask: 'Did you know him well?'

Frederick regained his composure. 'Through some charity work,' he said quickly. 'Gordon was a Rotarian – as am I. I don't know if you're aware but our aim is to "provide humanitarian service, encourage high ethical standards in all vocations and help build goodwill and peace in the world".' He shook his head. 'That's why it was such a disappointment when he got involved in this development and allowed it to create such conflict within the community.' He paused as he considered this. 'I don't know why he didn't see it coming . . .' His speech trailed off.

'See what coming?'

'Why, the conflict, of course.' Frederick looked at her and for a moment Pearl felt he was about to explain further, but a thought seemed to come to him, showing on his face as clearly as a cloud moving across the sun. 'Something bothered me at the pageant,' he said finally.

'Like what?'

'Well, that's just it,' said Frederick. 'I'm not really sure, I . . . just felt something was wrong . . . and that . . . something was going to happen.' He looked troubled and lowered his voice as he admitted: 'I never wanted us to lose the moral high ground. You see—'

At that moment, Martha called to him. 'Frederick?'

Glancing down to the clearing he saw Martha staring up at him. 'I'll be with you in a moment,' he called to her.

'No,' said Martha, insistent. 'The statement,' she called. 'Now.'

Frederick looked back at Pearl and reluctantly excused himself. Hurrying obediently down to Martha, he managed one last look at Pearl before Martha led him away, all the while her eyes fixed on Pearl.

Some ten minutes after leaving the camp, Pearl was approaching the Gorrell Stream when she saw a figure on the wooden bridge that spanned it. For a moment she thought it was Jason Ritchie, but as she drew closer, she recognised Adam Stone. She stopped in her tracks, wondering what he was doing, before she moved on towards him. Lost in thought, Adam hardly seemed to notice her until she had finally stepped on to the bridge itself.

'Are you on your way to the camp?' she asked.

Adam seemed dazed by the question but, after a pause, he shook his head. 'I . . . really don't think it would do much good, do you?'

'That depends on what you want.'

Adam failed to reply so Pearl explained. 'I just saw Simon. He seems to be getting something out of being there,' she said. 'As does my own son.' She paused and went on softly, as much to convince herself as Adam Stone: 'I'm sure they won't come to any harm.'

'No?' asked Adam doubtfully. He pushed himself away from the bridge and said: 'They're with Martha, aren't they? Her new blood?'

Pearl shook her head in confusion. 'I'm sorry?'

'Nothing's as it seems with her,' he went on. 'She's a ruthless woman.'

'Ruthless?'

'Pitiless. Without mercy. She never stops until she gets what she wants.' He turned away from Pearl, leaned on the bridge and looked down into the stream.

'Some people would say that's a good thing,' said Pearl, 'at least where this campaign is concerned.'

'Even if someone has to die?'

'You mean . . . Weller?'

Adam leaned back on the rail of the bridge then shook his head slowly as though trying to work something out. 'It's . . . almost as if the whole thing has been stage-managed – right from the judge's verdict . . . like one of her protests . . . her stunts. They're all calculated to the last move.'

Pearl frowned. 'You're not suggesting Martha's responsible for Weller's death?'

'That's exactly what I'm saying,' he said bluntly. 'She may not have killed him herself but I've no doubt she motivated the person who did.'

Pearl shook her head slowly. 'But she claims she only supports passive resistance. Peaceful protest.'

'It's all a façade,' Adam said softly. 'She'll stop at nothing to get what she wants.'

'An end to this development?'

'Victory,' he said sharply. 'She's like some . . . machine . . . a robot,' he decided. 'She's not programmed for defeat.'

Pearl took her time to process this, staring away towards Snowdrop Valley.

'How was he?' Adam asked. 'My son?'

Pearl tried to give a diplomatic response. 'He seems well. Happy.'

At this, Adam looked conflicted and Pearl spoke quickly, admitting, 'Look, I can't say I'm too pleased about Charlie being there either, not because of Martha, but . . .' She looked around as though feeling she was being watched – by every living creature in the wood. She thought of the walk she had taken only the other night – the hoot of a tawny owl warning of her presence – the flash of amber eyes on her path. Looking around at the picturesque scene, she saw the Gorrell Stream was lined on its banks with heavy flat rocks and yellow flag iris, and a haze of hoverflies appeared like a small cloud above the water, on which a pattern was forming out of tiny pinpricks of surface tension from the motion of water striders. She remembered the murmur of voices in the woods on the day of the pageant, perhaps not Tyler and Gloria Greenwood, but the ghosts of soldiers who had occupied Trench Wood, keeping watch over the estuary waters, holding back invaders . . . She shook her head. 'This place, it's . . .'

'What?'

Pearl remained speechless, unable to articulate her feelings but nevertheless sensing she was at risk, insecure and vulnerable, like the prey of the wild creatures she had seen in the area, so that when Adam Stone placed his hand on her shoulder she flinched beneath his touch.

'Are you okay?' he asked, concerned.

Pearl tried to gather her senses and glanced up at him.

He looked deep into her eyes and said, 'You may well be suffering from delayed shock.'

Pearl gave a nod, feeling she was becoming cold in the heat of the day.

'Have you got a car here?' he asked.

She shook her head.

'Okay,' he said, taking control. 'Then let me drive you home.'

It was almost dusk when Adam Stone pulled up in his rented Ford car outside Seaspray Cottage.

Pearl thanked him. 'This was very kind of you.'

'A pleasure,' he said softly.

'Would you like to come in? I could make some coffee?'

Adam Stone shook his head. 'I should get back. And I think you should rest.'

Pearl nodded. 'I'm . . . sorry if I took you out of your way.'

'You haven't at all. I'm renting a cottage in Marshside.'

Pearl reflected on this for a moment, remembering that the little hamlet, just two miles from Whitstable, lay on the Chislet Marshes, an area as picturesque as parts of rural France, so much so that perhaps Adam Stone could pretend he had never left home at all.

Adam reached into his pocket for a wallet and from it he handed her a business card. Glancing down at it, Pearl saw it bore his name and the contact details for a French clinical group in Toulouse. He scribbled a mobile number on the back. 'Would you keep me informed?' he asked.

'I know you have an agency and I'm happy to pay for your services. But I need to know if Simon's at risk – in any way.'

Pearl took the card from him and noted his helpless look. It chimed with the way she felt herself. 'I'll let you know,' she said. 'One parent to another. No need for payment.'

At this, and for the very first time, Adam Stone's expression softened. 'Thank you,' he said sincerely. He held out his hand to her and Pearl took it, feeling a strong grip that seemed, in that moment, much like a drowning man clinging to a lifeline.

Once Adam Stone's car had driven off into the night, Pearl moved to her front door and entered the cottage. Throwing down her bag, she suddenly noticed a thin strip of light beneath the door of her kitchen. A moment later, she heard the chink of glass . . . Heading quickly to the kitchen she threw open the door – and found McGuire pouring two large goblets of white wine.

He turned to face her. 'I . . . guess you could do with one of these?' He handed a glass to her.

Pearl took it from him then asked: 'How did you . . . ?'

McGuire glanced back at the kitchen door. 'You left it unlocked. You should be more careful.' He sipped his wine.

Pearl frowned. 'Yes,' she said, losing herself in his deep blue eyes. As she sipped her own drink she felt the tension of the day suddenly ebbing away like the tide on the beach outside. 'Lucky you were in the neighbourhood,' she said wryly.

McGuire moved closer. 'Just doing my job.' He allowed her to take another sip of wine, then took the glass from her hand and placed it on the table with his own. 'Feeling better?'

Pearl nodded.

'Good.' He moved in to kiss her. Pearl responded, pulling him closer. Somewhere in the distance, the bells of St Alfred's Church began to ring out the hour, but at that moment Pearl had no interest in the time of day.

CHAPTER THIRTEEN

Pearl stretched her body and reached a hand out towards McGuire but found only an empty space beside her. Opening her eyes, she saw that he was standing near the bed having just zipped up his jeans. As he grabbed his shirt from the back of a chair, her gaze lingered on him – tracing the contours of his strong arms and suntanned back. A moment later, she asked sleepily: 'What time is it?'

McGuire looked back at her, still lying in the bed he had just shared with her. The morning sunlight crept through the window, falling on her dark curls spread upon the pillow. He said softly: 'Time I left.' But then he lay down beside her, pressed his lips against hers and toyed with a ringlet of her hair as he went on: 'I still owe you dinner.'

'Can't you to stay for breakfast?' she asked. At that moment, the bells of St Alfred's Church rang out. 'Hear that?' she said. 'They're chiming for early Communion. It's Sunday. A day of rest.'

McGuire was clearly tempted but shook his head. 'Next time.' He got up.

'Scared to find out if my Eggs Benedict are better than yours?' she asked.

McGuire's smile quickly faded. 'I'm still in the middle of this investigation.'

At that moment, his smartphone beeped. Checking it, he remained silent for a moment as he carefully read an incoming e-mail. Noting his expression, Pearl leaned up on an elbow to get closer. 'What is it?'

'Autopsy,' he said. 'Cause of death . . . Cardiac arrest brought on by . . .' He trailed off as he read on.

'What?' asked Pearl impatiently.

'A neurotoxin,' said McGuire. 'Nicotine.'

Pearl shook her head, confused. 'But . . . Weller didn't smoke.' She frowned. 'He said so himself in the restaurant – he told Peter Radcliffe he'd given up.' McGuire looked back at her and she explained: 'Radcliffe's the councillor who's been championing the development?'

'You mean the same guy who brought Weller and Ritchie to the pageant?'

Pearl nodded. McGuire now showed her his smartphone, allowing her to read on.

'Administered by . . . "injection".' She looked up to see McGuire quickly buttoning his shirt, then she continued reading. 'Entry point was . . .'

'Back of the neck,' said McGuire, taking his phone from her hand.

'But I . . . didn't even know nicotine could be that toxic.'

'Clearly someone did.'

'Well, how on earth would you get hold of enough to inject?'

'Easier than you think,' said McGuire. 'Have you ever seen a reusable unit for electronic cigarettes? They're filled with concentrated solutions of liquid nicotine – as high as ten per cent in some cases – and readily available on the internet. A lot of it's coming from overseas without much in the way of safety standards. Readily available. Poorly regulated.' He raked his hands through his hair. 'And the killer wouldn't have needed that much. I've seen reports that just a teaspoonful of highly diluted e-liquid could be enough to kill a small child.'

As Pearl took this in, McGuire reached for his jacket. 'I've got to go.'

Pearl tried to make sense of what she'd just learned. 'So . . . Weller went to the downs to meet someone. They injected him with the liquid nicotine and then placed his body in the pillory?'

'Presumably someone he trusted,' said McGuire. He tapped his smartphone to refer to the autopsy. 'There were no defensive wounds.'

'Yes,' said Pearl. 'And why else would he go there at night, if it wasn't to meet someone he knew?'

'Or someone who had information for him?'

'He didn't seem the kind for a moonlight stroll.'

'And if he was, he could've done that at home,' said McGuire. 'His spread in Chestfield has over ten acres of grounds.'

As Pearl reflected on this, McGuire slipped into his jacket and said: 'Now I really *do* have to go.'

Pearl nodded and McGuire held up his smartphone. 'I shouldn't have shared this with you,' he said. 'So keep it to yourself – for now. And if you do turn up anything, let me know right away.' He slipped his phone into his jacket pocket then leaned forward and kissed her.

As he moved to the door, Pearl called to him. 'McGuire?'

He turned and saw her smile. 'Next time I'll make you breakfast.'

'Deal,' said McGuire.

Pearl spent the next few moments trying to absorb what she had just learned about Gordon Weller's death, but on hearing her kitchen door close, she got up and stood at her bedroom window, waiting for McGuire to appear in her seafront garden. He looked back up at Pearl, winked at her, then walked off along the prom in the direction of the car park at Keam's Yard. Once he had finally disappeared, she stared straight ahead, almost hypnotised by the thin skeins of cloud that were hovering above the sea. The tide was in and yet the morning seemed airless, the estuary waters stretched out before her like a swirling grey mist. She pushed the window open and dared to smile at the day ahead of her, but her face set as she saw a silver car parked on Neptune Gap. A moment later, a text sounded on her mobile. Two words appeared on the screen: *Let's talk.*

Ten minutes after receiving the message, Pearl was closing

her garden gate behind her and heading across the shingle beach towards a figure standing at the water's edge. Jason Ritchie was facing the sea, his arm raised as he tossed a pebble towards the water. It skimmed three times before disappearing beneath the waves. He continued to stare after it as though waiting for it to reappear. Finally he spoke. 'At this time in the morning, I'm guessing your friend wasn't here on police business.' He turned to face her but Pearl held her nerve.

'And I'm guessing that's not what you're here to talk about,' she replied. 'You don't seem to like answering phone calls.'

'In the circumstances, I'd rather we talked face to face.'

'About Gordon Weller's death?'

'His murder,' said Ritchie starkly. 'Because that's what it was.'

'You're sure about that?'

'My business partner is found dead, close to where our development is to take place, only days after the legal verdict for us to go ahead?' His eyes narrowed as he went on: 'One thing I'm not . . . is a fool.'

Pearl paused before responding. 'No,' she said. 'And that's why you arranged to have those "plants" in the crowd the other morning. To disrupt Martha's meeting and have them disagree with whatever she and Frederick Clark had to say.'

Ritchie gave a slow smile. 'Very good. I knew I was right about you. You're a smart woman. But now I need an update. It's what I'm paying you for.'

'No,' said Pearl, shaking her head. 'You're not paying me because I'm not working for you.'

Ritchie's face clouded. 'The cheque . . .'

'I haven't deposited it and I don't intend to. I ripped it up.'

Ritchie's hand moved quickly to his jacket pocket. 'Then I'll write another . . .'

'And you'll be wasting your time.' A pause followed before Pearl explained. 'Your money may buy you a lot of things but it doesn't buy me. *I* decide who I work for.'

Ritchie's hand dropped to his side. Pearl went on: 'If you'd answered my calls I could have told you that sooner. I even came to Black Mill, but I had a wasted visit. Now it looks like you've had the same.'

Jason Ritchie held her look for a moment as though testing her resolve. Finally he gave a thin smile. 'You'll change your mind.'

'I don't think so,' said Pearl, resolved.

Jason considered her for a moment before taking a step closer. 'Sooner or later,' he began, 'you'll come to me. Because I'll have exactly what you need.' He fixed her with a determined look, then turned and began walking slowly away from her, up the beach in the direction of the Old Neptune. As he climbed the stone steps across the sea wall and down into Neptune Gap, he gave one last look at Pearl before putting on his Ray-Ban sunglasses. After getting into his Lexus, the sound of its engine tore into the peaceful morning.

*

A few hours later, Pearl and Dolly were together in The Whitstable Pearl, busily packing hampers of food destined for the protest camp. It wasn't exactly a banquet and Pearl was short on 'loaves and fishes' so she had made stacks of sandwiches and included some large seafood flans and fruit which she hoped would provide a welcome change for Charlie from vegan soup.

Watching her daughter check the list in her hands, Dolly sensed Pearl's concern. 'I really wouldn't worry about him,' she said. 'Charlie'll be fine. He's a young man – sticking up for something he believes in. What he's doing, Pearl, is exciting. Rewarding!' She paused for a moment, a smile lighting up her face. 'You know, when I was at Greenham Common,' she went on, 'protesting against American cruise missiles—'

'Mum,' Pearl broke in wearily, but Dolly put up her hand.

'No, Pearl,' she said. 'I know I've told you stories before but you really should listen to this one.' Her look silenced Pearl and only once she knew she had her daughter's full attention, did she continue. 'It was the winter of eighty-two and a call had gone out to try to get enough of us women to surround the American base. None of us quite knew how many might turn up because the appeal for support had gone out by word of mouth.' She paused. 'Do you know how many came?'

Pearl shook her head.

'Thirty-five thousand.' Dolly looked at Pearl proudly. 'Thirty-five thousand women responded to that call. When they arrived, we linked arms, hands and . . . encircled nine miles of wire. That's what stood between us and the missiles, Pearl. Wire. So we decided we'd use it as a symbol. We pinned to it anything and everything that meant something to us. We had to stand among brambles to do that and we got cut to ribbons – but we did it, Pearl. We pinned up family photos, baby clothes, bottles, teething rings, teddy bears—' She broke off for a moment and smiled at Pearl. 'You were just a tot at the time so I wasn't able to take you with me. I had to leave you behind with your dad. And that wasn't easy – but Tommy understood.' She nodded. 'He agreed with me going. Said we hadn't brought you into the world for us to become the caretakers of weapons that could cause so much destruction. We had to do something and . . . well, that was the only thing we *could* do – go to where those weapons were and say no to them in front of the whole world.' She paused as she remembered: 'I'd taken one of your drawings with me and I pinned that up on the wire fence. There were women standing alongside us that day who'd come from all over the world – from Africa, Asia, America, New Zealand . . . We surrounded the base, and we blockaded it, too – we simply sat down in front of the gates and refused to go. The police arrived from inside, and we started singing: "You can't kill the spirit . . . You can't kill the spirit."' The smile on Dolly's face suddenly faded.

'What happened?' asked Pearl.

Dolly's expression darkened. 'They started dragging us away. Tossed us into the mud. Suddenly there was chaos. Screams. Cries. Orders being shouted by squads of police.

Curses as we hit the ground—' She broke off, biting her lip as she remembered. 'I saw one woman pulled away by her hair. But we just kept coming back.' She looked at Pearl. 'And we kept on singing. In the end, we lay down in front of the transport, all the while trying to explain to the police, and anyone else who'd listen, why we were doing this. We held on to one another, and we cried, but we kept on singing, "You can't kill the spirit."' She looked at Pearl. 'We felt like Suffragettes, Pearl, standing up to the establishment. Not for votes . . . but for peace.'

'I know,' said Pearl, torn. 'And I know how much it meant to you, and how you faced down the police that day, but . . . this isn't the same. McGuire's not policing a protest – he's investigating a murder. Somewhere in this town, maybe even in Snowdrop Valley, is the person responsible for Gordon Weller's death.'

Dolly frowned as she took this in. 'He really was murdered?' Pearl's look gave Dolly her answer. She took a moment to absorb this. 'Well, there's no reason to believe that whoever killed him might want to harm Charlie, or anyone else up there at the camp. Besides, Marty's there. He'll take care of him.'

'Will he?' asked Pearl, unconvinced. 'Marty's behaving weirdly,' she said starkly. 'You know how important his business is to him? He seems to have abandoned the shop – as though he's forgotten all about it. And that just isn't like him.'

Dolly reflected on this. 'Well,' she said, 'I don't think it takes much for a civilised man to revert to the primitive.

It happens when some men get close to nature. Look at Tarzan.'

Pearl sighed. 'Tarzan wasn't real, remember?'

'Oh yes.' Dolly frowned. 'Well,' she went on, searching for another reason, 'maybe it's good Marty's taking a break – he works too hard – like you, Pearl. It's no bad thing to feel so passionately about a cause that you're willing to make a few sacrifices – though that won't be the case where food's concerned.' She cast a knowing look towards the hampers she had been helping to pack.

'Sacrifices,' said Pearl, remembering something.

'What about them?' asked Dolly.

'That's something Martha Laker talked about today.'

Dolly shrugged. 'We all have to make them.'

'But you can't blame me for worrying,' said Pearl defensively. 'Charlie's my son . . .'

'And you're my daughter!' said Dolly. 'Which is why I've made a decision.' She paused, bracing herself before adding: 'First thing tomorrow, I'm joining the camp too.'

Pearl's jaw dropped open. 'What?'

'Don't look so surprised. I've been thinking about it ever since the camp was set up. Besides, if I'm there, I can keep an eye on Charlie.'

'Great,' said Pearl, with a fair degree of irony, 'now I'll have *two* of you to worry about.'

'You're forgetting,' said Dolly. 'I am virtually a professional. A proud geriactivist! Apart from Greenham Common, I've marched against the Vietnam War and the Poll Tax. For women's rights, I even burned my bra.' She smiled proudly.

Pearl looked down at her mother's ample bosom and couldn't help hoping that in those days Dolly had worn a smaller cup-size.

It was almost 7.30 when Pearl parked up on a side road on Borstal Hill and took from the boot of her Fiat a small trolley on which she placed the food hampers. Having made several trips to the downs in the last few days, she knew she could manage the short trek down into Snowdrop Valley using the timber steps from Laker's Field on to a well-trodden path. The evening was close and humid, with clouds of mosquitos gathering in the still evening air.

Her thoughts wandered to Gordon Weller and his last fateful journey to the Crown of the Down. Might he have been summoned that night by a message from his business partner? If so, how did that message come to him? Had McGuire found anything on Weller's phone records? Pearl reflected on the fact that Ritchie had told her how he wanted to hire her services to be kept informed of the local situation, but it was perfectly possible he wanted to do that in order to keep abreast of what Pearl knew – or could discover – about Weller's murder. She resolved to talk to McGuire about Ritchie – the person she suspected would have profited most from Gordon Weller's death – because the development deal was bound to have included an insurance clause.

Tipping the trolley down the timber steps towards the valley, Pearl paused as she heard something other than the flight of birds preparing to roost in the trees.

Further ahead, the strains of Charlie's guitar were floating on the air, voices singing the song he had been playing only the other evening in his room. Pearl listened hard, trying to hold on to the magic in her son's music, but it wasn't enough to displace the growing sense of unease she was experiencing. The song came to an end, followed by applause. The voices now drifted into silence until another sound served to startle her – a fat toad plunging into a nearby surface stream. Pearl moved on, aware that her nerves were causing her mind to play tricks on her, as they had done during the pageant, when she had thought she heard voices in the trees, before coming upon Tyler with Gloria Greenwood.

Taking a few more steps she finally found herself in a clearing and breathed a sigh of relief. She paused to enjoy her surroundings. Red campion was flowering alongside forget-me-nots and buttercups. The pungent smell of wild garlic hung in the air and she decided she would pick some on her way back and use it for tomorrow's menu at the restaurant. Behind her, raised up above this scene, the timber hide overlooked the whole area. Pearl smiled as she remembered something Dolly had once said: 'It's not only the birds that breed there.' It was true that the hide had long been used for lovers' secret trysts – even when it had been just a simple wooden shelter. Now it was a sizeable structure, having been extended some time ago, its walls log-lapped with a fair-sized observation panel that allowed any occupant to stare straight down to the area where Pearl was now standing. As her eyes focused up towards this gap, a feeling came over her that perhaps she, too, was being observed at that moment – but by whom? Looking around she saw no one and yet she knew she was surrounded by numerous creatures that inhabited the downs. A shiver ran through her and she decided to move on with her trolley, keen to get the food to Charlie and the other protesters before the evening light faded.

Taking a step forward, she heard a woman's piercing scream. Sharp and sudden it had sounded from somewhere close behind her, and looking back, Pearl saw two figures standing on the higher ground – a man and a woman silhouetted against the last of the sunlight filtering through the trees. Abandoning the food, Pearl headed quickly up to them. As she got closer she recognised Ben Tyler standing motionless; he was holding Gloria Greenwood protectively towards him.

'What is it?' Pearl asked. Gloria buried her face against Tyler's shoulder, as if trying to hide from something she had just seen. Tyler met Pearl's gaze and slowly raised an arm, pointing to the hide. Inside, a figure sat at the observation table, head leaning against the side of the log-lap wall, eyes staring straight ahead, mouth fixed in a smile – a rictus grin – born not of pleasure but pain.

Pearl took a step forward and felt for a pulse. In spite of the warm evening, her hand met only chilled flesh. A pair of familiar tortoiseshell spectacles lay on the table. A tiny puncture mark was visible on Frederick Clark's neck – a crimson pinprick of blood marking the entry wound of what Pearl felt sure had been yet another lethal syringe.

Looking back at Ben Tyler she shook her head. It was clear Martha Laker's loyal partner in the campaign had been dead for some time.

CHAPTER FOURTEEN

'I don't understand,' said Pearl to McGuire the next day on the phone. She was walking along the beach, the tide was out and a few spectral figures were dotted on the mudflats searching for bait. 'If Gordon Weller was murdered because of his plans for the Invicta development, why on earth would the same person want to kill Frederick Clark? Fred was an ally of the campaign and a supporter of the protest.'

'I can't answer that right now,' said McGuire on the other end of the line, unbuttoning his shirt collar as he entered his office at Canterbury Police Station. 'We've been busy securing the scene, conducting a search of the area—'

'And the murder weapon?' she asked expectantly.

'No sign of a hypodermic but it's possible it could have been discarded elsewhere on the downs.'

'Or taken away by the killer,' said Pearl. 'Surely it's more likely that the murderer came to the woods, killed Fred and then took away any evidence with him?'

'"Him"?' asked McGuire.

Pearl frowned. 'All right,' she said. 'The killer could be a woman and Martha Laker's house *is* close to the scene of the crime, but why would she want to murder Fred? He was working closely with her. It doesn't make any sense, but—' She broke off and paused for a moment. 'Ben Tyler's shepherd's hut is also close by,' she said, before adding: 'He and Gloria Greenwood were at the hide before me and found the body first.'

'The hut's been thoroughly searched,' said McGuire. 'No forensic links found. And you were right in your statement last night: initial examination of the body confirmed that Clark had been murdered at least an hour before Tyler and his girlfriend arrived on the scene.'

Pearl took this in. 'What about Jason Ritchie?' she asked. 'He's renting Black Mill – it's just a stone's throw from the downs—'

'Pearl, listen to me,' said McGuire firmly, cutting in. He paused before explaining: 'We found a note in Clark's pocket.'

'A note?' Pearl echoed. 'Well,' she continued impatiently, 'what does it say?'

From his desk, McGuire picked up a scrap of paper sealed in a plastic evidence bag and shook his head slowly. 'Your guess is as good as mine.'

'What are you talking about?' she asked, confused.

McGuire turned the bag around in his hand. 'It looks like some sort of . . . ancient script,' he told her. 'Makes no sense at all. I've put someone on to it but—'

'Can you get me a copy?' asked Pearl quickly.

'Oh, so you're an expert in hieroglyphics now, are you?'

'At least let me try.'

McGuire looked again at the note in the evidence bag, then tossed it on to his desk and gave in. 'Okay, I'll e-mail you a copy.'

'Thanks.' Pearl smiled. 'And now I've got to go.'

'To the restaurant?'

'No,' she said. 'I'm paying a visit to the *Chronicle*. Oh and . . . did you happen to find anything among Weller's phone records?'

'Like?'

'A message from his partner to meet him on the downs?'

'No,' said McGuire. 'Nothing of the kind – from anyone.'

Suddenly he heard what he thought was a click on the line. 'Pearl?' he asked. Silence. 'Pearl?' he asked more forcefully. But it was too late: she had gone.

The offices of the Chronicle Newspaper Group were situated in an area known as Estuary View, half a mile from the main roundabout at the top of Borstal Hill. Pearl drove into the virtually empty car park and admired the coastal view that gave the location its name. A few moments later, she headed towards a pair of glass swing doors. Expecting to find a bustle of staff on the other side, she was greeted instead by a teenage receptionist who was busy reshaping her eyebrows. Asking to see Chris Latimer on an important issue, Pearl waited for the girl to make a quick call before learning that the *Chronicle*'s news editor was out of the building and that someone else would see her in his absence.

Pearl found Bill Latimer in a large office surrounded by several empty but untidy desks. 'Excuse the mess,' were his first words, as he glanced awkwardly at newspapers piled on almost every surface. Attempting to gather some up, he then offered Pearl a seat. 'Nice to see you,' he said, 'though I'd have preferred to have done so under different circumstances.' He indicated a glass coffee-maker on an electric hob. Pearl shook her head but Bill poured himself a cup and explained: 'Chris is out covering Fred Clark's murder. I'm guessing you want to see him about that?'

Pearl nodded. 'My son and my mother are at the protest camp,' she explained. 'I wanted to know his thoughts about it.'

'I see,' said Bill sparely.

Pearl glanced around the empty office. 'Are . . . all your staff out chasing stories?'

Bill followed Pearl's gaze before he looked back at her and admitted, 'To be honest, the only staff the *Chronicle* has right now are Chris and a few trainees.' He shook his head. 'Extraordinary,' he went on. 'Once upon a time, we couldn't manage without a news editor, three staff reporters, two trainees, a sports editor and a sub-editor for headlines. Now I'm doing the latter as well as checking copy and producing photos.' He slumped into his chair and looked defeated. 'It's no secret our advertising revenue has dropped by more than twenty-five per cent over the last year. Classified-ad clients prefer cheap websites where their copy can be up and running in a matter of hours. It's a different game now.'

Pearl took this in, along with Bill's desultory mood, and asked: 'The paper's been in your family for some time, hasn't it?'

Bill nodded. 'True,' he said. 'But I've managed to make mistakes my father and his father before him never made.'

'Mistakes?'

Bill looked back at her. 'I'm what's known as the editor-proprietor so if anyone's responsible for this current situation – it's me.' He glanced around once more. 'I didn't see it coming,' he said, 'the shape of things to come.'

'I don't think you can blame yourself for that,' said Pearl. 'There can't be many who could have seen how much business would transfer online. And not only news. The same goes for food: there are restaurants in town that are doing a much better trade in online orders for deliveries than they are in-house. Sooner or later,' she went on, 'I may even have to join them. And I guess that's what Jason Ritchie would call . . . economic progress?' She saw Bill Latimer was considering a photo of Frederick Clark on his computer screen.

'Fred's idea of hell,' he said. 'But then if people like Ritchie had their way, the Fred Clarks of this world would all be swept away.'

'Would they?' asked Pearl, picking up on this.

'Sure,' said Bill. 'Fred never compromised. He was an honourable man. But he also preferred to live in the past.'

He paused before finally admitting: 'Maybe I do too.' His gaze now shifted to the wall where an old advertisement from an early edition of the *Chronicle* hung in pride of place – for a jamboree at Whitstable Castle.

'Did you know Fred well?' Pearl asked.

Bill shrugged. 'Maybe as well as anyone,' he said. 'We covered his campaigns in the *Chronicle* and printed his letters, in which he constantly complained about all manner of minor issues.'

'Like?'

'Cafés in the High Street littering the pavements with tables? He'd shop them to the council, then complain about local councillors not doing their jobs properly and awarding themselves unearned increases in allowances. He made enemies all round and there were plenty who asked just who the hell Fred Clark thought he was to have set himself up as unofficial policeman in this town? Fifty per cent of letters in the *Chronicle* complained about him being given any platform at all – but the other fifty per cent always agreed with him.'

'And you?'

'I looked at our circulation figures and acted accordingly.' He paused, then smiled, somewhat wistfully. 'I remember he once went on at me about giving him some space in the paper.'

'Space?' said Pearl, picking up on this. 'For a column, you mean?'

Bill shook his head. 'No. I think that would have been far too preachy for my liking – or anyone else's, for that matter. Fred was an earnest bloke and not exactly known for his sense of humour. He wanted me to run a small weekly section for chess buffs; you know the kind of thing: a diagram of a chessboard with a problem set for readers – how many moves to checkmate?'

'And . . . did you run it?'

Bill shook his head. 'I'm not sure how many chess fans we have among our readers but I'm guessing it's not many. Besides, I wouldn't have known how to check the solution – I'm not a chess player myself.'

'Martha is,' said Pearl thoughtfully as she remembered their recent conversation.

Bill shrugged. 'Well, that's something else she had in common with Fred,' he went on, 'apart from leading local campaigns.'

'But . . . I understand their tactics tended to be rather different?'

Bill sipped his coffee and said, 'Fred was always low-profile while Martha – well, you've seen for yourself, she's larger than life. The Queen of Whitstable.'

Pearl smiled at this. 'Wasn't that one of your front-page headlines?'

Bill nodded slowly. 'Yes. But she earned it after she saved those trees from the supermarket development.'

'So, you must have been grateful to her for filling so much empty space in your paper?'

'You bet,' he admitted. 'Campaigns are good for filling pages – sometimes for weeks or months at a time. And . . . *Gran Falls Down Stairs* or *Whitstable Child Loses Shoe* might be a tragedy for those involved, but as headlines they sure as hell don't sell many newspapers.'

'So, why would Martha complain that she can't get the coverage she needs for this campaign?'

'That's typical of Martha,' said Bill dismissively. 'I can tell you now, there were a few in Whitstable who had become bored with Fred Clark's complaints, but there are also plenty who've had their fill of Martha Laker. One of our letter writers actually warned that the paper was in danger of becoming the *Laker Chronicle*. Overexposure won't do Martha any favours – or her "burning issues" – and she'll never run out of those. Even if she wins this campaign, there'll be something else to take its place. No "happy ever afters" for Martha – just one long series of conflicts. That's what she thrives on; but after a while, it can become rather tedious – for the *Chronicle* and for its readers. It also devalues her campaigns.'

'It doesn't look like the protesters are getting tired of her,' said Pearl. 'There must be a hundred or more camped at Snowdrop Valley right now.'

'Yes,' said Bill. 'But since last night, there's one less – Fred Clark.' He looked at Pearl. 'News of his murder, and that of Gordon Weller, will continue to eclipse anything Martha has in mind for that camp.' He finished his coffee and pointed to a computer screen. 'Now, if you don't mind, I've got some copyediting to do.'

Pearl nodded and moved off, looking back at him, alone, in the empty office.

*

A few moments later, Pearl walked out of the *Chronicle*'s offices into bright sunlight and switched on her smartphone. She was just about to check her e-mails to see if McGuire had sent her a copy of the note found on Fred Clark's body when a call came in. The caller ID showed it was McGuire but, just at that moment, his voice was drowned out by a low-flying plane that was crossing the sky. Looking up, Pearl saw it was an old-fashioned biplane, just like the ones that used to fly over the beach during the local Regatta, but this one sported two wing-walkers who were drawing attention to a banner trailing behind it, which read: SAVE OUR DOWNS!

As the plane's engine chugged out a green trail, Pearl found herself smiling at this bold, creative, attention-seeking stunt; it had Martha Laker written all over it. As the plane disappeared into cotton-bud clouds, McGuire's voice sounded on the line. 'Pearl? Are you there?'

'Yes,' she replied quickly. 'Have you sent me that e-mail yet, with the copy of the note?'

'No. That's not why I'm calling . . .'

'But you said you would—'

'Listen to me,' said McGuire, breaking in. His tone was both urgent and firm. 'My DCs have been going through Weller's paperwork and all the Invicta Land accounts.'

'And?'

'And they've turned up a cheque made out to Nolan's Detective Agency.'

Brought up short by this, Pearl looked away in frustration, then explained: 'That had nothing to do with

Weller,' she said. 'It was Ritchie, just trying to get me on side.'

'What's that supposed to mean?' asked McGuire, terse.

Pearl walked on towards her car as she explained: 'He wanted me to do some work for him and left the cheque behind to tempt me.'

McGuire said nothing as he tried to compute this and Pearl felt obliged to fill the silence. 'Look, he just wanted me to do some "digging around", collecting information about the campaign? He made it sound legit and all above board – research for the benefit of all concerned. He's good at what he does – getting what he wants. But I saw the way he manipulated the crowd when Martha and Fred Clark held a rally at the beach. He used "plants" to disrupt things. He'd say in his defence that he was just trying to put out a balanced view of Invicta's proposals, but it was dishonest of him – a shady practice – and I wanted nothing to do with him.' Having reached her car, she opened the driver's door.

'And you didn't think to tell me any of this?'

'I hardly had a chance! But it had nothing to do with my finding Gordon Weller's body on the downs.' She got into the car and slipped the key in the ignition.

'Why don't you let me be the judge of that?' said McGuire.

Pearl heaved a sigh and gave in. 'Okay,' she said. 'In hindsight, maybe I should have mentioned it in my state-ment to the DC, but I wasn't deliberately hiding this from you. Nothing came of it. I never deposited the cheque. I ripped it up. The pieces are still in my fireplace.'

'And was this before or after you found Gordon Weller's body?'

Pearl took exception to his tone. 'What's that supposed to mean?'

'Pearl, this can't just be . . . forgotten. It's evidence.'

'Of what?'

'Of a link between you and Weller's company.'

'It means nothing!' Pearl protested.

'Then why didn't you tell me?'

'I . . . don't know,' she stammered. 'I didn't tell anyone . . .' She trailed off.

'Pearl?'

'All right, I . . . didn't want anyone knowing he'd come to see me, let alone thinking I might be working for the other side – for Invicta Land? I put Ritchie straight on that when he came back to see me the other day. I told you, I don't trust him.' She paused, unnerved by McGuire's silence, before she asked: 'You . . . do believe me?'

'Is there anything else you haven't told me?'

'No. I swear.'

For some time, McGuire remained silent – then: 'I'm going to clear the protest camp.'

Pearl frowned. 'Because of this?'

'No.'

'Then why now?'

'Because there are too many people there and I'm concerned about public safety.'

Pearl felt instantly conflicted: part of her was relieved that Charlie and Dolly would be out of danger but another part of her knew they would only blame Pearl and McGuire for putting an end to their protest. 'You'll increase local antipathy if you do,' she warned him.

'Maybe,' said McGuire. 'But I have other considerations right now. Talk to Charlie and Dolly and get them out of there.'

'Or what?'

'Or they'll be arrested,' said McGuire. 'And I don't want to have to do that.'

'Then don't,' Pearl ordered. Dolly's story about Greenham Common was still fresh in her mind.

McGuire took a deep breath. 'You know I can't show them any special treatment,' he said. 'Talk to them.'

'And what if they won't listen?' asked Pearl, her exasperation mounting. 'They have a perfect right to be there – it's public land.'

'No,' said McGuire. 'I have a murder investigation to deal with, and if that camp's not cleared by tomorrow morning – I'll clear it myself.'

'But—'

The line went dead in Pearl's hand.

CHAPTER FIFTEEN

Ten minutes after her conversation with McGuire, Pearl entered Seaspray Cottage, this time listening to another voice on her mobile. Dolly's message was unequivocal. 'We're not moving an inch.'

'But—'

'Look,' Dolly said, breaking in, 'in any campaign there's always a tipping point – a time when the authorities decide they'll try some new tactic, and usually just when you're beginning to get somewhere. That aeroplane stunt of Martha's has raised more awareness of the cause and brought more than a hundred new recruits to the camp. The more of us there are – the more powerful we'll be.'

'And what about Fred Clark and Gordon Weller? Two men have been murdered.'

'I know,' said Dolly, torn. 'We all know. And we're sorry – especially Martha about Fred. He was one of us, but . . . have you considered that he may have been done away with just for this to take place – for the camp to be broken up? We can't do that, Pearl. Fred wouldn't have wanted it. Martha said as much this afternoon in a speech to us.'

'Did she?' asked Pearl, picking up on this.

'Yes,' said Dolly. 'She said Fred had told her how he'd always doubted the power of protests and demos – until now. But since the camp was set up, he could see how this campaign could be won – especially as all other means had been exhausted – apart from a legal appeal, which could cost tens of thousands.'

Pearl mused on this. 'That's what a court would consider to be hearsay.'

'What?' asked Dolly, confused.

'You only have Martha's word that Fred said any of that.'

'And you don't trust her?'

Pearl decided not to answer but instead to change tack. 'How's Charlie?'

'He's fine, Pearl. I promise you. He's made good friends with Martha's son, Simon, and he's keeping himself busy around the camp. He sends his love but—' The line suddenly began to break up.

'Mum?'

Dolly's voice returned. 'He agrees with the rest of us, Pearl. We're not going anywhere—' Her voice disappeared once more.

'Reception's bad,' said Pearl.

'Then I'll call later. Don't worry!' yelled Dolly finally.

Pearl ended the call and slipped her phone into her

pocket. Glancing across the living room of Seaspray Cottage, she moved to her laptop, switched it on and checked among numerous e-mails in her inbox for one in particular. Finding it, she clicked on it. Its title was *The Note* and it had been sent earlier that morning by McGuire. There was no message, just an attachment – which she opened. Looking at only a single line of characters on the page, she now understood why McGuire had used the word 'hieroglyphics': the symbols used in the note found on Fred Clark's body had an Egyptian style to them, resembling something that might be found on a pharaoh's sarcophagus. Thinking back to her earlier conversation with Bill Latimer, Pearl then put in a search for a chess site. The page showed aerial diagrams of chessboards with a sequence of possible moves to checkmate – and the latter was denoted by a hash sign: *1.Qg5+ Ke4 2.Rf4+ Ke3 3.Qg3+ Ke2 4.Rf2+ Ke1 5.Qg1#*. Checkmate. She punched the word into her search engine and learned that Martha was quite right: the Arabic term '*Sheikh Mat*' or 'the king is dead' had arrived with the game of chess from the Islamic world, but she also noted that the modern Arabic word, '*mate*', could also be used to describe someone who had been rendered helpless by confusion – something Pearl now felt herself to be about these murders . . .

Pearl slept fitfully that night. The air felt muggy, like a suffocating blanket. She tossed and turned, troubled by dreams filled with surreal images of pyramids and chess pieces while roaring planes turned somersaults in the sky.

The hieroglyphic symbols from Fred Clark's note jumbled themselves into various chess moves and hash signs as Bill Latimer's voice echoed a warning: *If people like Ritchie had their way, the Fred Clarks of this world would all be swept away* . . . The words seemed to be a premonition . . .

Pearl looked out of her bedroom window: the usual peaceful seascape had become a dark line on the horizon. A black squall of stormy weather was rising up into a massive wave and a wall of sea water was coming closer – an unstoppable tsunami growing ever taller, thundering towards her until the crest of its wave finally curled and began crashing down— Pearl woke with a start, gasping for air. Looking quickly around her moonlit bedroom, she realised the tsunami was still there, formed from the fear and anxiety that engulfed her in that moment. She got quickly out of bed and dressed.

Less than half an hour later, Pearl had made her way into the camp at Snowdrop Valley. Everyone appeared to be asleep, tucked up in sleeping bags and tents. Pearl spotted the familiar sight of Charlie's guitar lying close to an unlit fire, but heading across to it, she saw that a nearby sleeping bag was unzipped. One of Charlie's T-shirts was lying on top of it.

'Pearl?' Close by, Dolly had just woken. 'What is it?' she asked, trying to make sense of Pearl's presence in the camp.

'Charlie,' said Pearl. 'He's not in his sleeping bag.'

Dolly rubbed her eyes and took Pearl's view across the camp. 'He was up late,' she said, 'with Simon. Playing guitar.' She pointed across to another sleeping bag. Pearl saw that Simon Stone was fast asleep. Heading across to him, she shook him gently awake.

'What is it?' he said sleepily.

'Where's Charlie?' Pearl asked urgently.

Simon raised himself on one elbow, pushed his long fringe back from his eyes and saw the empty sleeping bag and abandoned guitar. 'I . . . left him up,' he explained. 'He wasn't tired but I needed to crash out. The fire was getting low and . . . he said he'd go and get more wood.' He looked around. 'He can't be far.'

Pearl stared around in the darkness, overwhelmed by a mounting sense of dread.

'Don't worry,' said Dolly quickly. 'I'll get up and help you find him.' She began struggling with the zip of her sleeping bag, but before she could free herself, a hand clamped firmly on Pearl's arm. She looked back to see Ben Tyler. He held Pearl's gaze for a moment, then picked up Charlie's T-shirt.

'What're you doing?' she asked, unnerved.

Tyler nodded to Scooby at his side. 'The dog's part bloodhound,' he explained. He held the T-shirt tightly against Scooby's nose then signalled for the dog to go on ahead. Looking back at Pearl, he nodded determinedly. 'Come on.'

After making their way out of the camp Pearl found herself struggling to keep up with Tyler. 'Two murders on these downs and now my son's missing.'

Tyler failed to respond but followed Martha's dog further into Gorrell Wood.

'If he's come to any harm . . .' Pearl went on, her words trailing off as she found herself unable to contemplate that possibility.

Tyler fixed his gaze straight ahead and said only: 'We'll find him.' He moved on quickly and purposefully, following the dog's trail.

'Does Martha know about you?' Pearl asked with suspicion.

Tyler remained silent as he paused for a moment, noting Scooby sniffing around in the undergrowth. Pearl studied his face, searching for an emotion – but found none.

'You killed a man,' she said starkly. 'In Ireland. That's true, isn't it?'

Tyler's was mouth set. Still he failed to respond.

'Is that the reason you're here?' she asked. She was baiting him, frustrated by his silence. 'You're running away—'

At this, Tyler's head finally snapped in Pearl's direction, as surely as if he'd been punched.

'I'm not running,' he said in a low voice. 'And I'm not fighting. Not any more.'

Unnerved by his look, Pearl steeled herself and called out into the darkness for her son: 'Charlie!'

Only silence followed. Then a sigh escaped Pearl's lips. Her fear continued to mount and Tyler knew it.

'I told you,' he said, 'the dog will find him.'

As he started to move off, Pearl pursued him. 'Alive – or dead?' she asked suddenly, desperate for an answer. 'This is all down to you and Martha Laker,' she went on.

'What is it? Does she give you protection in return for your support? And why did she go to see you the other day?' She found herself chasing after Tyler, waiting for a reply that failed to come.

'Why won't you answer me!' she cried. On the cusp of tears, she now stopped in her tracks. Tyler turned and saw her pain. Moving back to her, he set his hands firmly on her shoulders and said: '*Nothing* is going on. You hear me?' He paused, staring deep into Pearl's eyes, and then said, 'Martha's the only person in a long time who's treated me like a human being and not . . . an animal.' He glanced away as though needing to escape but realising there was nowhere to run. 'She found out what happened to me at the last place I stayed. She got the farmer's permission for me to keep my hut on the field near Benacre. She let me take the dog for company . . . after . . . she heard what happened to my own dog. My Shadow.' He struggled with a memory then continued: 'Shadow went missing. Two nights later, I found her – with her throat cut.' He swallowed hard. 'It was a sign. For me. A sign that no one wants a traveller for a neighbour – especially one with blood on his hands.' His dark eyes took on a haunted look. 'And mine are soaked with it.' A muscle tightened in his jaw. Raising his hands from Pearl's shoulders he stared at them as though they might have belonged to a stranger.

'That's what happens when you fight the way I've done. With these.' He turned his palms to his face. Pearl saw how they were trembling. 'Bone cracking bone,' he whispered. 'You hear it with every punch.' He clenched his hands into tight fists and Pearl now saw their power. 'And you're right,' he whispered. 'These *are* the hands of a killer.' His breathing had become shallow. A silence settled until, somewhere in the wood, an owl hooted. Tyler's black eyes shifted back to Pearl and for a timeless moment, he and Pearl simply stared at one another before a dog's bark broke the moment – like a sheet of glass shattering between them.

Tyler grabbed Pearl's hand and pulled her towards him, dragging her onwards, staggering through the under-growth until they finally caught sight of Scooby, silhouetted in the moonlight, head lowered, haunches raised, front legs braced straight out before him – gaze fixed on some-thing near the wooden bridge that spanned the Gorrell Stream. Tall yellow flag irises swayed idly in the breeze around the water's edge.

Pearl's heart quickened, blood pulsing in her ears as she and Ben caught sight of what the dog had found . . .

Fair hair was floating gently out on the surface bloom of the water. Pearl let out a scream of pain and launched herself forward but Tyler's strong grasp pulled her back. Instead, he leapt into the stream in her place and waded across to the figure on the other side. Quickly lowering his head to Charlie's, he then looked back at Pearl, and in that moment her world stood still before darkness descended.

CHAPTER SIXTEEN

Pearl had sat for some time in the hospital waiting room. The walls were covered in faded posters offering helplines for various conditions. Flow charts explained the roles of hospital personnel and gave advice on how to keep infections at bay. The posters disappeared as she closed her eyes and wished she could do the same for her fears for Charlie. A water cooler bubbled. The hands of a clock clicked the hour. Footsteps in the hallway outside approached – then retreated – reminding Pearl that she had never felt so alone. Then, the door suddenly opened and a moment passed between Pearl and McGuire before he opened his arms and she rushed to him. As he held her tight, she pressed her cheek against his shoulder, aware that, in that moment, he gave her everything she needed: comfort, protection and the knowledge she wasn't alone.

'What happened?' he asked.

'Tyler . . . pulled Charlie from the stream. He must

have slipped,' she went on. 'Struck his head on the wet stones that line the banks.' She paused, then: 'His face was lying above the waterline.' She looked up at McGuire who gave a long slow exhalation. 'And now?'

'Now they're doing X-rays . . . scans . . . checking for fractures.'

He laid the palm of his hand gently against her cheek. 'I'm so sorry.'

'No,' she said, cutting in. 'You were right.' She shook her head slowly. 'That was no place for anyone to be and I should have listened to you. But . . . I'm not sure I could've stopped Charlie if I'd tried.' She looked up at him as she asked: 'The camp?'

'Disbanded,' he said. 'Everyone went quietly in the end. Martha's decision. Your mum's on her way here.' He hesitated before bracing himself to broach something. 'Look, Pearl—'

'I know what you're going to say,' she said quickly. 'Stay out of this? Leave it to you?'

He held her gaze. 'Yes,' he said softly. 'It's my responsibility, not yours. And I don't want you coming to any harm. Do you understand?' A moment passed between them before a voice sounded.

'Mrs Nolan?'

Pearl turned and saw a young nurse standing at the door. As she came forward, Pearl noted the name written on a plastic tag on her uniform – Azra Choudhury.

'Charlie's fine,' said Azra. 'But we'd like to keep him here overnight – we'll take good care of him, I promise.'

She smiled and Pearl looked back at McGuire, feeling as though her heart had just begun beating once more.

Hours later, once Pearl had returned home from the hospital, a visitor arrived at Seaspray Cottage. Adam Stone looked troubled as he explained: 'I was very sorry to hear about Charlie. How is he?' He waited anxiously for Pearl's reply.

'He's doing okay,' she said finally. 'My mother's with him at the hospital right now. I just came back to check on the restaurant and to get Charlie's room ready. I'm hoping he'll be discharged later today.'

Adam's expression instantly relaxed. 'Thank God,' he said. 'I know it was all Si's idea that he joined the protest—'

'That's true,' said Pearl. 'But it wasn't Simon's fault that this happened. It was Charlie's decision to join the camp so there's no need for you to feel any responsibility. Or Simon.'

'Nevertheless, I do,' Adam insisted. He looked pained before admitting: 'To be honest, I didn't want Si to be here at all right now – in England, I mean. But I can't stop him seeing Martha, much as I'd like to.'

'She is his mother,' said Pearl.

'Yes, of course,' Adam said tersely, 'though she's hardly been in his life much until now.' Looking at Pearl, he explained: 'We broke up when Si was just two years old.'

Pearl nodded at this and gestured to the sofa behind him. 'Why don't you sit down?'

Adam hesitated, then saw Pearl's smile as a further

invitation and took a seat. He went on: 'Martha and I were . . . never really suited . . . but I suppose it was a *coup de foudre*. I was enthralled by her, fascinated by her energy . . . her passion.' He paused. 'But I made the mistake of thinking that the passion was for me alone. I was wrong,' he said. 'Martha gets . . . swept away by things.'

'Things?'

'Events, issues, people.' He paused, then: 'She was studying PPE when we met.'

Pearl nodded. 'Politics, philosophy and . . . ?'

'Economics,' said Adam. 'But she soon tired of that and switched to sociology – then she did an art course. It was the shape of things to come.'

'Her . . . adaptability?'

'Her inability to settle – or to stick with anything – or anyone.' He looked at Pearl. 'I know you'll think this is just sour grapes from a former partner, and in part you'd be right, but while Martha was busy exploring new subjects and relationships, I had a Ph.D. ahead of me – and our young son to take care of.'

'You mean . . . she left you?'

'More than once,' he said. 'The first time . . . she took Si off to a commune in California. Let's just say her judgement about the whole episode was faulty. I flew out and rescued him. He was only two years old. After that, I tried to make sure that the one thing he had in his life was stability.'

'And a responsible parent?' asked Pearl hesitantly.

'I've done my best.'

'And now?' Pearl asked. 'Just like Charlie, your son's free to make his own decisions.'

Adam frowned at this. 'Yes,' he agreed. 'And it's true that Martha's now more stable than before. At least, her relationship with Jane seems to have helped.' He took Pearl's silence as a cue to carry on. 'I'm . . . sure you're curious about Martha's sexuality but far too polite to ask.' He paused. 'Would she have been happier in a relationship with a woman from the start? Perhaps. Does that mean our relationship – what we had together – was a mistake?' He shook his head. 'No. I refuse to accept that. Once upon a time we loved one another, and if we hadn't been in love, we would never have had Si.'

Pearl considered this. 'Well, whatever Martha's short-comings as a parent might have been, Simon still has two parents and it's clear Martha loves him very much. It's there in her every look.'

Adam looked conflicted at this, then nodded. 'And he loves her too,' he admitted. 'Though she may not have . . . earned that love.'

Pearl noted Adam's hands clenching and unclenching as he steeled himself to continue. 'However stable Martha may appear to be right now, there's always an element of drama in her life – usually of her own making.'

Pearl hesitated. 'I . . . do understand how you feel,' she said. 'If anything serious had happened to Charlie, I'd be looking around for someone to blame but . . . as much as he'll always be my child, Charlie's also his own man, and what I've learned through this is there's nothing

I could have said or done to have stopped him doing what he wanted to do – protecting that piece of land? I can see how you want to protect Simon, but ultimately we all have to take responsibility for our own decisions. I didn't want Charlie to join the camp – and I certainly didn't want him to stay after Fred Clark's murder. But, now it's all academic because the camp's been disbanded. And I understand that was Martha's decision – not mine – or that of the police.'

Adam nodded slowly. 'Has there been . . . any progress about the murders? The police have told the press that poison was used.'

'A fatal injection of liquid nicotine,' said Pearl, taking careful note of Adam's shocked reaction.

'Are you . . . sure about that?' he asked.

Pearl nodded. Adam appeared stunned before explaining: 'I've done work in this field,' he said. 'I specialised in it.'

'Then you'll know just how powerful a small amount of nicotine can be?'

He nodded. 'Of course. And it wouldn't need to be injected either,' he said. 'A concentrated solution of liquid nicotine can easily be absorbed through the skin. In fact, there have been cases of life-threatening cardiac arrest just from contact with the contents of a broken electronic cigarette.'

'So, you . . . know all about it?'

'I just told you,' said Adam. 'I specialised in neurotoxins. And if you're thinking this might single me out as a suspect for a murder case, you'd be right. But for that reason alone, I'd be a fool to kill someone this way. Besides,' he went on, 'I had absolutely no reason to have wanted either of those men dead.'

In that moment, as he held Pearl's look, she felt she had no possible reason to doubt him.

A few hours later, after a phone call from the hospital, Pearl was back in the driver's seat of her car, heading along the Blean Road to Canterbury, on a scenic route that carved its way through lush green fields. Finally, the spires of the great cathedral became visible, rising above a heat haze suspended over the city. Approaching Canterbury Police Station on the busy Longport road, Pearl imagined McGuire would be imprisoned in his office, poring over statements, forensic reports and information gathered by his small team, but she drove on beyond the police station, heading instead towards the Kent and Canterbury Hospital where she parked up outside its art deco façade.

In an observation ward, Charlie was dressed and waiting for her as a nurse helped to empty the contents of his bedside cabinet. 'Here, let me do that,' said Pearl, taking over efficiently to allow the nurse to move on.

Charlie smiled as he watched his mother pack a few toiletries into a small holdall she had brought along, together with some magazines and notepads that had kept him occupied during his stay.

'Where's Gran?' asked Pearl.

'She had to leave for an art class,' Charlie explained. 'I told her I'd be okay.'

Pearl returned her son's smile. 'And how are you feeling now?'

'Absolutely fine.' He sat down on the hospital bed. 'Though I guess this'll take a while to go down.' He lifted his blond fringe and indicated a dark bruise on his temple. Pearl looked at him, pained, but before she could say a word, Charlie broke in quickly: 'I know,' he said. 'I should have been more careful. But I guess I got carried away with the whole thing. I should have seen the risks but . . . it was like we'd all been swept along with the cause.'

'Swept along . . .' echoed Pearl, noting this was the same phrase Adam had used about Martha's passions.

'Yeah,' said Charlie. 'And I know the camp's gone but I'm still supporting the campaign, okay? And I still want to do what I can to help.'

Pearl noted her son's determined expression and decided not to argue. Instead, she nodded in agreement. 'I respect that, Charlie. But don't forget, two men have been murdered.'

Charlie frowned. 'I know,' he said. 'Poor Fred Clark. Why would anyone want to murder him? He was just a quiet guy trying to do the right thing. He told me he'd never been involved in anything like this before.'

'Did he?' said Pearl, picking up on this as she continued to pack Charlie's things.

'Yeah. We had a game of chess together the other

night and he said the Whitstable Preservation Society had fought plenty of local issues using legal means, and by lobbying councillors and other politicians, but he'd never actually got involved in a protest before.'

'When you say "lobbying councillors",' said Pearl, 'did he happen to mention any names?'

Charlie thought about this. 'He said that Peter Radcliffe had helped in the past, but usually only when a local election was coming up. Fred said that Ratty had been no use at all this time because he supported the development. So that's why Fred had joined the protest. He also said Martha had been right about tactics – it was like a game of chess – you need to know all the moves but you also have to know your opponent and be prepared to do the unexpected to take them by surprise.'

Pearl thought about this before asking: 'Who won?'

'Sorry?'

'The chess game you played together.'

'Oh – Fred did.' Charlie smiled at this. 'He admitted he'd been playing for years. He'd even belonged to a chess club. He was a bit of a grandmaster, if you ask me.' He smiled. 'Or maybe a chess hustler?'

On Pearl's silence, Charlie looked up to see she was staring down at some loose sheets of paper she had just found among his magazines.

'What's up?' he asked, curious.

Pearl held up the sheets of paper on which were various scribbles. 'What're these?' she asked.

Charlie shrugged. 'Oh, that's just me and Gran,' he

explained. 'We were playing a few games together to pass the time.' He nodded towards the papers. 'Noughts and Crosses,' he went on. 'And Hangman. Why?'

'No reason,' said Pearl thoughtfully. But as she stared back at the series of patterns on the pages, and the symbol of a matchstick man hanging by his neck, an idea had suddenly begun to form.

CHAPTER SEVENTEEN

'So, Charlie's okay now?'

'He's fine,' said Pearl quickly to McGuire on the phone in her hand. She was at home at Seaspray Cottage while McGuire was in the Incident Room at Canterbury Police Station.

Pinned to a whiteboard in front of him, a single photograph of murder victim Gordon Weller had now been joined by one of Frederick Clark. Emanating from these images were numerous other names and photographs – Martha Laker and Jane Orritt, Jason Ritchie, Marty Smith and a newly included set of photos of Adam and Simon Stone. There were also a number of local news stories and press photos from the *Chronicle* showing Marty's altercation with Gordon Weller at the pageant – and finally, a photo of Ben Tyler, taken from his driving licence, beside a copy of Frederick Clark's note showing the strange hieroglyphic symbols.

'Something at the hospital got me thinking,' said Pearl.

'About what?' said McGuire, drawing his attention away from the images before him in the hope that Pearl's 'thinking' might possibly help with a lead.

'The note found on Frederick Clark's body,' she said. 'Have you managed to get anywhere with it?'

'Not yet,' McGuire admitted, though he hadn't given up hope on that either.

'Something jogged my memory today,' she went on.

'About?'

'Charlie passed some of his time in hospital playing games with Mum – like they used to do when he was little and . . . then I remembered how he used to be into codes.'

'What sort of codes?'

'Cryptograms. They're a . . . kind of puzzle using encrypted text?'

'And?'

'Well, I just wondered if perhaps the symbols on Fred Clark's note aren't ancient text after all – but a code of some sort. Charlie used to chat to his mates that way.'

McGuire took this in. 'Did you show it to him?'

'Yes, none of the symbols registered with him and he needs to rest, but Fred Clark used to be a good chess player so I thought maybe the note might relate to the kind of code used in chess problems.'

'Chess?'

'Yes. The sign for checkmate is a hash symbol, for instance . . .'

McGuire waited expectantly.

'But I think I may have just got waylaid with that idea.'

McGuire sighed in disappointment.

'Nevertheless . . .' said Pearl.

'Yes?'

She paused and frowned before finally asking: 'What if it really is a coded cryptogram that the murderer used, knowing only Fred himself would have understood it?'

McGuire considered this. 'It's possible,' he said. 'Can you work on it?'

'Me?' said Pearl. 'You've got far more resources at your disposal—'

'You've got to be joking,' said McGuire. 'I've barely got enough PCSOs, let alone codebreakers!'

'Stop coming up with excuses and try,' said Pearl. 'After all, you want me to butt out and leave this case to you, don't you?'

'Yes, but . . .'

'Good luck,' she said. 'I need to take care of Charlie.' Putting down the receiver, she smiled to herself.

Later that evening, Pearl tiptoed into Charlie's room and checked on him as he lay sleeping on top of his bed, curled on his right side so that the bruise on his left temple was fully exposed. Pearl reached out to him, her fingers hovering just above the lesion, a reminder of all her recent fears and concerns since Charlie had joined the protest. Not wanting to wake him, she nevertheless hoped that by some strange transcendent power she might heal him – so she traced the contours of the dark stain and its yellow border. Charlie's fair hair was pushed back from his face and he looked peaceful, beautiful and, apart from his injury, as perfect to Pearl as on the day he had entered this world more than twenty years ago. But Dolly was right; Charlie was no longer a child – he was a young man – his own man – though he would forever remain his mother's child.

Giving birth to him all those years ago had altered the course of Pearl's life – putting an end to her dreams of becoming a police detective and occupying the role McGuire now performed at Canterbury CID. Since meeting the police detective, there had been times when Pearl had questioned whether half the attraction she felt for him was due to his position. Would she still feel the same for McGuire if he wasn't a DCI? There were certainly other times when she resented the fact that he had the job she had always wanted for herself. It was also true she had competed with him during his cases, but none of that had seemed to matter one jot when she had feared for Charlie's safety last night. She had simply been grateful to be able to rely on him - when she had needed him most – when confronted with the possibility of losing Charlie.

Ultimately, Pearl had no regrets about the course her life had taken – because it had resulted in her son. She continued now to look down at him, saw his lips part and a thin film of perspiration gather on his brow. She reached up and pushed the window open a little to allow the salty sea-fresh air to enter the room. She had already unpacked his bag, put away his clothes and set a jug of water and a beaker beside him, together with his mobile phone. Now she reminded herself of what the young nurse had told her: Charlie would be okay.

Creeping downstairs, Pearl was just about to head to the kitchen when she saw the flap of her letterbox slowly opening. Curious, she opened the front door. Standing on her doorstep was Olivia Latimer – an envelope in her hand.

'I'm . . . so sorry,' Olivia stammered. 'I didn't want to disturb you at all. I was just going to post this through your door.' She hesitated before handing the envelope to Pearl. It was addressed to Charlie Nolan c/o Pearl Nolan.

'Feel free to open it,' Olivia went on. Pearl did so and found a greetings card showing a tranquil beach scene on its front. Inside, a short message read:

With best wishes for a speedy recovery.
From Olivia and Bill Latimer and all at the
Whitstable Chronicle.

Pearl looked back at her. 'This is very kind of you,' she said before slipping the card back into the envelope. 'Would you like to come in? I was just going to make some tea.' Olivia looked torn but Pearl went on: 'You're not disturbing me, I promise. Charlie's fast asleep and I could do with some company.'

At this, Olivia Latimer gave a smile. 'Okay.' She stepped inside Seaspray Cottage and Pearl led the way into the kitchen where she quickly put on the kettle and showed her guest into the garden. 'It's a lovely evening,' she said.

Olivia nodded. 'You're right.' She smiled as she looked towards the sun lowering in a sky that was streaked rose pink above an opalescent sea. Olivia sat down at a bistro table while Pearl moved back into the kitchen and finally emerged with some freshly made tea.

'So,' Olivia said, 'your son will be all right – after his accident last night?'

Pearl nodded. 'Yes. There's slight concussion so the doctor said he needs plenty of rest and to avoid any stressful situations. I've been keeping a careful eye on him.'

Olivia nodded as she took this in. 'I'm sure,' she said. 'It must all have been a great worry for you.'

Pearl looked up at this, unsure if she was referring to Charlie's stay at the camp, his accident or the fact that two men had been murdered on the downs just a stone's throw from Snowdrop Valley.

Olivia went on to clarify: 'I know if it had been Chris, I'd have been beside myself, but then—' She broke off before confiding: 'Well, I've always been an over-anxious parent. Perhaps because Chris, like your Charlie, is an only child? I think I know how you must feel.' She gave a weak smile and stirred her tea.

Pearl sighed. 'I'm not sure the protest camp was a good idea,' she said.

'No,' Olivia agreed. 'But that wouldn't have stopped Martha if her mind was made up.' She looked up at Pearl. 'Don't get me wrong,' she said quickly, 'I have nothing against her. In fact, I have reason to be grateful to her: she once helped with gaining petition signatures for our objections to a nightclub close to our home and she did us proud – not least because she has quite a mailing list.'

'And a lot of sway with local people?'

'Yes,' said Olivia. 'And maybe because she has no political ambitions, people trust her. She's never put herself up for councillor and she was also very supportive when I had my accident.' She paused for a moment, cup in hand, as she explained: 'A car accident – some years ago.' Pearl nodded at this. Olivia looked pained, toying with a teaspoon as she explained. 'I . . . had to give up my career. I was a dancer, and for a time, it felt like my life had ended but—' She broke off for a moment, then carried on: 'I suppose, ultimately, we're all programmed for survival. I survived. Martha helped. She has a great "can do" spirit about her. All things are possible with that attitude. She and Jane gave me my very first commission – as a portrait painter.' She paused again as though revisiting this period. 'That was a real turning point for me,' she said finally.

She sipped her tea as Pearl thought to herself how much she had in common with Olivia Latimer: they were mothers of sons, two much-loved only children, but they were also two women who had set out on one course in life – only to change direction and live another. For Olivia, that had involved art; for Pearl, it had been a restaurant that bore her name – and a career that had brought none of the accolades or promotion McGuire had enjoyed, just the satisfaction of customers who enjoyed her food.

'Does Charlie know what he wants to do?' asked Olivia.

'He's in the middle of a graphics course at university,'

said Pearl. She smiled. 'And Chris seems to enjoy his work on the *Chronicle*?'

'Oh, yes,' said Olivia. 'Chris is a good reporter, and he has great respect for the paper but...'

'But?'

Olivia struggled with something but maintained a brave face. 'He'll take over the paper,' she said, 'and I'm sure he'll make a great success of it.' She offered a broad Pollyanna smile and Pearl felt obliged to agree.

'Of course,' she said, joining in with Olivia Latimer's optimism.

Some time after Olivia Latimer's visit, Pearl answered the phone to Dolly, who asked: 'Is Charlie okay?'

'Fast asleep.' Pearl smiled to herself. 'We were so lucky.'

'Yes,' said Dolly. 'Lucky that Ben Tyler was awake and knew how to prime that dog to find him.'

Pearl realised she had hardly given a thought to Tyler since Charlie's rescue.

'Have you managed to thank him?' Dolly asked.

'No,' said Pearl guiltily. 'Not yet.' She bit her lip, remembering how she had goaded Tyler last night, accusing him of killing another man and acting in concert with Martha for mutual protection.

'He seems a good man,' said Dolly. 'Attractive, too. And he's certainly got a way with animals. Martha's dog will do anything for him. I saw that first-hand at the camp.'

'You're right,' said Pearl, thinking about Ben's own dog, Shadow, an innocent creature, slaughtered by a coward who didn't dare take on a traveller like Tyler face to face.

'I really think we should come up with a way of thanking him,' said Dolly.

Pearl considered this. 'Yes,' she said. 'Yes, you're right.'

CHAPTER EIGHTEEN

It was still light when Pearl settled a basket on to the back seat of her car. It contained a bottle of Malbec, some home-smoked salmon and samphire and a thank-you card. It took less than ten minutes for Pearl to drive up Borstal Hill and park her Fiat before heading off across Laker's Field. As she did so, Dolly's words echoed in her mind: *He seems a good man.* Certainly it was true that Ben Tyler was a loyal supporter of Martha and the campaign but, more than that, Pearl now felt she owed her son's life to him.

Arriving at his shepherd's hut, she was disappointed to find no light in the windows. A log fire outside the door was dead. Still hopeful that Tyler might be inside, Pearl knocked on the door. *Silence.* She called softly: 'Ben?' Still no response. Looking around, she saw a pile of logs nearby with a small axe propped alongside them. She moved away, then hesitated and decided to turn back. This time, she mounted three small steps and tried the hut's door handle; to her surprise it turned beneath her hand.

Pearl entered Tyler's modest hut to find it unexpectedly homely. An upholstered built-in seating area surrounded a pine tabletop, the flap of which dropped flat against the wall to create more space when it wasn't in use. At one end of the hut was a wood-burning stove, for heat, and a kitchen area consisting of a basin and a two-burner meths stove for cooking. At the other end, a cast-iron bed was covered with a patchwork quilt. Looking around, Pearl saw few possessions other than some oil lamps, lanterns and books stacked on shelves. Leaving the door open behind her for light, she moved further inside. The small collection of books included one on wood carving and another on the history of Benacre Wood. In front of them lay some bird feathers and what looked to be the tooth of a wild cat.

An old tome, missing its spine, piqued Pearl's curiosity. She picked it up and thumbed through it, fascinated to find it was a well-used guide to hedgerow food and foraging. She was about to replace it when she noticed something else on the shelf: several old photographs tucked away at the back of the books. Pearl took them from their hiding place and moved to the door, allowing the fading light to spill on a few images of Ben Tyler as a younger man. He stood in a boxer's pose, but without gloves and wearing only red straps around his wrists. His bare chest was emblazoned with the image of a hawk in flight, wings outstretched towards Tyler's powerful shoulders. The bird seemed to share the same intense look as Tyler – a piercing gaze filled with menace – a look she remembered well

from last night when Tyler's dark eyes had stared straight
into her soul, commanding attention, striking fear.

But he had not harmed her – instead, he had saved the
life of her son. Flicking through the photos she found an
old clipping from a Kerry newspaper, reporting on the
fate of a man called Michael Casey, who had died during
a bare-knuckle boxing fight with an English traveller, a
man by the name of Ben Tyler. Pearl read on, learning
that while the sport of bare-knuckle fighting had died out
in many places after the advent of licensed boxing, it had
continued as a tradition in Southern Ireland – the country
in which it had begun. Fight organisers maintained that
their matches were legal and that adequate safety measures
were always put in place. Spectators reported that Tyler
and Casey's match had consisted of three two-minute
rounds with a twenty-second count on a knockdown,
but after a knockout punch from Tyler, Casey had failed
to regain consciousness, and a subsequent post-mortem
had discovered a ruptured aneurism in the dead fighter's
brain. Police at Ballyheigue Garda Station were asking for
further help with their inquiries.

Pearl took a moment to assimilate this before refolding
the newspaper clipping and slipping it back among the
photos on the shelf. Turning towards the pine table, she then
set down her basket, containing the wine and smoked
salmon – and left.

Stepping down from the hut, Pearl glanced back at it
as she considered what she had just read. Tyler had killed
a man – but was he a murderer? She looked around to

find night had quickly fallen. Surely Tyler would not have strayed too far leaving his hut unlocked? Admittedly, he didn't appear to have much to steal but from what he had told her about the slaughter of his dog, as a traveller he would surely be careful to avoid further acts of discrimination, or even retribution for having taken another man's life – though it was clear, from the photographs Pearl had seen, that he was more than capable of defending himself. Pearl felt torn. Unable to leave things as they were, she decided to go in search of him to Benacre Wood, no longer feeling vulnerable – but protected by the silvery glow that was being shed by the rising full moon.

It filtered through the canopy of trees, lighting her way, though she had no firm idea where she was heading. Somewhere within these ancient woods she felt sure Tyler would be walking Martha Laker's dog, as was his routine at this hour. She thought once more about the fairy tales of her childhood, and of the two children, Hansel and Gretel, who had been consigned to the woods by an evil stepmother, only to fall prey to a wicked witch. But Pearl also now remembered the ending to that story; how the children had survived due to their own ingenuity and how they had gone on to view the menacing forest quite differently once they were no longer at risk. In the same way, Pearl realised that she, too, was beginning to see things from a different perspective. The woods did not have to be viewed as a place of danger but a magical setting for enchantment and transformation. Perhaps the whole recent episode, which included the death of two local men, executed with precision for reasons that still remained unknown, was bringing about a change in Pearl's preconceptions.

Until now, she had considered this unfamiliar territory with fear and suspicion but tonight she began to sense she was as much a part of the ancient woodland as the creatures that inhabited it: the tawny owl that would soon be hunting its prey, the amber-eyed fox on its nightly prowl and the smaller more vulnerable creatures who would need to remain alert in order to remain alive. Pearl continued to follow the silvery trail before her, testing her resolve, confronting her fears and facing them down, reminded now of what Frederick Clark had told Charlie during their game of chess: about the importance of knowing your opponent and being prepared to do the unexpected in order to take them by surprise.

Martha had mentioned the need to make a sacrifice in order to achieve a final victory. *Checkmate.* Pearl also now remembered what Martha had told her about the origins of that term – how it was said to be derived from the two Arabic words *Sheikh Mat* - Dead King. The game never ended until the king was finally cornered but it now occurred to Pearl that, in chess, it was actually the queen that held all the power. The king moved only one square at a time while the queen could move as any piece, apart from the knight. Pearl now remembered Marty dressed as a knight in full jousting armour on the day of the pageant on the Crown of the Down. Then she saw Frederick Clark in her mind's eye, dressed as a medieval king. Martha had been the Queen of Spades and Jane the Queen of Hearts. No bishop in evidence, though Rev Pru, from St Alfred's Church, had been present on the day. Perhaps, thought Pearl, the rook, or castle, signified the Crown of the Down itself, while Pearl and every other local person who had attended the event, or joined Martha's protest camp, were mere pawns in the battle to save the local downs from development – Martha's own 'castle'.

This analogy appealed to Pearl, though it offered no further clues as to the identity of the killer who had injected Gordon Weller and Frederick Clark with a toxic dose of liquid nicotine. Weller and Clark – two men ranged at either end of the pitched battle for the downs. Frederick had mentioned being disturbed by Weller's death, particularly since they had both been involved in some charity events. Fellow Rotarians, Pearl remembered, though she wondered now if their relationship could possibly have run deeper than that. As Dolly had pointed out, Frederick had made an unlikely ally for Martha – an upright civil servant and pillar of both the local community and the Whitstable Preservation Society – who had become drawn into Martha's plans – 'swept along' by them perhaps, as Adam Stone had once been by Martha's passion.

Could Martha be responsible for murdering Weller? Certainly she had told Pearl she would shed no tears over his passing. But could she then have gone on to murder Frederick Clark? And if so, why? Had Clark become suspicious of her following Weller's murder? And what about the note that had been found on his body? What could the cryptogram mean – if it was indeed a coded message? In her heart, Pearl knew it was unlikely McGuire would ever fathom the sequence of symbols to make sense of the message. And yet, she felt sure there were, by now, enough clues for her to be able to make sense of all that had happened.

Had she really allowed circumstances to confuse her thought processes to such an extent that they did now resemble the tangled undergrowth of Benacre Wood? If so, the silvery moon was suddenly casting light, not only upon the ground before her, but on this particular case.

Martha could only rely on a mutual alibi with her partner, Jane, for her whereabouts on the night of Weller's murder. After the pageant, she could certainly have tempted the developer to return to the downs, ostensibly to discuss a way forward – a compromise of some sort – only to lure him to his death. It was perfectly possible that if she had been sitting on the bench of the pillory with Weller she could have administered the injection, and manoeuvred him easily enough into the pillory and headed home within minutes. On the evening of Clark's death, she had been close to the murder scene, dividing her time between the camp at Snowdrop Valley and her home. She could have disposed of a hypodermic syringe as easily as she could stash away a supply of deadly liquid nicotine. And perhaps, Pearl now considered, it was possible that for all her apparent innocence, Jane Orritt might even be her lover's accomplice.

Sometimes, the most obvious solution to a problem was the real solution all along – and Pearl realised she might have allowed herself to become blinded by more complex alternatives – until now. With this sudden realisation, light began to dawn at the edge of Benacre Wood. Pearl saw that she had walked the entire length of the wood from its axe-shaped 'head' to the end of its 'handle', which bordered the area on which she now stood – a piece of open land where the group of standing stones had been erected. Pearl had failed to find Tyler but now she felt convinced she was closer to the truth – though proving it all to McGuire would be another matter.

She paused, staring out across the field as the full moon shone directly down on the standing stones. They had been put in place a few years ago by someone connected to the Friends of the Downs – a new monument, this time not to a local campaigner but to the ancient woodland itself. Pearl wandered across to them, noting how they formed a semicircle around a central slab. Drawing nearer, she began to feel like an actor, stepping out on to a stage – perhaps one on which an important drama was about to play out . . .

Pearl's breath caught in the back of her throat as she saw something lying on the central slab. For a moment, she remained paralysed, rooted to the spot, imagining that some sick individual had sacrificed a creature and left it there – slaughtered – like Ben Tyler's dog. A river of blood was dripping down on to the ground. *Could it be Martha's dog?* The loyal creature, Scooby, who had found Charlie the night before. Bracing herself, Pearl only needed to take a few more steps forward for her question to be finally answered.

It wasn't an animal – it was a human being lying flat on the cold stone. The full moon was casting a silvery spotlight upon the body of Martha Laker – an axe thrust deep into the bloody cavity of her chest.

CHAPTER NINETEEN

Early the following morning, Pearl was sitting with Dolly and Charlie in her sea-facing garden. An online story from the *Chronicle* was visible on Pearl's smartphone lying on the bistro table – with a glaring headline.

Murder on the downs: Campaigner Martha becomes third victim in latest murder to rock town

Tributes paid to fearless campaigner slain on the downs last night

By News Editor Chris Latimer

Wednesday 24 June 2020

Tributes have been flooding in following the death of Whitstable resident Martha Laker, 53, whose body was found murdered last night on land near Duncan Down in Whitstable.

Ms Laker, a well-known local environmental campaigner, had recently been fighting a proposal from Invicta Land to build housing on green space near Laker's Field, close to the home Ms Laker shared with her partner, Jane Orritt.

The discovery of Ms Laker's body comes only days after the twin murders of Gordon Weller, 51, a co-director of Invicta Land,

and Frederick Clark, 61, spokesman for the Whitstable Preservation Society (WPS). The WPS had recently joined forces with Ms Laker's Save Our Downs campaign group to fight the Invicta Land development.

Mr Weller's body was discovered last Thursday on the Crown of the Down after a medieval pageant. The event had been staged by the Save Our Downs campaign, of which Ms Laker was spokesperson. Frederick Clark was found dead in a hide close to Snowdrop Valley where a protest camp had been in place until earlier this week.

Ms Laker's partner, Jane, a local homoeopath, said: 'I cannot believe this has happened and that Martha is no longer with us. She was the most vibrant and vital person I have ever known, always ready to help members of our local community with ways of preserving our precious environment. She firmly believed we could all make a difference if we tried, and her favourite campaign slogan was: "Many fleas make big dog jump." I pray that her murderer is caught soon.'

A Book of Condolence has been set up at St Alfred's Church in Whitstable High Street. Reverend Prudence Lawson said,

'We are deeply shocked by the news of a third victim in these brutal murders. Our thoughts and prayers are with Martha Laker's family and friends, and also for those of Mr Weller and Mr Clark.'

Senior Investigating Officer, DCI Michael McGuire of Canterbury CID, said, 'Police were called to land close to Duncan Down last night at approximately 21:10 hours after a report was received from a member of the public who had found the body of a female. Officers and Kent Ambulance Service attended and the victim, identified as Martha Laker, was pronounced dead at the scene. No arrests have been made in connection with this murder and we are appealing to anyone who can assist with our investigation into any of the suspicious deaths that have recently occurred in the area. A crime scene remains in place.'

Whitstable resident Councillor Peter Radcliffe said, 'I knew Martha Laker well and though we were not always on the same side of the battles she fought, she did so bravely and effectively. Martha will never be forgotten.'

What are your recollections of Martha Laker? Contact the Chronicle on newdesk. whitchronicle.co.org

'Old hypocrite!' said Dolly.

Pearl looked up quickly from the news feature, which included recent photos of Martha in her Queen of Spades costume, to see Dolly pointing accusingly at the paper.

'Ratty,' Dolly explained. 'Martha was a thorn in his side, an obstacle in his path . . .'

'Any more clichés?' asked Pearl.

'You know what I mean,' Dolly said. 'If you ask me, he's only too pleased that she's out the way. And to think you allowed him in the restaurant last week with *both* of those developers!'

'One of whom is now dead,' Pearl reminded her.

Dolly fixed Pearl with a look. 'And you could have ended up the same way,' she said.

Charlie looked pained. 'Gran's right,' he said.

'Yes,' Dolly continued. 'Why on earth did you go up on the downs last night, after everything that's happened?'

'I told you—' said Pearl wearily.

'You went to thank Ben for rescuing Charlie,' said Dolly, cutting in.

'Yes,' said Pearl. '*You* were the one who said I should do that.'

'And I'd have gone with you, if only you'd told me!' said Dolly. 'I never once expected you'd go up there on your own – and at night.'

'Murders can take place any time of day,' argued Pearl.

'Maybe,' said Charlie, 'but there was no need to put yourself on the line like that. You were worried enough about us at the camp, so you must understand how we feel?'

Pearl looked at Charlie and Dolly presenting a united front – and capitulated. 'I do,' she said, reaching a hand out to them both. 'And I'm sorry.'

With Pearl's sincere apology, Dolly softened and patted her daughter's hand. 'It's all right,' she said. 'I know you haven't had much sleep.'

'What does McGuire say?' asked Charlie.

Pearl shook her head. 'I haven't had a chance to talk to him yet. The police officers who responded to my Emergency call last night came straight from a road traffic accident. They took my statement.'

Dolly nodded. 'Must have been a terrible shock for you, finding Martha's body like that.'

'Yes,' said Charlie. 'What kind of person puts an axe in someone's chest?'

'A lunatic,' said Dolly.

'Or,' said Pearl, 'someone who hated Martha Laker with a real vengeance.'

Dolly and Charlie remained silent as though reflecting on this for a moment before Dolly finally said: 'Sometimes people can be too clever for their own good.'

Pearl looked at her mother. 'What d'you mean?'

Dolly went on: 'A farmer once told me that every once in a while, one young sheep in his flock would be smart enough to work out that if it lay on the ground at a cattle grid, it could roll across and make its way to freedom.'

'And?' asked Pearl.

'That was the sheep that he would have to slaughter first – or the rest of the flock would learn from it and escape too.' She paused and fixed Pearl with a look. 'Don't be too clever for your own good, Pearl.' Her words seemed to resonate in the silence that followed before she went on. 'Promise me you won't do anything like that ever again?'

Pearl recognised the looks of concern and fear on Dolly and Charlie's faces. She nodded. 'I promise.'

*

A few hours later, Pearl was heading to The Whitstable Pearl when she decided to take a short detour to St Alfred's Church. Although she was not particularly religious and had never been a regular churchgoer, Pearl would sometimes find herself drawn to the local place of worship, which had become part of the very fabric of the town. When members of the fishing community had been lost at sea, St Alfred's clergy had provided solace and a suitable memorial service – just as Rev Pru did at times such as these. Offering traditional Anglican worship and a relaxed and friendly atmosphere, the church in the High Street seated several hundred people, and for over two centuries had positioned itself in the heart of the community, both geographically and in relation to those it served. It did so not solely for religious purposes, and to commemorate births, deaths and marriages, but also by offering itself for public meetings on a variety of issues concerning the town – many of which had been hosted by Martha Laker. On most days, the narthex, or antechamber of the church, was a popular meeting place for local people as it served light lunches of soup, sandwiches, tea and cake at reasonable prices.

Today was no exception and Pearl entered to find tables filled with senior citizens and mothers with young children. A Book of Condolence had been placed in a conspicuous position at the entrance to the nave and a morning service was about to come to an end, voices of the congregation and choir singing the words of a hymn that seemed wholly appropriate for a campaigner like Martha Laker: *Fight the good fight with all thy might! Christ is thy strength, and Christ thy right; Lay hold on life, and it shall be . . . Thy joy and crown eternally.*

Opening the book, Pearl saw it was already filled with scores of comments from local people, some of whom had used predictable phrases such as 'Gone but not forgotten', while others had actually referred to Martha Laker's murder: 'Cut down in your prime – the devil who did this must be found. Soon.' One message captured Pearl's attention with its poignancy. Affixed to the book, it was framed by a colourful hand-drawn image of wildlife and read: 'Thank you, Martha, for saving the supermarket trees for all our birds, bees and butterflies. With love from the children at St Alfred's School.' Running a finger down all the entries in the Book of Condolence, Pearl noted one from Marty Smith: 'I wish you were still here to lead us to victory against the DFLs.' Another from the Whitstable Preservation Society read: 'We took our inspiration from you. You will be greatly missed.' Chris Latimer, of the *Chronicle*, had written the simple tribute: 'A trouper', while in bold, ostentatious handwriting, a message from Councillor Peter Radcliffe declared: 'A leading light in our town is dimm'd. A voice we know is still'd.'

Pearl was just considering how the use of the archaic verbs, still'd and dimm'd, seemed to underscore the pretentiousness of this self-important councillor when she noticed two other messages, written consecutively on the page. The first, from Simon Stone, was an affectionate valediction to his mother – 'You will always be in my heart' – while the next comment, from Adam Stone, appeared ambiguous in sentiment: 'Goodbye Martha'. Was it a stark farewell, wondered Pearl, or a final expression of relief at Martha's death?

After leaving St Alfred's Church, Pearl managed to take only a few steps before she stopped in her tracks: Chris Latimer and Councillor Peter Radcliffe were exiting Marty Smith's fruit and vegetable shop, Cornucopia. She watched for a few moments as the two men exchanged a few brief words outside on the pavement before they finally moved off together.

Pearl then headed on to the shop, entering to find Marty arranging bundles of asparagus into a neat display. Coming up behind him she said sharply, 'So you've heard the news?'

'Of course,' said Marty. 'The whole town's heard.' He picked up his empty asparagus crate, took it to the rear of the store and tossed it into the back yard.

Pearl followed him there. 'What were Latimer and Radcliffe doing here just now?'

Marty said nothing for a moment, then: 'What do you think? The press man's after another headline – and Radcliffe's trying to get in on the act.'

Pearl frowned. 'What do you mean?'

'Ratty loves being in the paper, doesn't he? He was in here going on about what a tragedy this is?' He gave a snort. 'He couldn't care less about Martha as long as that development gets built. Crocodile tears,' he sneered. 'He brought the developers to the pageant, didn't he? Thinking about it, I should have thumped *him* too!'

As he strode back to his counter, Pearl admonished him. 'Keep your cool.'

But Marty turned to her, scowling petulantly. 'Why should I? Three murders in this town and what's your copper friend doing about it, eh? How can it take so long to catch the killer? Surely it's obvious who's responsible.'

'Is it?' asked Pearl flatly.

'Jason Ritchie,' said Marty, jutting his chin towards Pearl. 'He's done away with the two people leading this campaign—'

'*And* his business partner?' queried Pearl, reminding him about Weller.

'Exactly!' said Marty, unfazed. 'So he'll be getting the lion's share of this development!' He gave a self-satisfied look. 'I may not be a . . . DCI at the CID,' he said, 'and I may only sell fruit and veg for a living, but I know two and two makes four!' He went behind his counter, lips tightening.

As some customers entered the store, Pearl lowered her voice and agreed. 'All right,' she said, 'admittedly, Ritchie stands to benefit from these murders – but the police still need evidence in order to charge him.'

'Then why isn't your copper out finding it? What exactly is he doing now, eh? Filing his nails? Or taking a back-hander from Ritchie? I notice he's always got time to give quotes to the paper – but none to catch a murderer!'

As customers' heads began to turn at this, Pearl lowered

her tone and said: 'McGuire needs proof. And there's nothing to say that the murders weren't committed by more than one person. After all,' she continued, 'if the same person is responsible for all three murders, why didn't they use the same method? Why resort to an axe to kill Martha?'

Marty looked at Pearl, unable to answer, but at that very moment, Pearl's mobile phone sounded an incoming text. Looking down at it, she saw a short message: *Could you possibly come to see me?* The sender was Jane Orritt.

Half an hour later, Jane Orritt answered the door to Pearl. She was dressed in a bright pink summer dress, her hair unplaited and newly styled so that it fell across one shoulder. Pearl could have sworn she was wearing a slick of pale pink lipstick.

Thanking Pearl for coming, Jane led the way out of a large square hallway and into a room that looked out on to Laker's Field. Pearl had prepared herself to find Martha's partner distraught and vulnerable; in fact, Jane seemed in perfect control, adopting a far more mature persona than the girlish role she had always seemed to take on around Martha. Pearl entered the room, brought up short to see a large portrait on the wall above a long sofa. It showed Martha, looking considerably younger, wearing a crimson blouse, a wry smile playing on her lips. Jane noted Pearl's shock and her gaze followed Pearl's to the portrait.

'It's very lifelike, isn't it?' she said. 'And very special.

It was done some time ago by Olivia Latimer. A commission. Her first, I believe. I think she captured Martha perfectly.' She allowed herself to smile as she went on: 'There's a . . . regal bearing about her, but there's also a hint of Martha's true nature in her eyes – mischief and rebellion? I think that's been captured perfectly.'

For a moment, as both women continued to look up at the portrait, Pearl imagined the terrible poignancy of the moment might suddenly overwhelm Martha's bereaved partner. The painting, though magnificent, was a poor substitute for the real thing. Jane, however, remained calm, perhaps, thought Pearl, tranquillised against the loss of her lover in such a brutal murder.

As if reading Pearl's thoughts, Jane finally turned to her and said: 'I'm sorry. It must have been a terrible thing for you to find her murdered in such a shocking way.' She frowned now, seemingly more concerned for Pearl than herself.

Pearl nodded slowly. 'It was a . . . vicious killing,' she said, knowing that 'slaughter' would have been a more accurate term – though she could not bring herself to use it.

'Yes,' Jane agreed. 'The person responsible must be seriously mentally ill – not that I believe killing could ever be viewed as a sane action.'

Pearl hesitated before asking: 'What about a man killed in a fight?' She paused. 'A bare-knuckle fight?'

At this, Jane glanced away to the window then looked back at Pearl and said finally: 'So you know about that.' She got up, perhaps, thought Pearl, simply to avoid her gaze. When she reached the window Jane looked out on the contested land and spoke again. 'Martha and I knew, of course. But we agreed to keep it a secret – for Ben's sake. He was trying to start again, in a new environment.' She looked back at Pearl and went on, 'A little like us, too.'

Pearl gathered her thoughts before commenting: 'The method used by Martha's killer was quite distinct from that used to murder Gordon Weller and Fred Clark.'

Jane nodded slowly. 'That's true,' she said, pondering this for a moment. 'Could there be . . . two killers, do you think?'

'What did the police say?' asked Pearl, avoiding Jane's question. 'I'm presuming you've been interviewed?'

Jane nodded. 'I just answered the detective's questions, that's all. He was quite sensitive.'

'DCI McGuire?'

Jane nodded again. 'He didn't give much away, though – about any findings . . . evidence.' She paused again and asked Pearl: 'You must have given a statement too?'

Pearl nodded. 'I did. Last night, while the police secured the crime scene.'

Jane took this in. 'Can I ask what you were doing at the standing stones last night?'

Pearl looked up. 'Is that the reason you wanted to see me?'

At this, Jane looked edgy so Pearl compensated. 'Look, I do understand you needing to know as much as possible about what happened but . . . to be honest, I'd actually gone to the woods to talk to Ben.'

'Ben?' said Jane quickly. The look on her face seemed to betray both shock and suspicion in equal measure.

'Yes,' Pearl continued. 'I don't have a phone number for him,' she explained, 'but I know where his shepherd's hut is.'

'And what did he have to say?' asked Jane, curious.

'Nothing,' said Pearl. 'He wasn't home.' At this, Pearl detected some relief from Jane and went on. 'I walked the entire length of Benacre Wood. There was a full moon. It was a nice evening . . . until I came upon Martha's body.' She broke off for a moment: 'I'm so sorry for your loss.'

'So am I,' said Jane. 'But that's not the reason I asked to see you. What I have to say won't be secret for much longer, so there's no reason why you shouldn't know now.' She paused for a moment then moved to an antique desk and opened a drawer. 'Martha left a copy of her will here – and one with our solicitor, Barrett and Chambers in the High Street. I believe the police have contacted them.'

She handed Martha's will across to Pearl, who began reading. After a few moments she looked up – but said nothing. Jane filled in the silence. 'Martha left the whole of her estate to me.' She paused, then went on: 'I was never sure what her intentions were. We never spoke about dying. Why would we? Martha was so full of life.' She smiled, almost wistfully, then quickly broke off, and bit her lip as though trying to stifle some distress. Eventually she went on: 'It was a brutal way for her to die but . . . at least it was quick.' Pearl frowned, shocked at this, but Jane went on: 'Martha hated illness and anything to do with it.

She couldn't even bear having a cold, or having to take care of anyone else in ill health. In fact, I think it was the one thing she truly feared – to lose her strength, her vitality and stamina – and to become old and . . . infirm? At least she's escaped that.'

Astonished by Jane's ability to find positives in her partner's death, Pearl remained silent while Jane reorganised her thoughts. 'It was actually Simon I wanted to talk to you about,' she said finally, adopting a businesslike tone.

'Simon?' asked Pearl.

'Yes,' Jane went on. 'He's Martha's son but . . . as you can see, she's named me as her sole beneficiary so everything comes to me.' Her eyes fell on the will once more. 'Which makes things very awkward. I don't want Simon to be disappointed, though I'm sure he never thought in any way about gaining from Martha's death.' Jane looked around her. 'Martha and I spent so much time and money on this house; we expected to be here for decades—' She broke off again, this time as though lost for words.

'And now?'

Jane shook her head slowly. 'Now, I'm not sure I want to be here without her. There would be too many . . . difficult memories.'

Pearl was brought up short by the word. 'Difficult?'

Jane took a deep breath and then admitted: 'I have a great deal of respect for the truth,' she said. 'That's why I'm being honest with you right now – and why the police will get nothing but the truth from me. I loved Martha deeply,' she went on. 'She was the kind of human being you meet only once in a lifetime. I'm glad we did meet. We had fifteen wonderful years together but . . .' She frowned then went on, choosing her words carefully. 'Martha was a very complex woman. With complex needs.' She looked directly at Pearl as if expecting to be understood.

But Pearl admitted: 'I'm . . . not sure what you mean.'

Jane looked away and then tried again. 'We had an informal agreement,' she said. 'An understanding. We . . . enjoyed an open relationship.'

'I see,' said Pearl finally. 'You mean, Martha . . . had lovers?'

'Relationships,' said Jane quickly. 'She was capable of strong attractions – towards men and women. I always knew this and I felt that if these . . . relationships weren't allowed to run their course, they could become,' she paused again then said, 'obsessions.'

Pearl took this in and said tentatively, 'I . . . suppose it might be difficult for one partner in a relationship to get used to such an arrangement?'

Jane shrugged. 'Perhaps,' she agreed. 'But I put up with it,' she went on, 'and I was able to tolerate Martha's affairs.' She added: 'I understood them. Sometimes I could even gain a vicarious thrill from them.' She looked at Pearl. 'Does that sound perverse?'

A pause settled before Pearl replied. 'It's not for me to say. But you've been amazingly honest.'

At this, Jane managed a smile. 'Well,' she began, 'I told you: the truth is important to me – perhaps even more so now.' She took the will back from Pearl.

'And I presume,' Pearl began, 'that Simon's father, Adam, wasn't as understanding as you were of Martha's affairs?'

'It's not something we ever discussed,' said Jane briskly, 'so you'd have to ask him. But I'm sure he's going to be disappointed by the contents of this will – at least, as far as provisions go for his son. He loves Simon. As do I.'

'Then . . . it's in your power to make the provision for Simon that Martha failed to?'

The question hung between the two women for a moment before Jane looked pained. 'Yes,' she said. 'I have thought about that, but . . . it wouldn't be respecting Martha's wishes to go against the terms of her will. There was a reason she made it out the way she did. And Adam isn't exactly short of money. He owns a large property in the centre of Toulouse and a farmhouse in the countryside in a village called Escanecrabe. We have to be honest about the will's contents, but I was thinking it might help if I were to offer some of Martha's possessions to Simon – including this portrait. That might be acceptable, don't you think? You're a parent yourself. You met Martha and saw how she was with Simon. I'd appreciate it if you could give me your honest opinion.'

Pearl considered the question she had just been posed. Apart from Simon and Charlie being roughly the same age, there seemed few other parallels between Martha and Pearl. In fact, the more Pearl learned of the late Martha Laker, the less she found to like about her – in life or in death.

She framed her reply carefully. 'I'm sure you'll reach the right decision.'

*

A short while later, as Jane Orritt was showing Pearl from the house, she turned to her and said, 'Can I ask why you were going to see Ben last night?'

Pearl noted Jane's troubled look. 'I wanted to thank him,' she said, 'for saving my son's life. And I . . . also wanted to find out if there was something he may have seen or noted at the protest camp – or the pageant – that might be important.'

'Well,' said Jane, 'I'm sure he would have told the police if that was the case.'

'Not necessarily,' said Pearl. 'Because sometimes we see things . . . but don't realise their true significance at the time.'

Jane nodded slowly. 'Thank you,' she said. 'I think I understand.'

Jane Orritt opened the front door and Pearl stepped outside. It was only then – as she glanced down at a pile of logs stacked outside the front door of the house – that she suddenly realised something herself.

Back in her car, Pearl dialled McGuire and waited patiently for the call to connect. 'Please listen,' she said quickly.

McGuire noted the urgency in her voice. 'What is it?' He had just got out of his own car and was heading on foot towards Canterbury Police Station, negotiating his way around groups of students who had just exited a lecture at nearby Christ Church University.

'The murder weapon,' said Pearl. 'The axe.'

'What about it?'

'The first day I met Martha Laker, Ben Tyler brought an axe to Martha's house. He lent it to her to chop logs for her wood-burning stove.'

'And?'

'And I just remembered that the one I saw outside his shepherd's hut last night was much smaller.'

McGuire was using his security pass to gain access into the police station. In the foyer, he now stopped in his tracks. 'What are you saying?'

'I'm saying that the axe used to kill Martha must have been the same one she had borrowed from Tyler. It was engraved on the blade—'

McGuire spoke over her. 'You couldn't possibly have seen that when it was lodged in Martha Laker's thorax.'

'True,' said Pearl, 'but I did notice it had a carved handle . . . carved by Ben himself. He has books on carving in his hut and he was giving lessons at the camp when I went to visit Charlie. If that same axe had been left at Martha's home, and never returned, it's possible Jane Orritt could have used it last night. And,' she continued, 'there's a very good reason why she may have wanted Martha dead.'

CHAPTER TWENTY

'Come to give me a quote for my next story?' Chris
Latimer took a sip of coffee from the mug in his
hand, though Pearl considered he hardly needed it. He
was already hyped up, beads of perspiration on his brow
and shirtsleeves rolled up, as if for action, though all he
was doing was waiting for the last sheet of paper to emerge
from a printer at the *Chronicle*'s offices.

'No,' said Pearl firmly. 'And I've closed The Whitstable
Pearl today, out of respect to Martha, and,' she added
pointedly, 'to avoid any journalists trying to track me
down for quotes.'

'Good idea,' said Chris. 'Journos can be a pain in the
neck.' He winked and offered a mischievous smile then
picked up his sheets of printed paper and took a seat at his
desk to check them. 'So,' he continued, 'if you're not here
to help me with the news, what can I do for you?'

'Have you had any further press statements from DCI
McGuire?'

'Why?' asked Chris. 'Haven't you?' He gave her a knowing look before taking another sip of coffee and then explaining, 'Look, I'm here to get the news out, Pearl, not to offer informal bulletins to all and sundry.'

Pearl's mouth dropped open at this. 'All and—'

'If you must know,' he said, speaking over her, 'Jason Ritchie's only just left.'

Pearl frowned. 'And what did he want?'

'Same as you,' said Chris, without taking his eyes from his work. 'Information.' He took a biro from behind his ear and began making corrections to his story.

'What sort of information?' Pearl persisted.

'Does it really matter?' asked Chris wearily. 'We're all in the same boat: fishing around for clues as to who's committing these murders.'

'And you think that's what Jason Ritchie's doing?'

'Ah!' said Chris with some revelatory zeal. 'I see where you're heading: if he was responsible for the murders, he wouldn't need to ask questions, right? Is that what you think?'

'Not necessarily,' said Pearl. 'He's quite capable of putting on a front – and handling the press – with a bluff.'

'Well,' said Chris, 'we in the press also have a knack for knowing when we're being spun a line. So . . . if he wasn't fishing for clues, why else would he want to see photos of the pageant?'

'I've no idea,' said Pearl, picking up on this. 'You tell me.'

Chris shrugged. 'Your guess is as good as mine,' he said. 'But he wanted copies.'

'And did you give them to him?'

'I said I'd send the file by e-mail.' He paused to look at Pearl. 'Not that it'll do him any good. I've already been through them all myself.'

'Looking for what?'

Chris looked up at her. 'Anything and nothing,' he said cryptically. He indicated the papers in his hand. 'Now, if you don't mind, I really do have to get on with this.'

'Another news story?'

Chris heaved a weary sigh at Pearl's persistence.

'Editorial,' he said, turning the first page around so she could see it. Pearl began reading.

Execution of a Queen

Whitstable is a feisty little town, more than capable of holding its own against any commercial forces that might threaten its loss of character.

Over the years it has managed to fight off these threats but sometimes it has needed help to do so. In many of the high-profile campaigns we have featured in this newspaper, one person repeatedly came to its aid: Martha Laker.

Although Martha was not a Whitstable native, the Chronicle believes she earned the right to become the town's honorary 'queen'.

Martha Laker fought tirelessly on numerous issues on Whitstable's behalf, and as a firm believer in 'people power' she inspired many local people to find their voice.

Martha was an irritant to some – a heroine to others – but her passion was always in evidence in all the causes she took up, including her recent battle to oppose building on local green space on the downs.

Last night, Queen Martha was deposed – executed in the most violent manner on the land she campaigned so hard to save for this generation and those to come.

Martha Laker has become the third victim in a string of murders which have rocked our town in recent days.

The Chronicle says it is time for us all to step up to the plate and help the police find the person responsible for these heinous crimes – the person who has brought Queen Martha's proud reign to a premature end.

Pearl finished reading and mused: '*Execution of a Queen* . . .' She paused for a moment, then: 'I take it that was written by your dad.'

Chris looked up, surprised. Pearl explained: 'That's how he viewed Martha.'

'So did a lot of people.'

'Perhaps,' said Pearl. She turned for the door now. Chris watched her go, then saw her turn back to him. 'I take it you won't be sending those photos to Ritchie free of charge?'

At this, Chris Latimer looked shifty. 'He made a donation to the paper,' he said finally.

Pearl smiled. 'I thought he might.'

Chris pointed a finger at her. 'Look,' he said, 'you probably think, as everyone else does, that Jason Ritchie had more reason than anyone to kill Martha Laker – but I understand he has a sound alibi for last night.'

'Really?' said Pearl, taken aback. 'And what would that be?'

'He was in a meeting.'

'Meeting?'

'With Councillor Peter Radcliffe.'

Pearl looked away as she absorbed this. Chris went on: 'By the way, how's your son doing?'

'He's fine,' said Pearl. 'Spending the afternoon with his gran.'

Latimer gave a nod. 'Good.' He got back to his work as Pearl headed for the door.

*

Ten minutes later as Pearl was driving back down Borstal Hill, she called McGuire on the speaker phone in her car, surprised that he answered.

'Look, I know you're busy,' she said, pre-empting any excuse from him, 'but is it true Jason Ritchie and Councillor Radcliffe were in a meeting together at the time of Martha Laker's murder?'

'According to their statements,' said McGuire, on the computer in his office, as he tried to concentrate on making notes for a meeting of his team.

'You mean there's nothing else to corroborate this?'

'There's CCTV,' said McGuire. 'They met at the Long Reach pub last night at eight-thirty and were recorded leaving just after ten. Waitress stated that they sat at a table in the restaurant and ordered a snack and some drinks.'

'And?'

McGuire looked away from his computer screen and gave his full attention to Pearl on the phone. 'Car park cameras clocked Radcliffe leaving in his car around ten past ten,' he said.

'And Ritchie?'

'He left on foot – just as he'd arrived. Remember,' said McGuire, 'that windmill he's renting is less than a ten-minute walk away from the Long Reach roundabout.'

'But you've no one to corroborate when he arrived home?'

'No.' McGuire became suspicious and asked: 'What's all this about?'

Pearl ignored his question and continued with her train

of thought. 'So he . . . could have gone straight to Benacre Wood,' she said. 'There was enough time for him to get there on foot—'

'And then he just happened upon Martha Laker?' said McGuire, doubtful.

'Maybe he arranged to meet her there.'

'How?'

'I don't know,' said Pearl testily. 'But that's for you to find out.' She paused as she considered various possibilities. 'Have you checked his phone company records?'

'Of course.'

'And?'

'No record of any calls between Ritchie and Laker last night. Or any other night, come to that. Besides,' he continued, 'if Ritchie managed to put an axe through Martha's chest, how d'you imagine he got back to Black Mill from Benacre Wood without leaving a trail of blood for my forensic team to find?'

'I don't know,' said Pearl, frustrated. 'But it's still possible,' she insisted.

'Why?' asked McGuire.

'Because he told me himself: he's no fool. In fact, he's a very smart guy – so he could've thought of a way.' She thought to herself. 'Maybe Radcliffe picked him up?'

'Pearl . . .'

'No, listen! He could have set off in his car and then parked up in the same field as Tyler's shepherd's hut – that's only a short distance from the Old Thanet Way. Have you made a forensic inspection of Radcliffe's car?'

'It went straight to a garage this morning for an MOT.'

'Then check it out there,' Pearl insisted. 'It's perfectly possible that the first two murders were premeditated and the last was opportunistic. Jason and Radcliffe could have decided at their meeting they should go and talk to Martha . . .'

'And then they just happened to find her – in the wood – with Tyler's axe nice and handy? Come on, Pearl, how likely is that?'

Pearl paused, then: 'You've interviewed Tyler?'

'Of course.'

'And where was he last night? Because he wasn't at his hut.'

'Says he was out with the dog.'

'Doing what?'

'Your guess is as good as mine,' said McGuire. 'But if you ask me, considering his nocturnal jaunts, he had more chance of murdering Laker than Ritchie or Radcliffe. I checked with Jane Orritt – the axe he lent Martha was never returned. She maintains it was left with a log pile near the front door, so Tyler could easily have taken it last night and used it to kill Martha.'

'But why?' asked Pearl. Before McGuire had a chance to respond, an idea came to her. 'He and Martha could have been having an affair.'

'Could they?' asked McGuire, unconvinced.

'Jane told me only this morning that they had an "open relationship". That means—'

'I know what an open relationship is,' said McGuire

testily, aware that time was running out before his team would be back for the meeting.

'Do you?' asked Pearl, curious.

'Yes,' said McGuire. 'So get to the point – please?'

'Martha had sexual relationships with both men and women,' said Pearl. 'And Tyler's an attractive man.'

'Is he?' asked McGuire, uneasy.

'Yes, he is,' Pearl said. 'He's tall, dark, unpredictable—'

'All right,' said McGuire, having heard enough.

'Martha could have been giving money to Tyler – maybe to pay for his support with the campaign? Maybe he was after more—'

'Hold on,' said McGuire, trying to keep track of his thinking. 'The person who stood to benefit most from Martha's death was Jane Orritt. There's an insurance policy and that house is worth a cool million.'

'But only with its view,' said Pearl, thoughtful. 'It's probably worth half that if it ends up overlooking a new housing complex.' She remained silent for a moment, considering yet more possibilities, none of which were yet fixed in her mind.

'There's also Adam Stone,' she said.

'What about him?'

'He's worried about the influence Martha had over their son.'

'Enough to kill her?' asked McGuire. 'If so, he could have done that any time in the past twenty years.'

'But he's a doctor. He did research into neurotoxins?'

'We know that,' said McGuire. 'So why would he set

himself up as an obvious suspect by using nicotine to poison Weller and Clark? And what was his motive for wanting them out of the way?' McGuire paused. 'Remember your training,' he said finally. 'Method, opportunity, motive.'

'Yes,' said Pearl, deflated.

McGuire checked his watch. 'Look, I have to go. I've got a briefing in five minutes.'

'Press?'

'My team,' said McGuire. 'I need to see what they have for me. I'll talk to you later, Pearl, but please . . . stay out of trouble?' He replaced the receiver and stared down at it for a moment, his head filled with new ideas about the case, but none of them leading him where he wanted to go. He checked his watch again, then gave his attention once more to his unfinished report.

Straight after McGuire rang off, Pearl drove on towards the busy town, through streets lined principally with holidaymakers. In spite of a series of horrific murders, tourists were still heading towards the beach carrying lilos and coolboxes or queuing at an ice-cream tricycle that bore the name, Lickett & Smyle.

Was it possible, thought Pearl, that visitors didn't bother reading the local papers while on holiday? Of course they didn't. They had better things to do than to scrutinise cub-reporter accounts of Whitstable's tedious council meetings or to read letters from residents like Frederick Clark who felt passionately enough about paro- chial issues to complain about the increase in councillors' allowances or the reduction in local rubbish collections. Perhaps Whitstable figures like Clark and Martha Laker would only ever be viewed by DFLs as colourful small-town eccentrics – even in death. Three murders in Whitstable was a tragedy to local people, but for those visiting from the capital, or from other big cities, they represented only a tiny percentage of a greater national crime statistic. Perhaps this was the reason McGuire was able to keep an emotional distance and adopt a formal, measured approach to his detection work, while Pearl took local crimes personally – as an assault on her own community – a wrong that had to be righted.

The recent murders may have resulted in a small boost for the *Chronicle*'s local sales figures, but whether those could be maintained had yet to be seen. Certainly, if the paper relied on heinous crimes to survive, things had reached a dire level.

Turning off the High Street and on to Island Wall, Pearl parked her car, before noticing a figure standing on the front porch of Seaspray Cottage. As she got out of her Fiat, a young man turned to face her. She saw it was Simon Stone.

CHAPTER TWENTY-ONE

Tension was etched on Simon's young face. It was clear to Pearl he had hardly slept and she ushered him inside.

'I got a missed call from Charlie earlier,' he explained. 'I tried to call him back but couldn't reach him, so I thought I'd come round. Is he . . . home?'

Pearl called out to her son, but the silence that followed came as no surprise.

'He's spending today with his gran,' she explained. 'I think they were heading to Tankerton Slopes where phone reception's not so good.' She paused, noting Simon's disappointment. 'I'm so sorry about your mother,' she added softly.

Simon gave a nod to acknowledge this. 'We all are,' he said.

'Can I get you something?' Pearl asked. 'Tea? Coffee?'

Simon shook his head but remained rooted to the spot.

'Why don't you sit down?' she asked gently.

Simon did so, taking a seat on the sofa. Pearl sat

down beside him and saw his gaze wander around the room, finally lingering on some small framed photos of Pearl with Charlie as a small boy. Her heart went out to the young man – a boy without his mother – and in that moment, she wondered whether Simon's own home in France was scattered with similar photos of him with his father, Adam. Martha had been the absent parent in Simon's life, just as Carl was in Charlie's – though Carl had never returned as Martha had done. Simon looked at Pearl and managed a brave half-smile.

'I was always so proud of what she did,' he said. 'Maybe because she did it . . . with passion?' Pearl nodded but said nothing, allowing him to go on. 'She was . . . vibrant, alive and . . . never ever boring,' he said. 'She fought for other people and plenty of good causes but, in many ways, she was a stranger to me.' He looked lost at this realisation and shook his head helplessly. 'I . . . can't say I ever really knew her – or at least, knew her well. I suppose that was half the fascination for me. She was a mysterious figure – an enigma?'

'How old were you,' asked Pearl, 'when she came back into your life?'

Simon thought for a moment. 'Ten,' he said. 'She'd met Jane and they were living in Whitstable. I think she'd become more stable then. Her life, that is,' he qualified. 'I . . . think she and Jane liked to think of me as the child they never had together? Anyway, I started getting presents sent over, then letters, Skype calls and . . . she bought me a smartphone and we'd use it for FaceTime.

All of a sudden, she was back in my life. It felt good. I felt wanted – by Martha, I mean.'

'You always called her by her name?'

Simon gave a small shrug. 'It never felt right calling her "Mum" – she was more like a friend. A fun friend.' He gave a tight smile.

'And she was proud of you.'

Simon looked up at this.

'She loved you very much.'

'Did she?' Seeing Pearl's confusion, Simon sought to explain. 'I mean, well, she always seemed to enjoy having me around,' he said. 'An extension of herself? She liked the fact we looked so alike and talked about having a portrait painted of us together.'

'And how did you feel about that?' asked Pearl.

Simon shrugged. 'I was happy to go along with it – to please her,' he said, 'but I don't think Dad much liked the idea.' He looked conflicted. 'You have to remember, he's done everything for me, and I'm really grateful but . . . To be honest, sometimes it feels like I've been locked away in our place in France. We're in the middle of the countryside most of the time, and it's beautiful but . . . There are times I've felt like I was . . . caged, and suddenly there was Martha offering me a key to the rest of my life. I wanted to take it. I still do but . . . it's going to be hard without her.' He broke off again.

Pearl allowed a silence to sit between them before: 'You still have that key,' she said. 'Martha gave it to you, but you don't need her to open the door for you. You can do that yourself.'

'Yes.' Simon nodded. 'But I'm not sure I want to – if she's not here any more?' For the first time he looked genuinely overcome with sadness and got up as if to escape it.

At that moment Pearl's landline phone rang. 'Excuse me,' she said gently, before moving quickly to answer the call. It was Charlie.

'Listen, Mum,' he began, 'Gran and I are having a good time. We're down at JoJo's restaurant right now and wondered if you wanted to join us?'

'That's great,' said Pearl quickly, 'but you go ahead without me. I've got someone here with me right now and . . .' She turned quickly to Simon, a smile on her face – but it faded as she saw he had vanished.

Much later that evening, Pearl sat alone in the cottage, light fading beyond the window as she sipped a glass of wine while looking at her laptop screen, checking all she could find on Jason Ritchie. Business directories gave his contact details and professional qualifications, and a detailed online search provided full information on all the companies he had been involved in. Invicta Land showed only Gordon Weller as a fellow company director. All appeared above board, just as Ritchie himself had declared to Pearl at their first meeting. She thought back to that day, how persuasive his arguments had appeared, how she had been tempted to take up his money and his challenge to her – to provide some background information so he could be fully updated about local opinion and the progress of the campaign against his development.

And then – murder – with Gordon Weller found dead in the pillory on the Crown of the Down – a medieval form of torture and public humiliation. Shortly after, a new victim – Frederick Clark – also injected with nicotine, this time in the hide on the downs, followed by Martha Laker, brutally executed by a hand-crafted axe belonging to Ben Tyler, but lent to Martha some days ago.

Pearl was well aware from her police training that most murders are not committed by strangers but by people who have close relationships with the victim. Violent crimes could generally be categorised as either 'instrumental', where the offender seeks a material advantage, as in a robbery, for example, or 'expressive', whereby the perpetrator is driven by a powerful emotion, such as jealousy, hatred or resentment. Domestic homicides usually provided examples of 'expressive' violence. Considering this now, Pearl could see that each of the murders, apart from that of Frederick Clark, bore the stamp of expressive violence and of all three, Martha's killing exhibited the most violent force. Nothing had been stolen from the victims – but their lives – and whereas the murder of Gordon Weller could be viewed as the elimination of an enemy of the campaign to save the downs, there was no such parallel motive for the killing of Fred and Martha. Viewed in this way, Pearl could see only one person who might wish for the campaign to come to an end – and for Weller to disappear for good: Jason Ritchie. But then she also remembered Simon Stone sitting in her living room earlier that day, as he had talked of being 'caged' by his father's love. Both the

Save Our Downs campaign and the woman who had led it stood in the way of what Adam Stone wanted for his son – an education at the Sorbonne and a professional career in France – away from Martha Laker.

Pearl glanced towards her copy of the *Chronicle* and considered Chris Latimer's enthusiasm for his news reporting. Could it possibly be that he was not only responsible for his recent stories but the contents within them – the murders of three local figures? It seemed too far-fetched to be true. But Pearl had become so deeply engrossed in considering these possibilities she physically jumped at the sound of her landline ringing. Picking up the receiver she spoke tersely: 'McGuire, where have you been?'

At that moment, he was alone in the Incident Room, close to the whiteboard, his mobile to his ear. 'Listen to me—' he said.

But Pearl cut in: 'No, I've been thinking . . . I know Ritchie has an alibi for last night but there's nothing to have stopped him paying someone else to kill Martha. Like we said, the "method" – the use of the axe – was totally different to the other two killings, and if Ritchie hired infiltrators for the rally on the beach, he could surely hire someone to kill Martha Laker.'

'The note,' said McGuire firmly.

Pearl was brought up short. 'What?'

'The coded note found on Frederick Clark's body,' said McGuire. 'You were right.'

'Was I?'

'Partially . . .' added McGuire, before he went on: 'Check the e-mail I just sent you.'

Pearl brought up her inbox and found an e-mail from McGuire. Opening an attachment, she viewed a set of symbols that resembled those on the note left on Fred Clark's body.

'It's a Masonic code,' McGuire explained. Pearl took a moment to absorb this. 'Freemasons, you mean?'

'That's right. It seems, for centuries, they've used crypto-grams in ceremonies and for secret messages. This one's known as the pig-pen cypher – don't ask me why – but it corresponds to the note found on Clark's body, which translates as: "The hide. The downs. Tonight. 1800."'

Pearl reflected on this for a moment. 'That easy, eh? A secret message summoning Fred Clark to his death . . .' She made a sudden realisation. 'Weller and Clark were both Rotarians; they could easily have been Freemasons, too. Perhaps Weller got the same message?'

'If he did, it's yet to be found. Maybe he disposed of it. What do you know about Masons?' McGuire asked.

'Apart from funny handshakes and rolled-up trouser legs? Not much,' Pearl admitted. 'It's all very covert, although there's a Masonic Temple right here in Whitstable and I did once see a sign outside it, saying "Open Day".' She smiled. 'Seemed rather a contradiction in terms.' She paused before asking: 'What about you?'

'A few years ago,' McGuire began, 'I was involved in an investigation into a Masonic Lodge in London. I managed to get myself into a special reception – undercover. Believe it or not, they actually throw them sometimes in order to attract new blood.'

'Men only?'

'Of course. I found out there are over a quarter of a million Freemasons in over eight thousand lodges in the UK. And guess what? Many of them are either in the police force or retired from it. Just over ten years ago, the Government tried to put together a voluntary register of Masonic police officers, but less than half responded to enquiries and of the ones who did, only one per cent admitted to being Masons. Meanwhile, the Home Office reckoned the real figure was probably ten times higher.'

'So why did they want a register in the first place?' asked Pearl. 'Possible corruption?'

'A Government report suggested Freemasonry couldn't be totally discounted as a factor in historic miscarriages of justice by a particular Serious Crime Squad.'

'And?'

'Plans for compulsory registration of Freemasons were abandoned after a challenge on Human Rights grounds.'

'So . . . if it's all so innocuous why the secrecy?'

'Originally? Tradition,' said McGuire. 'Freemasonry goes back to the men who built King Solomon's temple. The secret handshake was a covert sign for medieval stonemasons to prove to one another they had been properly trained.'

'And the rolled-up trouser leg?'

'Part of the ancient initiation ceremony to prove they weren't carrying a weapon. As you progressed through the ranks you got to wear funny aprons and become involved in secret ceremonies.' He paused before: 'Thinking about it, I wouldn't be at all surprised if Welch wasn't a Mason.'

'Your superintendent?'

'Yeah. I can just see him in all the regalia, holding court at a lodge dinner.' He paused again. 'As to being "innocuous", I once heard rumours they threatened a slashed throat for breaking Masonic secrets.'

'No!' said Pearl, shocked. 'Using an axe?'

'Of course not,' said McGuire. 'Now it's a noose around the neck. A loose one, of course. Just for fun.'

'But I don't understand,' said Pearl. 'What's the point of it all?'

'Some would say it's a good way to climb the greasy pole. A great opportunity for networking, apparently.'

'But you haven't been asked to join?'

'Now, that would be telling,' he said. 'Actually, I can think of better ways to pass an evening – given half the chance, that is,' he added knowingly.

Pearl ignored his comment and asked: 'Is there anything else you can tell me about the Masons?'

McGuire shrugged to himself. 'It's hierarchical,' he said. 'And there are lots of links with the past. The Middle Ages. The Bible. Once you're a Master Mason, I believe you can join something called the Knights Templar – a subdivision of the Masons, based on the original twelfth-century knights.'

'Knights . . .' mused Pearl.

'What about them?'

'There are knights on a chessboard and . . .' She trailed off.

'And?' prompted McGuire.

Pearl said nothing but was thinking back to Marty's costume at the pageant and wondering whether, as a successful local businessman, he could possibly have been invited to join a local Masonic lodge. 'Nothing,' she said finally – until: 'Ritchie could be a Mason?'

'Yes,' said McGuire. 'So could Chris Latimer, his father Bill and Councillor Peter Radcliffe—'

Pearl spoke over him: 'But Ritchie, more than anyone, could have tempted Gordon Weller to meet him on the downs. He mentioned to me that he doesn't like speaking on the phone and much prefers face-to-face contact.'

'With you I can understand why,' said McGuire.

'Concentrate,' she said, admonishing him. 'So he meets Weller on the Crown of the Down and . . .'

'Kills his business partner.'

'Days later he gets the coded note to Fred Clark, who goes along to the hide expecting to meet a fellow Mason, someone he can trust, and—'

'But why the hide?' asked McGuire quickly. 'Ritchie could have met him anywhere.'

'Think,' said Pearl. 'The hide was so close to the protest camp it would implicate those involved, including members of the campaign, like Martha, Jane and . . .'

McGuire was shaking his head. 'No. It doesn't stack up, Pearl. How does it implicate the campaign group if Clark was part of it? He was fighting the same development – on the same side.'

'I know,' said Pearl. 'But there was tension between Martha and Fred Clark. I witnessed that at the camp the other day and Fred told me himself that he was troubled by something – Martha's tactics, perhaps? Maybe they were becoming more extreme and Fred, after all, was a quiet, methodical, practical man. Mum said she was surprised they'd ever teamed up in the first place. She said they were "chalk and cheese". Cracks were beginning to show in their relationship. The other day, for instance—' She broke off for a moment as an idea came to her. 'But thinking about it now, perhaps the tension at the camp was manufactured . . .'

'What do you mean?'

'Protest camps often attract infiltrators.'

'You heard that from Dolly?'

'Yes. And I don't think it's just paranoia on her part. It makes sense. Someone at the camp could have been feeding information back to Ritchie. I told you, that's the way he operates. He put "plants" in the crowd at that rally on the beach after the court case. Disruptors. And if news got back to him about any possible infighting between Martha and Fred Clark, he could have used that by murdering Clark, a few hundred metres from both the camp and Martha's home – a way of implicating her?'

McGuire considered this then shrugged. 'Ultimately it didn't work – because Martha was murdered too. And you've got nothing to go on but your own suspicions about Ritchie.'

'Gut instinct,' said Pearl. 'It serves private detectives very well.'

'I'd rather have something more concrete,' said McGuire.

'I know,' Pearl said, resigned. 'So you'll need to gather more evidence, won't you?'

'Do you know how long it took to crack this code?' said McGuire.

'The important thing is we did it.'

'*Who* did it?' said McGuire.

'One of your DCs, no doubt,' Pearl said finally. 'And you never know, this code may still be of use to us. I can't help thinking you need to put a tail on Jason Ritchie.'

'Or Jane Orritt,' said McGuire. 'Or your friend Marty Smith or anyone else involved in this campaign—'

'No,' said Pearl firmly. 'Not everyone is capable of murder. Marty included.'

'That's just your opinion.'

'I know Marty.'

'Do you?' For a moment the question hung between them before McGuire continued. 'There are some things you don't see, Pearl. The guy's besotted with you. And to be honest,' he paused before continuing, 'I don't blame him.'

'Then why doesn't he kill *you*?' asked Pearl with a smile. 'You're his rival.'

'Am I?' asked McGuire.

'You know you are.'

'So . . . maybe he's on a killing spree just to give me a case I can't solve.'

'Don't worry,' said Pearl. 'I'll solve it.'

McGuire's voice lost its playful tone. 'I told you before,

Pearl: stay out of this. I don't want you coming to any harm.'

'I know,' she said. '*You* told me that. And so did Mum and Charlie.' She was smiling now at the thought, but her smile slowly faded as she saw something beyond her window.

'Pearl?' asked McGuire on her silence.

'I've got to go.'

'Where?'

'I'll explain later!'

With a sudden click on the line, McGuire looked down at the receiver in his hand then replaced it. He was just about to move away from his whiteboard when his face set on noticing that some joker on his team had scribbled a message below the photos of the three murder victims. It read: *And then there were none.*

Pearl headed quickly through her garden and reached the gate leading on to the promenade just as Councillor Peter Radcliffe and his wife Hilary were approaching.

'Taking an evening stroll?' asked Pearl.

'Giving the pooch a walk on the beach,' said Radcliffe sparely. He nodded to where Hilary's little dog was sniffing around some cerise-flowered mallow that was growing wild amongst the shingle. 'He's not a "pooch",' said Hilary, offended. 'He's a bichon frise. And he much prefers grass to the beach,' she explained. 'But, sadly, the local downs are a place to avoid right now.'

'Yes,' said Radcliffe ominously. 'Two good men murdered.'

'And Martha,' Pearl reminded him.

'Of course,' said Hilary ruefully. 'Another dreadful tragedy for you to stumble across, Pearl.'

'Seems strange,' said her husband, his eyes narrowing as he looked at Pearl. 'You always seem to be around when corpses are dropping.'

Hilary shook her head despairingly. 'It's truly shocking,' she said. 'Luca and I love the downs but this is like a bad dream – I keep thinking we'll all wake up soon. Can you believe it's only a few days ago that we were all at the pageant?'

She looked from Pearl to her husband, who said dismissively, 'Martha Laker's stunt, you mean?'

'Which Fred Clark fully supported,' said Pearl. 'They made formidable partners.'

'But the partnership's now over,' said Radcliffe firmly. 'They're both gone. Eliminated.'

'Yes,' said Pearl, 'that's one way of looking at it.'

Radcliffe gave a snort and continued, 'I just hope the police are concentrating on the gipsy.'

'Gipsy?' asked Pearl.

'The one in the caravan near Benacre,' said Radcliffe.

As Luca trotted across, Hilary slipped the dog's lead on. 'I think you'll find it's a shepherd's hut, darling.' She smiled sweetly at him.

'And how would you know?' He scowled.

Hilary looked a little awkward before explaining, 'I told you, Luca and I love the downs – for our "walkies".' At the mention of the word, the little dog began panting. 'I'll . . .

go on ahead to the Neptune,' she said. 'Luca could do with a drink and so could I, for that matter.' She managed a weak smile. 'Goodbye, Pearl.'

And with that, Hilary minced off towards the Old Neptune pub. Her husband was just preparing to join her when Pearl said: 'I got the impression something troubled Fred Clark on the day of the pageant.'

'Like what?' asked Radcliffe, looking back at her.

'I'm not sure,' Pearl replied honestly. 'Something that happened that afternoon.'

'The brawl, you mean?' said Radcliffe. 'That was Smith not being able to hold his drink.'

'After you brought the developers along to the event.'

Radcliffe frowned. 'So what if I did? It was a public event.'

'And last night?' said Pearl. 'I understand you met with Jason Ritchie.'

Radcliffe's frown deepened. 'Who told you that?'

'You were seen at the Long Reach pub.'

'So what?

'It's not a million miles from the downs, is it? And on the same night Martha Laker was murdered?'

Radcliffe's features screwed into a tight ball. 'Be very careful what you're suggesting, Pearl Nolan. I have excellent legal representation and slander is a heinous crime.'

'Not as heinous as murder,' said Pearl.

For a moment she held Radcliffe's gaze, aware that the warm sea breeze had just developed a sudden bite. The councillor's hand moved quickly to hold on to his toupee and he glanced towards the coastline as he said, 'I'm going to join my wife and I suggest you go inside, Pearl. One thing we can both be sure of is the weather's taking a turn for the worse.'

With that, he quickly moved on up the beach towards the Neptune. Pearl watched him go, then looked out to sea. The wind was stiffening and a black line of cloud had just appeared on the horizon – as it had in her dream. A squall was approaching.

Pearl's landline was ringing as she went back inside Seaspray Cottage. She picked up the receiver to hear Dolly's voice.

'How's the weather there?'

Large specks of rain were splattering across Pearl's leaded window. 'Not good,' she said. 'Where are you?'

'Herne Bay, and it's pouring. Seems to be coming from the north-east,' she said. 'It's bound to be with you soon – but Charlie and I are going to stay here for a while. I just thought I'd let you know.'

'Sounds sensible,' said Pearl. 'Everything's fine here. Have fun; don't get too wet and I'll see you later.'

A moment later, her phone rang again. 'What is it now?' she asked, expecting it to be Dolly, having forgotten something.

A man's voice sounded: 'I know what happened.'

Pearl recognised the voice as Jason Ritchie. 'The murders?' she asked.

Silence.

'Tell me,' said Pearl, impatient.

'I don't want to talk over the phone.'

'Have you contacted the police?'

'No.'

'Why not?'

'I can't,' Ritchie said finally. He left a pause, then: 'I told you once before: you'll come to me – because I'll have exactly what you need.'

'Answers?'

'Photos.'

Pearl took this in and fought a battle with herself before she asked: 'Where are you?'

'At home.' Ritchie paused. 'I'll be waiting for you. Come alone.'

The line went dead in Pearl's hand.

CHAPTER TWENTY-TWO

Pearl sat in her Fiat, parked in a side street off Borstal Hill, her windscreen wipers seemingly tapping out a message for her – a warning perhaps: *Go home . . . go home. . .* She took her mobile from her pocket and dialled McGuire – waiting for the call to connect. But when it finally did so, she heard only a recorded message: *'This is DCI McGuire. I'm sorry I can't answer your call right now, but leave a message for me and I'll get back to you.'* Frustrated, Pearl waited for the tone and said only: 'Call me.'

Staring out of the driver's side window, she looked up at the towering structure of Black Mill. At sixty feet high, its octagonal form loomed above the surrounding properties. She counted the mill's floors from the number of windows visible: five – with the cap set on the very top floor above these, leading out to the fantail. Perhaps if the mill's weatherboarded exterior had never been tarred and had remained its original white, it might have appeared less menacing than it did at this moment.

Pearl remembered her promises to her family and to McGuire. But then she began to reason with herself: it wasn't as if she was in some remote spot; she was in Whitstable, just off the main road into town, and close enough to neighbouring homes to seek help – if any was required. She had brought her mobile phone with her, fully charged, and she knew McGuire would pick up her message and call as soon as he could. She was the sole proprietor of a private detective agency and had just been offered a major lead in the hunt for a local murderer. Was she going to ignore Ritchie's invitation to a private meeting and leave things to McGuire, who right now was probably involved in a meeting with his team? She contemplated that question for only a few seconds before switching off her car engine and grabbing the keys from the ignition. The windscreen wipers – and their warning – were silenced.

Once out of the car, Pearl pulled up the hood of her raincoat and headed along Miller's Court to the spot on which an earlier mill had once existed as far back as two centuries ago. Black Mill's four sweeps had once borne shutters that could be adjusted to cope with varying wind strengths. Judging by the force of the north-easterly gale which was now blowing in sheets of cold rain, Pearl imagined that any of the seven millers who had once worked the old corn mill might have made a productive night of it. Climbing a few steps leading to a decorative brickwork pathway, she found herself standing in front of a wide timber front door. Painted a welcoming red, it seemed to Pearl like something out of a fairy tale itself. She reached out to grab the iron knocker and felt the door opening beneath her hand . . .

A spacious hallway, hung with paintings, offered a welcome shelter from the summer storm. Pearl closed the door behind her and took a few steps forward.

'Jason?'

Silence.

Looking around for a moment, she decided to head off along the hallway of the mill's extension towards what she knew to be the property's main living quarters. Entering a large dining room, she saw that a beautiful Arts and Crafts table and chairs failed to conceal an old foot bell that had once summoned staff to serve courses for Laurence Irving's dinner parties. She called out again. 'Jason?'

Again, silence.

Moving on, she discovered a kitchen and breakfast room – equally deserted. A staircase led to two other floors of the house but Pearl decided to retrace her steps along the hallway in order to investigate the rest of the ground floor. Opening a door at the foot of the mill structure, she found it housed a stylish grand piano. Wandering across to it, she opened its lid and pressed a key. The note resounded in the empty room as though bouncing off the old timber beams in the ceiling. She was just about to call out once more when the wind suddenly gusted, bearing down against the walls of the mill. The branch of an old fruit tree slapped against the window as if admonishing her.

Heading back towards the door of this room, she hesitated, as she noticed that a timber staircase followed the curve of the wall, leading up to the next floor of the mill – and a room, said to have an amazing view, that had been used by Laurence Irving as an artist's studio. Curious, Pearl climbed the stairs, emerging on the first floor of the windmill, to find herself in an elegant sitting room. Three large millstones were set in the ceiling between two old timber beams but Pearl's attention was drawn towards a set of French doors. Looking out of their window panes, she took in the view across Borstal Hill to the estuary waters in the distance. The turbines of the local wind farm were spinning against the fierce incoming wind – just as the sweeps of old Black Mill would have been spinning centuries before. A streak of sheet lightning shot against the sky, illuminating white-capped waves rolling in fast towards the shoreline. It was indeed a spectacular view but Pearl felt only a sense of increasing frustration about the wild goose chase on which Ritchie had clearly set her.

Grabbing her mobile from her pocket, she dialled his number. The call went straight to voicemail. At the tone, she decided against leaving a message and rang off. Her stomach tensed with anxiety as she realised that Ritchie's own call may have been just a ruse to get her here – to the mill – so that something could take place elsewhere. *Another murder?* If so, this time, she would not be around to discover it – or prevent it. *How could she have fallen for such a trick?*

Moving quickly away from the French doors, she decided to head home and call McGuire once more, this

time to ask him to put out a search for Ritchie. Then she
noticed something. A set of photographs were spread
out on a coffee table near a sofa. Ritchie had mentioned
photographs in his phone call. *Had he left these for her?*
Pearl sat down and sifted through the shots, realising that
these were surely the photos for which Ritchie had paid
Chris Latimer. But why? What could they possibly show
that might have caused him to summon her to Black Mill?
And if they had been the reason for his call – where was
he? Not wanting to waste more time, she quickly flicked
through the shots and saw that each photo bore a date and
time code.

The first, timed at 11.47, showed the *Victuals and Ales*
tent and the circus-school acrobats performing near the
beacon with Robin Hood's band nearby. From 11.49, a
few more photos showed The Whitstable Pearl's stall with
Charlie, Ruby and Dolly in fancy dress. At 11.51 they
were joined by Pearl and Marty in his knight's armour. At
11.52, Rev Pru was posed in her surplice. Then at 11.53,
Martha and Jane Orritt were featured as the Queens of
Spades and Hearts, respectively, standing near the pitch-
pot beacon. Pearl remembered Chris Latimer reminding
both women that Martha was due to give her speech at
midday. Jane was smiling, looking in the direction of the
crowds, but Martha was staring directly at the camera –
with a look of intent that Pearl hadn't noticed at the time
because, as she recalled now, Marty had needed help with
his clumsy knight's helmet before he had finally abandoned
it. At 11.56 more photos showed Martha with Simon

and Adam Stone. Excellent studies followed of Martha giving her speech from 12.03 and then more of Frederick Clark taking up position to give his own speech at 12.05 before he lit the beacon. At 12.36, several shots had been taken of the fracas caused by Marty, with McGuire intervening – then nothing more. *Nothing illuminating. Nothing incriminating.* Pearl chewed the inside of her lip before deciding to reinspect all the photos – those before Martha's speech, those during it and the ones of Frederick Clark and Marty's arrest.

Thinking back to the sequence of events, she remembered that it was after Fred's speech that McGuire had arrived at the pageant and she had headed into nearby Trench Wood with him, to the secluded clearing and patch of meadow – until they had been disturbed by the sound of a woman's scream. Had there been something else that had happened at that time? *Had she really heard the sound of voices in the trees?* Or had Pearl's imagination been playing tricks on her that afternoon? Could there have been others in the same part of the woods at the same time, apart from Ben Tyler and Gloria Greenwood?

Sheets of rain lashed across the panes of glass in the French doors, as though demanding her attention. Pearl responded by moving back to the window. Peering directly below, she now saw something she had failed to spot before: Jason Ritchie's silver Lexus was parked in an area at the back of the mill near a courtyard. Surely he hadn't ventured far, on foot, in this weather? But if he wasn't in his car – where was he? Glancing around the room, she saw a flight of timber steps leading to the second floor – and took them.

Pearl's hand remained firmly on the rail as she moved slowly and carefully up the steep stairs. In spite of her fear of heights, if Ritchie was somewhere in this mill, she was determined to find him. The stairs led to a narrow opening on to the next floor. Pearl barely caught sight of some mill workings before there was a flash of lightning and a bolt of thunder struck almost immediately overhead. The room was suddenly plunged into darkness, and the black stairwell beneath her told Pearl the whole mill seemed to have lost its electricity supply. Only a dim light entered through a small rectangular window against which rain hammered as the storm continued to rage. A stench of dampness hung in the air.

Pearl heard her own breaths coming fast in the darkness. Fear was beginning to overtake her. She tried to calm herself and take stock, before fumbling in her pocket for her mobile phone. Her trembling fingers closed around it and she grabbed it from her pocket – only to feel it slip from her hand – clattering down the dark stairwell, bouncing, one step after another, until it finally landed on the floor below. Pearl let out an involuntary sigh, which seemed suddenly to echo in the room. Or was it the voice of another person? *Was there someone else there?* Inching her way around a timber structure in the centre of the room, her foot met with something. Instantly, she withdrew it, then braced herself and squinted in the darkness.

Something was lying propped against the cold mill wall. *An old sack of flour?* Crouching down, Pearl recognised the unmistakable cedar-wood fragrance of Ritchie's brand of aftershave. Reaching out, she found his head slumped against his chest. His body was still warm to her touch. She felt for a carotid pulse at the side of his neck – and found it. *Ritchie was still alive.* As Pearl quickly got to her feet, thunder cracked loudly overhead and another bolt of lightning pierced the room through the tiny window to fall on another figure in the shadows.

'Thank God it's you!' breathed Olivia Latimer with relief. Her hand went quickly to her throat as she explained: 'He tried to kill me. I . . . struck out with this, I—' Her rapid staccato speech broke off and she tossed something heavy towards Pearl's feet.

Pearl searched among bat droppings before picking up a piece of cold metal – an old mill tool, she guessed – a hammer at one end and a spanner at the other. 'What were you doing here?' she asked.

Olivia shook her head as if finally coming to her senses. 'Chris told me that Jason had gone to talk to him and had paid him for photos of the pageant. But he shouldn't have done,' she insisted. 'They're the property of the *Chronicle*. I . . . didn't trust Ritchie so I came to return his money but—' She broke off as Pearl set the heavy mill tool back down on the floor and crouched again towards Ritchie, hearing his heavy breaths.

'He's still alive,' she said. 'We must call the police.'

'Yes,' said Olivia, nodding in agreement. 'But . . .

I can't,' she stammered. She handed a mobile phone to Pearl. 'Battery's gone.'

Pearl checked the phone and handed it back to her. 'Mine's on the floor below,' she explained. She looked back at Ritchie, still unresponsive, then turned back to Olivia: 'Go down and find it, will you? I'll keep an eye on Ritchie.'

Olivia looked torn. 'Couldn't you go?' she asked. She looked around and clutched at her throat. 'I'm . . . scared of the dark.'

'And I'm scared of heights,' Pearl admitted, managing a smile at the thought.

Olivia Latimer, however, remained unamused. Her features were impassive but something in her beautiful dark eyes unnerved Pearl in that moment, reminding her of something Dolly had said, about having once seen Olivia dance in *Swan Lake*: not the white swan, Odette, but the evil double, Odile. Pearl felt a rising surge of fear as a thought occurred to her: 'Why . . . didn't you go back downstairs before the lights failed?'

'I heard someone down there,' Olivia explained. 'I didn't know it was you.' She took a step forward. Ritchie gave a low moan. Another bolt of lightning entered the window and shone directly on him.

Pearl shook her head as she realised something. 'You . . . didn't hit him with this,' she said, indicating the mill tool. 'There's no blood on it . . . and no wound . . . and—' She broke off as thunder cracked overhead. Lightning brought enlightenment. 'He's been drugged.'

She steeled herself for a response but Olivia Latimer was silent for a moment before finally a long sigh escaped her lips. She then spoke, softly and calmly: 'It had to be done,' she said. 'After I'd got him to call you.'

A sudden gust of wind pummelled the walls of the old mill. The moon was rising beyond the window, casting a silvery light in the gloom. Pearl heard blood pumping in her ears as Olivia went to take a step forward.

'Stay where you are,' Pearl ordered. Olivia remained rooted to the spot and for a brief moment, she appeared to be appraising Pearl. Finally, she spoke. 'It's no use,' she said, her hand moving slowly to her pocket.

'I'm warning you,' said Pearl, stepping back to feel out the curve of the cold mill wall behind her with her palms.

'What I've planned for you and Ritchie is very quick,' Olivia continued. 'An easy death. That's what I've found.' A thin smile appeared on her lips.

Pearl shook her head slowly. 'Easy perhaps for Weller and Clark,' she said. 'But not for Martha.'

'No.' Olivia shook her head. 'Martha deserved something special.'

'For what?' asked Pearl. 'For meeting your husband Bill in the woods on the day of the pageant? Is that why there were no photographs taken for over thirty minutes that day?' she went on, as the truth began to dawn for her: 'Bill was the photographer, wasn't he? So the look on Martha's face in those photos was for him. She was summoning him.' She paused now. 'Her lover?'

Olivia shook her head slowly. 'You're clever, Pearl,

but not quite clever enough.' She took a deep breath and released it before explaining: 'Some men are destined for greatness – but not Bill. It took his grandfather a lifetime to create the *Chronicle* – from nothing. My husband managed to destroy it in just a couple of decades. But I couldn't allow the only legacy I have for my son to just disappear. Surely you, as a mother, can understand that?' Her head tipped to one side, inviting empathy.

But Pearl continued to edge back. 'I don't understand,' she said. 'Why murder Gordon Weller?'

'Why else?' asked Olivia. 'He was putting pressure on Bill to gain the paper's support for the development. Paying for headlines.'

'Bill told you that?'

'Of course not,' said Olivia dismissively. 'I found out. I made it my business to find out – everything – from the very first day I discovered that Martha Laker and my husband were—' She broke off, unable to voice the truth. 'It was years ago,' she said finally. Looking back at Pearl, she went on, fuelled now by anger. 'Martha used him, toyed with him. And he allowed her to do that because . . . Bill's a fool. The paper was losing readers and he began drinking. Wallowing in self-pity. A prime victim for Martha Laker. So she began an affair with him . . . boosted his ego – and not because she was attracted to him or because she loved him.' She shook her head. 'No,' she went on. 'She used their . . . relationship . . . to help win her pathetic battles. I suspected what was going on. And I knew, for sure, once I'd put a detective on to them – a snoop like you. I had all the evidence I needed. All the sordid details. And photographs. And then?' She looked pained, struggling to explain as she went on: 'Just as I was planning to leave him, to divorce him and to take what was rightfully mine of the business . . . I had a car accident. One stormy night. Just like this.' She looked around the rain-whipped mill, then continued: 'Suddenly I had nothing *but* him. I was dependent on him. I needed Bill just to survive.' She paused. 'I know how guilty he felt. I could see it in his eyes. He stopped drinking. I told myself that perhaps we could start again – pretend none of this had happened. I desperately needed to have what I had once had but . . . it was all gone. I tried so hard – months and months of physio . . . training . . . but I couldn't dance as I'd done before . . . We were short of money and once we took Chris out of boarding school, I knew I had to find a way to carry on – for him. I had to draw a line under the past. D'you understand?'

She fell silent, allowing the storm to articulate her desperation before continuing, 'Martha and Jane were full of sympathy and kind words. They even gave me my very first commission as a painter.'

'A portrait of Martha . . .' Pearl whispered.

'Yes,' said Olivia bitterly. 'And yes, I should have refused. But I couldn't. No matter how hard I was trying to move on, I was drawn to her, just like Bill, like . . . waves to the shore. Martha sat for me for weeks as I studied every line of her face, every contour of her body, listening to her, going on and on about her causes . . . and all the while I was trying to find what it was about her that had been so lacking in me?' Olivia shook her head as though confused. 'She wasn't beautiful. She had no grace. And yet . . . after she and Bill—' She broke off. 'He never once looked at me in the same way again – only with pity. It was as though he was searching the ruins of my face to find the thing he once loved.' She paused for a moment. 'Art became my therapy. My life. It enabled me to carry on. And that's all I've done ever since – for my son. For Chris. But then . . . this development was to take place – right on the downs – right under Martha Laker's nose – and I knew she would put pressure on Bill – even though Chris has been virtually running the paper. She began blackmailing my husband. And this time she wasn't the only one.'

Pearl took this in, searching for an excuse to keep Olivia talking. 'So . . . Martha and Gordon Weller deserved everything they got?' said Pearl. 'But what about Fred Clark? What had he ever done to you?'

'Fred was a clever man,' said Olivia. 'He put two and two together. He heard something on the day of the pageant.'

'A conversation between Martha and Bill?'

Olivia nodded. 'She took Bill into the woods. I saw her do it. He was taking photos of her. And I followed. I saw Fred there, listening. Days later, I realised it wouldn't be long before he said something to the police – or to you. And I couldn't let that happen.'

'So you summoned him to his death with a coded note,' said Pearl. 'Just as you'd done with Weller.'

287

Olivia shrugged. 'I couldn't risk being identified with a handwritten note, an e-mail or a phone message. But Gordon and Fred were in the same Masonic lodge as Bill. I knew the codes they used. And I knew Fred would always trust another Mason.'

'Except it wasn't a Mason he met in the hide that night. It was you.'

'Yes,' said Olivia starkly. She offered a proud smile.

'And now?' asked Pearl.

'Now, you'll be found here,' Olivia explained. 'The victim of the prime suspect in all of this.' She glanced down at Jason Ritchie. 'He's only slightly sedated but the police will know that he summoned *you* here – with that phone call. The facts will speak for themselves . . .' She slowly withdrew something from her pocket and took a step forward. A bolt of lightning fell on the syringe in her hand. Pearl quickly reached down to the bat-soiled floor and snatched up the old mill tool before taking the only way out left to her.

Rushing up two short flights of steps, she found herself in the mill's cap, trying to seek an escape route in fresh darkness. Heavy machinery blocked her path and only a single shaft of moonlight pierced the room from a tiny window. Pearl grasped the mill tool tightly for defence but something made contact with her face. A tiny pipistrelle flew up into the ceiling, causing Pearl to strike out blindly in fear. The mill hammer struck the great timber brake wheel then flew from Pearl's hand and disappeared down the stairwell. Suddenly, with a loud groan, the old mill workings cranked into operation. The single shaft of moonlight momentarily disappeared as one of the mill's four sweeps obscured the window. As it sailed past once more, Olivia Latimer was now revealed, as if she was on a stage, like the dancer she had once been – Odile – in the arc of a spotlight.

Pearl slowly backed away. The mill's sweeps turned, faster this time, powered by the creaking fantail outside, their shutters creating a slow strobe of light against the tiny window – just enough for Pearl to spot a single door in the cap. She kicked it wide. A blast of wind and rain almost knocked her back off her feet, but beyond it she saw a wooden platform leading to the white fantail – and a sixty-foot drop below. Freezing rain soaked her clothes as she inched out on to the platform, her vision masked by torrents of rain, reminding her of the windscreen wipers that had sounded out a message for her: *Go home . . . go home . . .*

In the distance, the lights of the wind farm were barely visible, blinking red on the horizon against the dark sky. The sweeps turned once more and the light bleeding in from the cap's window revealed a dark silhouette in the doorframe. Olivia Latimer stepped out on to the platform as though oblivious to the storm. Once again, she withdrew the syringe from her pocket; this time she discarded the needle's cover. With a sudden lunge, she made her move but Pearl grasped her wrist, shocked by the older woman's physical power as she resisted. Olivia now took hold of Pearl's other arm, forcing her back with great strength.

For a former dancer, like Olivia, there was always muscle memory to be called upon. Pearl found herself being pushed back further, her spine buckling, compressed against the wooden rail of the platform as the fantail blades whirred close above her head, driving the mill's cap and the sweeps into the high wind. Determination was etched on Olivia's face – the last thing ever to have been seen by Weller, Clark and Martha herself – but now Olivia Latimer's dead eyes were trained on a new victim.

Pearl dug deep to find her own strength and kicked out in desperation, her foot jamming against Olivia's knee before the dancer's swift reflexes allowed her to wrench her leg aside, forcing Pearl to sink further down against the rail, which now cut so deep into her spine she felt as though her back was breaking. Still she held fast to Olivia's wrist but the tip of the needle was coming closer – so close, Pearl could almost feel it touching her skin. Her neck muscles strained to keep her head bent forward, eyes fixed on the syringe in Olivia's hand, but it was no use.

Pearl's strength was finally deserting her as the adrenalin that had been coursing through her body was fading. Her heart still hammered against her chest as her head snapped back against the rail, and she found herself looking up as a flash of forked lightning illuminated the night sky above her, allowing her to believe that this would now be the last thing she saw, and not the face of her killer . . .

It took only a split second for the pressure to release, and for Olivia Latimer to be drawn back suddenly, as though by the gusting wind. The dark look in her hollow eyes became one of shock – perhaps even surprise – and she seemed to hover for a moment before finally lunging forward again, this time not upon Pearl, who had slipped to one side, relieving the pressure on her spine. Latimer had become unbalanced by an unknown force behind her and was being propelled towards the rail as the fantail continued to revolve, its blades spinning towards her, as though offering her a lifeline. Olivia took it, grasping a wooden blade which took her up towards the night sky, supporting her like a partner in a ballet, high on the wind, before the fantail headed back down again. Another crack of thunder seemed to signal the end of the performance. Olivia's hand was now slowly losing its grip on the wet blade.

Pearl made a move towards her but, in the next instant, the fantail tossed Olivia Latimer mercilessly aside. Abandoned to the elements, her dancer's body seemed to sail for a moment on the wind, before plummeting down to crash on the courtyard below. There she lay, like the chalked outline of a murder victim. But this was the body of a killer, its outline formed by a pool of blood spreading out towards a silver Lexus.

It took Pearl another moment to finally register that she, herself, was still alive – and safe. Jason Ritchie was standing beside her on the platform, his hands grasped tightly to the rail as he tried to steady himself. He looked back at her and, in that moment, Pearl knew she owed her life to him.

CHAPTER
TWENTY-THREE

Some weeks later

A perfect summer's day. The sun burned down out of a sky so clear it had transformed the estuary waters into a deep cobalt blue. It might have been a Dufy painting that Pearl was admiring – but it was the view from the sea wall at the foot of her garden – and she was sharing it with Jason Ritchie. Reacting to something he had just told her, Pearl turned to him and asked: 'You're actually pulling out of the development?'

Ritchie nodded. 'I've always been a winner,' he said. 'But this town of yours has me beaten.'

Pearl frowned at this, confused. 'But . . . there's nothing standing in your way any more. Jane Orritt is putting the house up for sale. The council have issued the formal approval notice for your development. The town still needs housing—'

'Affordable housing,' Ritchie cut in. 'You were right – and so was the campaign – the properties Gordon and I were going to build on Laker's Field would have been snapped up by DFLs – homes traded as assets. You know as well as I do, something else is needed for Whitstable. Something special – though Gordon won't be around to see it.' His expression darkened.

'That's true,' said Pearl, staring out to sea once more. 'He and Martha were enemies, but in one way, at least, they were very much alike. They both knew the power of the media, and thought they could control it – through Bill Latimer.'

Ritchie shrugged. 'Newspapers need controversy as much as campaigners need newspapers.'

Pearl nodded. 'The *Chronicle* had always run editorials in support of local campaigns, but it also invited responses from residents—'

'Of which,' said Ritchie, 'there are no fewer than forty thousand in Whitstable.'

'That's right,' said Pearl. 'People think of us as a small fishing town but including all the local environs, we're actually a considerable force. Until this development, our local campaigns had been fairly innocuous: fighting a one-way system, keeping shops independent, saving the local post office or preventing tree clearances during the bird breeding season. But now there was a vested interest – Invicta Land – threatening to build on local green space. Olivia Latimer was right: Bill was a fool. His affair with Martha Laker was something Martha could always use against him when she needed it most – perhaps for her most important campaign.'

'Her final campaign,' said Ritchie.

'Yes,' said Pearl. 'Though it brings a new beginning.' She reached into her bag and unfolded a copy of a newly printed newspaper. Its front cover read:

A new day dawns for your Chronicle

by Editor Martin Trubshaw

Thursday 23 July 2020

For almost a hundred years, the Chronicle newspaper has provided news for the people of Whitstable.

From today, the news will continue, the name will remain the same, but the form of the newspaper will change because the Chronicle is now under new ownership.

Your weekly Chronicle will continue to bring you comprehensive coverage of local events while maintaining the highest standards in our reporting.

We look forward to continuing a proud tradition of campaigning journalism for which the Chronicle has always been greatly respected. That tradition will continue.

We are here to serve you – our readers – so feel free to contact our News Desk with any stories or suggestions for what you would like to read in your local newspaper. Be part of the Chronicle's new dawn.

Ritchie looked at Pearl, who explained: 'Bill Latimer has sold out to a new media group and, I gather, for a song. But perhaps that will still be for the best – if Bill and his son can move on from all this.'

Ritchie looked troubled. 'I . . . honestly didn't know that Gordon had been paying Bill Latimer for press coverage. There was nothing in the accounts—'

'Because he'd used cash payments from his own bank

account,' said Pearl. 'They've been found by the police. Gordon knew the power of local media – especially the *Chronicle*. He'd used it in the past for his own ends – but then so had Martha. The difference being that she'd also used the paper's owner, Bill Latimer. His was a fading empire but his wife wasn't about to allow her son's future to be destroyed by Bill's mistakes.'

'And Fred Clark?' asked Ritchie.

'The truly innocent victim,' said Pearl. 'I believe Gordon was also putting pressure on him to withdraw his support for the campaign. I've discovered that if the Whitstable Preservation Society had appealed against the court decision – and lost – the Society's trustees would have been personally liable for all the legal costs. Fred was under a lot of pressure but he knew he was on the right side – until the day of the pageant, when he must have heard Martha attempting to blackmail Bill about their relationship.'

'Why the hell didn't he speak out?' said Ritchie in frustration.

'Against an old affair?' asked Pearl. 'He couldn't have been aware that Olivia Latimer already knew about it, but Fred was a clever man and he recognised Martha's words had taken on a special resonance when she told the media that day that if they didn't tell the truth – she would. That was surely a veiled threat to Bill Latimer. Then, just moments later, both she and Bill disappeared. No photos were taken for the *Chronicle* until over thirty minutes later, even when Gordon was being attacked by Marty Smith. There were only a few shots of Marty being arrested. Bill had missed the rest because he had been in Trench Wood – with Martha.'

Jason Ritchie took a moment to consider this, then reached into his jacket pocket and took out his chequebook.

'I told you before,' said Pearl quickly. 'I'm not for sale.'

'And I'm no fool,' said Ritchie. 'I learned that lesson. But I'm leaving two cheques with you – to pass on.' He scribbled on each of them with a fine pen, then tore them from the book and slipped them into an envelope, which he handed to Pearl. She looked at him. 'You saved my life.'

Ritchie shrugged. 'Circumstances,' he said. 'And an old mill.'

'Perhaps,' said Pearl, 'and a pipistrelle bat? If it hadn't flown up when it did, I might not have struck out at it and knocked the mill's brake.'

Ritchie smiled slowly. 'Sometimes it pays to disturb the local wildlife.'

'Bats are a protected species,' she reminded him.

Ritchie looked at her. 'You're right,' he said. He got to his feet and pointed a finger at her. 'I've learned not to argue with you, Pearl.'

'Where are you off to?' she asked.

He took a few moments to reply. 'Somewhere far away,' he said. 'I've always been . . . the man with a plan? But for the first time in my life, I don't have one. All I know is: I need a break. And a rethink.' He looked back at her. 'How about you?'

Pearl got up from the sea wall. 'I've got a restaurant to get back to.'

'And the agency?'

Pearl paused at this. 'We'll see what comes up.'

Jason watched as she picked up her bag. Taking his keys from his pocket he asked: 'Can I give you a lift?'

Pearl smiled. 'Thanks, but I could do with a walk.'

Ritchie nodded then turned and walked away, up the beach towards the old white clapboard pub at Neptune Gap. There, he opened the door to his silver Lexus, slipped on his Ray-Ban sunglasses and looked back against the sun towards Pearl. This time, she raised an arm – and waved goodbye.

Later that same day, Pearl was with Charlie in his Canterbury flat, which had been fully repaired – and approved by the city council for reoccupation. Pearl had unpacked a bag of clean laundry for her son, and having found only a limp lettuce in the salad compartment of his fridge, she had fully restocked it with a selection of delicious food items from The Whitstable Pearl. She had also prepared a light lunch of grilled tiger prawns with coriander and ginger, marinated peppers and artichokes and a crispy green salad, followed by some vanilla ice-cream lightly doused with a twelve-year-old Spanish Amontillado sherry.

As Charlie settled back and put his feet up on the sofa, Pearl noted that the bruise on his temple had finally faded. He was suffering only a slight hangover acquired at the Old Neptune pub, where he had spent the evening before saying goodbye to some old Whitstable friends. Pearl cleared away the dishes and arranged some sunflowers in a vase before deciding that now was a good time to broach something that had been on her mind for some days.

'Charlie,' she began, 'we both know there's a shortage of reasonably priced accommodation for rent locally, but if the restaurant has as good a summer as we had last year, perhaps I could help you with the deposit on a flat closer to home.'

'In Whitstable, you mean?' asked Charlie.

Pearl nodded. Her son looked shocked. 'You don't need to do that, Mum,' he said.

'I'd like to,' said Pearl. 'I didn't exactly get much time to spend with you, did I?'

'I know,' said Charlie, 'but it's not as if you and Gran are really far away, is it? We're only twenty minutes down the road from one another.'

'True,' said Pearl.

'And I've been thinking,' Charlie went on. 'When the new term starts in September, I might start sharing this place again – with a friend.'

'Oh?' Pearl's curiosity was piqued.

'Yeah,' said Charlie. 'I told Si he could come and stay for a while.'

'Simon Stone?'

Charlie nodded. 'We met last night at the Neppy,' he said. 'His dad's going back to France but Si says he needs more time to figure out what he really wants to do.'

Pearl took a few moments to absorb this. 'And . . . is his dad okay about that?'

Charlie gave another nod. 'It's Si's life,' he said. 'His

dad can't live it for him, and he . . . can't really stop him doing what he wants to do?'

'No,' said Pearl, thoughtful. 'You're right.' She managed a smile now then wandered to the window and pushed it open. Looking down on the busy pedestrian thoroughfare of St Peter's Street, she saw crowds of tourists investigating market stalls. Charlie was right: Canterbury was just eight miles from Whitstable – though it always seemed to Pearl like a completely different world. Nevertheless, she now understood that it was a world her son enjoyed inhabiting. The smell of street food wafted upwards on the air and a young busker took up position on the opposite side of the street.

'Gran's coming over next week,' said Charlie. Pearl looked back at him and he went on to explain: 'There's an exhibition being planned at the café down the road – the Boho? Gran and I thought we'd get some pieces of work together for it and share the space? We were talking about it the day we went to Herne Bay.'

Pearl knew Charlie was referring to the day the freak storm had blown in, though he had been careful not to mention what had occurred later that night. A line had been drawn. The murders on the downs were now a thing of the past. Life was moving on – for everyone.

'That sounds good,' said Pearl. 'I can't wait to see them.' She raised a smile for her son and Charlie returned it. 'Thanks for having me around, Mum,' he said, his voice barely audible above the noise of the city as the busker started strumming an electric guitar – the opening bars of a slow song by Ed Sheeran. The smell of savoury noodles, combined with sweet candyfloss, was entering the room with the music. Charlie began nodding along to this soundtrack, his eyes closing.

Pearl picked up her bag and crossed the room to him. 'Any time,' she said softly, planting a gentle kiss on her son's forehead, though she knew, in that bitter-sweet moment, that Charlie wouldn't be in need of his old bedroom for some time.

Over an hour later, Pearl had exchanged the city streets of Canterbury for the local downs. Staring down at her walking shoes, she moved on steadily through tangled undergrowth, using the same rhythm to recite an old poem:

> 'They shut the road through the woods
> Seventy years ago.
> Weather and rain have undone it again,
> And now you would never know
> There was once a road through the woods
> Before they planted the trees.
> It is underneath the coppice and heath,
> And the thin anemones.
> Only the keeper sees
> That, where the ring-dove broods,
> And the badgers roll at ease,
> There was once a road through the woods.'

For a few moments, Pearl fell silent. Then she smiled slowly. 'I knew I'd get there in the end.'

'You always do,' said McGuire, walking slowly beside her. He stopped in his tracks. 'Come here.' Pulling her towards him, he held her tightly in his arms. After all that had happened, he knew how lucky he was to be able to do so. As they broke away, she looked up at him and her beautiful grey eyes scanned his face.

'You . . . said you wanted me to be honest with you from now on?'

McGuire nodded, then watched as she reached into her pocket and produced an envelope which she handed to him. He hesitated before opening it, then took out two slips of paper.

'Cheques,' said Pearl, 'from Jason Ritchie.'

McGuire studied each of them and noted five-figure sums. Pearl continued: 'One is for the Whitstable Preservation Society and the other for a volunteer group that looks after the downs. Funny,' she continued, 'I never really appreciated this place until now.' She looked around, taking in the sparrows brawling among the trees, but McGuire's gaze remained on Pearl.

'Me neither,' he said. He tipped her face back towards him and went on. 'We made a promise, Pearl: never to let work come between us, remember?'

She nodded. 'That seems like an age ago.'

'I know,' said McGuire. 'But I'm still prepared to keep it – if you are.'

Pearl looked up at him – part of her wanting to explain why it was so important to hold on to her independence and to a dream she had cherished for so long – perhaps too long – because she still couldn't allow it die. Not yet. She would always be her own woman and in that moment she suddenly remembered a sentiment from Canterbury's poet, Chaucer: no man would ever say to her: 'checkmate'. Rather than taking the time to explain, she simply nodded slowly to McGuire.

He leaned in and pressed his lips against hers and as they broke apart, he kept his face close to Pearl's, as he held up her pearl earring in his hand. His voice dropped to a whisper as he asked: 'So… where's that meadow you wanted to show me?'

Pearl smiled, took the earring from him and slipped it into her pocket before grasping McGuire's hand. 'Come on,' she said. But they had hardly taken a step before a black shape bolted from the trees.

Martha Laker's dog, Scooby, nuzzled Pearl's palm, while a small bichon frise appeared, as if from nowhere, jumping up at McGuire.

'What's going on?' he asked, registering that both dogs were familiar to Pearl. She opened her mouth to explain but a small scream was suddenly heard straight ahead. Heading quickly to a bank of trees, Pearl remained speechless for a moment, before: 'Well I never.'

McGuire followed her. 'What?'

'Not "what" – "who"?' Pearl indicated through a gap in the trees. McGuire took her view to see Ben Tyler offering a hand to help someone up from the grass. Pearl whispered: 'That's Hilary Radcliffe. Councillor Radcliffe's wife.'

At that moment, Tyler and Hilary emerged on to the

footpath, brought up short by the sight of McGuire and Pearl before them. Hilary quickly brushed down the summer dress she was wearing and called abruptly to her dog: 'Luca!' The bichon turned and scampered obediently back to his mistress, quickly followed by Scooby.

Ben put on his leather hat – after tipping it politely to Pearl – and then he and Hilary headed on along the path with their dogs. Pearl looked back at McGuire and smiled. But in the next instant, McGuire's mobile suddenly sounded. Taking it from his pocket, he noted the caller was Superintendent Maurice Welch. Pearl saw him struggling with something.

'Aren't you going to get that?'

McGuire looked at her, made a sudden decision and switched off his phone.

'It can wait,' he said. 'A promise is a promise.' He smiled, pocketed his mobile and now took Pearl's hand firmly in his own. As they stepped into the clearing, which became a small patch of meadow, Pearl looked up at the deep blue sky. McGuire followed her gaze to see a kestrel soaring high above, gliding on the thermals across scores of acres of precious downs – land that would remain wild and beautiful for as long as there were those who cared enough to keep it that way. It was Whitstable's own Eden, and in that moment, it belonged to Pearl and McGuire.

AUTHOR'S NOTE:

The importance of location in the Whitstable Pearl Mysteries

Many authors invent fictional locations for their detectives, but I chose a real place – my adopted home town of Whitstable, where I've lived for the past twenty years.

W. Somerset Maugham wrote about the town in two of his novels, *Of Human Bondage* (1915) and *Cakes and Ale* (1930), but he referred to it as 'Blackstable', and it's been suggested that he did so because he had an unhappy time there. I don't know if that's true, but I do know that, in writing the Whitstable Pearl Mysteries, I wanted to pay tribute to the town I love and to celebrate it by using its own name.

Whitstable is a quirky place with an independent, anti-establishment spirit, which I feel may be due to its old smuggling history. But it's also quintessentially English and full of interesting characters – the perfect location for my books.

Growing up as a child in a very rundown part of the East End of London, the world was opened up to me by reading books in our public library – particularly those of the Golden Age of Detective Fiction, which made use of exotic locations and fine country houses.

My upbringing may have helped me to go on to write the fictional TV world of *EastEnders*, but it was from reading crime novels such as Agatha Christie's *Murder in Mesopotamia*, *Death on the Nile* and *A Caribbean Mystery* that I came to appreciate the importance of location and how readers can be transported to other worlds simply by turning the pages of a book.

For that reason, I remain a fan of writers who make great use of location in their work, notably Donna Leon, whose Commissario Brunetti novels are set in Venice, and the American writer Stephen Dobyns, who brings alive the Saratoga Race Course in his Charlie Bradshaw crime novels.

I love the idea of location becoming almost another character in a novel, and I'm lucky to be able to feature not only a seaside location here in Whitstable, but also beautiful local countryside and the great city of Canterbury just a few miles away.

I know many readers will never be able to visit Whitstable in person, but I hope that reading my books will allow them to feel they can still enjoy a welcome break here on our mysterious coast . . .

ACKNOWLEDGEMENTS

I always wanted to write a Whitstable Pearl Mystery that strayed from the beach locations I have used in other books to include our more rural haunts. Of those, we do not have many in the centre of Whitstable but we are very lucky to have an area of fifty-two acres of land known as Duncan Down, at the entrance to our town, which I have thoroughly enjoyed researching and featuring in this book.

I became properly acquainted with this area, and the nearby ancient woodland of Benacre Wood, following the invaluable help with research that I received from local city councillor Ashley Clark. Ashley should in no way be confused with the entirely fictional councillor, Peter ('Ratty') Radcliffe, who has been featured in other books as well as this one. Cllr Ashley Clark does a tremendous amount of work in conserving local green open space in Whitstable and has been instrumental in gaining Village Green status for Duncan Down. This status means that, unlike the fictional areas I have mentioned in Murder on the Downs, our own 'downs' are protected against development.

Ashley very kindly gave up his time to take me on fascinating and informative recces across our rural areas and even helped me to pinpoint the area I have fictionalised as Laker's Field. He also helps the group of volunteers known as the Friends of Duncan Down, whose work has been so important there in maintaining this space.

I would also like to thank Howard and Deb Stoate for their generosity in allowing me to feature their beautiful home, Black Mill, in this story and for giving me a most exciting tour, right up into the very top of the windmill, the cap, including the fantail platform – all of which inspired the ending of the book. Thanks also go to all the volunteers at Herne Mill where I enjoyed a guided tour one sunny Sunday afternoon.

Throughout the past year, I have been fortunate to have had the kind support of Dominic King at BBC Radio Kent, and also the former local newspaper editor, John Nurden, whose experience of the news industry helped to inspire sections in the book. I will always be grateful to the late Keith Dickson and all his hardworking staff at Harbour Books in Whitstable; and my friend Victoria Falconer, for her invitations to me to stage events at WhitLit – Whitstable's own literary festival.

My thanks also go to authors Lisa Cutts, William Shaw and Jane Wenham-Jones for partnering me for author talks throughout the year, and to Lisa especially for also giving me valuable advice on police procedure.

I'm also very grateful to all the wonderful book stores and festivals that have invited me to stage events – at which I have been lucky enough to meet many of my readers.

And, as ever, my thanks go to publishing director, Krystyna Green, and her team at Constable at Little, Brown Book Group, as well as to my agent, Michelle Kass, and all who work with her at Michelle Kass Associates.

Finally, to my readers, without whom there would be no Whitstable Pearl Mysteries – thank you!